# A SLAVE OF THE *Shadows*

BOOK ONE

NAOMI FINLEY

Huntson Press
Inc



ISBN: 978-1-7750676-0-3

Cover Designer: Victoria Cooper Art
Facebook: www.facebook.com/VictoriaCooperArt

Editor: Scripta Word Services
Website: scripta-word-services.com

In memory of Jimmy

Thank you for always believing in me. I am forever changed because of all the things you taught me in life.

# Reading Order for Series

Novels:

*A Slave of the Shadows*: Book One

*A Guardian of Slaves:* Book Two

*A Whisper of War:* Book Three (Coming Soon)

Novellas:

*The Black Knight's Tune:* Novella One

*The Master of Ships:* Novella Two

*The Promise Between Us:* Novella Three

*The Fair Magnolia:* Novella Four

Novels can be read alone or with the novella series.
The author's shorter works are best read in the suggested order.

# Prologue

## Olivia

***CHARLESTON, 1832***

THE DOGS WERE GETTING CLOSER. TERROR WAS SLIPPING INTO panic. She held her swollen belly as she ran through the woods, the hand of the small slave child clasped tight in hers. She knew if they were caught her secret would be out. Many lives would be in danger, and who knew what would happen to the child?

They reached the swamps and blundered in, the sucking mud of the marsh grasping at their legs. The child's pace slowed. Night was closing in around them and she was tired.

"Missus, I can't!" she cried.

"We have to, sweetheart. We can't stop!" she urged, breathless. She felt as if her lungs were going to collapse. Determined, she pushed on into the deadly swamp, even as her mind screamed, *We will never make it!*

Fear ate away at her mind as fatigue took over. She was going to give birth right there in the middle of the swamps if they didn't find cover to rest soon. Blinking sweat from her eyes, she desperately searched for a hiding spot. There! She pushed into dense brush several yards in front of them, almost diving in, tugging the little girl with her. She crouched and pulled the foliage around them.

The howling of the dogs grew deafening as they pulled their

handlers through the swamp. She imagined the wet, muddy ground suctioning at the slave traders' feet as they moved. The child's fright overtook her and she began to sob. Olivia covered her mouth with her hand, watching the light from the torches bobbing through the swamp, growing from bright dots to drive the darkness back as they got closer. She could hear the dogs sniffing, trying to catch their scent. Pulling the child to her, she tried to calm her trembling body, willing her to be silent.

She had come across the half-starved child hiding in the woods by her plantation. There'd been no time to plan a better escape. She couldn't follow the usual channels. With the slave traders on their heels, she reacted without thinking. As she'd sprinted across the fields with the child, she heard one man yell behind them, "It's a bloody white woman with the child!"

*We need to get to the swamps. It's the only way we stand a chance,* she'd thought.

Now—it was only minutes before they would be caught. If by some miracle they escaped detection, they would starve to death or become prey to the low country predators. Her mind ran wild with these paralyzing thoughts, not realizing for a brief moment that the lights had dimmed, and the dogs' barking drifted farther away. The child started to speak, but Olivia silenced her with a finger to her lips. They sat completely still, unsure if any of the slave catchers had stayed behind.

The light from the full moon bathed the swamp in an eerie glow. She lay waiting, wrapped in the veil of vines hanging from the cypress tree looming above them. Her skin recoiled from the chilling dampness setting in. She pulled the child closer and they huddled together for warmth. Exhaustion carried the child away into sleep. Olivia followed, descending into a restless sleep plagued by baying hounds and cruel slavers.

Morning wrapped the swamp in mist, making visibility

unreliable. Cautiously, she parted the vines and stepped out of their hiding place. Her skin itched, and the child scratched feverishly—the mosquitoes had made a meal of them as they slept. She stopped, her ears tuned to the noise around them. There, the trickling of a distant creek. And all around, the croaking of frogs.

They must turn back. It was suicide to go farther into the swamps without food and water. The slave catchers had likely given up, thinking they had gone deeper in, sacrificing themselves to the environment.

She doubled back, pulling the child with her to the main road, where she paused and peeked up and down the road before stepping out. Clear. She ran to the cover of the trees on the other side, her head turned, peering over her shoulder to make sure they weren't being followed.

A scream escaped her lips as she collided with the solid chest of a human.

"Olivia, for God's sakes, what were you thinking?" The man grabbed her shoulders, giving her a shake.

"Ben!" She breathed a sob of relief.

"For the love of God, woman. You're so impulsive!" he scolded, his expression a mixture of concern and affection.

"I didn't think. But now that's neither here nor there." Knowing the answer, she asked, "Does he know?"

"Yes. They came by the plantation in hopes of obtaining your husband's and my help. They said it was a pregnant white woman they spotted with the child."

"He is already beside himself with anger over us. Now he will surely turn me in." She wrung her hands together in worry.

"He loves you, Olivia; he will help you."

"I don't know, Ben," she fretted. But then she turned her attention back to the matter at hand. "We need to get her out." She looked down at the little girl.

Opening the saddlebags on his horse, Ben pulled out some clothes. "Little miss, put these on," he said, handing the girl the pants and shirt.

The child slipped the clothes on, frowning with displeasure at the boys' attire.

He lifted his hand, which held a razor blade. "This is going to hurt a little."

The child's wooly mane fell to the ground as he shaved her head. She squirmed and grimaced in pain at the dry shave, but never let out a peep. Olivia gathered the evidence and hid it beneath a nearby rock, along with the discarded blade.

After spreading a blanket on the ground, Ben smiled down at the child and gently stroked her cheek. "We have to play hide and seek for a little longer, all right?"

She nodded.

Olivia knelt before the child and kissed her cheek, then drew her in for a hug. "Be safe. May we meet again when you are grown," she whispered into her ear.

Ben had her lie down on the blanket, and he rolled her up in it, then draped her within the blanket across the rear of his horse and tied it securely in place. He quickly kissed Olivia's forehead. "We have delayed long enough." He mounted his horse. "Now go!"

Gathering her muddy, torn skirts, Olivia hurried toward the plantation. As the big oak trees came into view, her nerves surged with anticipation of what lay ahead.

# CHAPTER One

## Willow

***CHARLESTON, 1850***

A SHIVER WENT THROUGH ME—I COULDN'T SHAKE THE EERIE feeling of being watched. I scanned the hillside overlooking my father's plantation before slipping my foot into the stirrup on my buckskin Arabian mare—a recent gift from my father—and hoisted myself up. Casting another glance around and seeing no one, I summed up my case of the jitters as my imagination.

The month of March had rolled in and brought with it a heat wave. The sun beat down on me, and sweat trickled down my back as I sat in the saddle, drinking in the beauty of Livingston Plantation. I admired the ancient oak trees framing the lane leading to the front of the plantation. Evergreen vines with fragrant yellow flowers climbed the massive iron gates guarding the entry. Great white pillars expanded the front veranda, extending through the second-floor balcony with its wrought-iron railings. Well-manicured gardens surrounded the main house. It was one of the grandest sea-island cotton and rice plantations in Charleston, and I felt a sense of pride in its splendor.

I glanced out over the fields and noted that our overseer, Jones, was making his rounds. A few of the slave children were also moving through the fields, offering the field hands water to quench their thirst. Our dog Beau had found himself some shade under a moss-covered live oak tree, where he lay panting.

My horse stirred and stomped an impatient hoof. "All right, let's go," I said, lightly kicking my heels into her sides. She took off at a full gallop.

I'd left my hair loose and the warm, refreshing breeze blew my chestnut tresses out behind me, teasing the tips up from my waist and tugging the rest out to follow. As we sped over the countryside the tension in my neck and shoulders slowly released. My jaw, clenched since the morning argument with Father over the discipline of a slave, relaxed.

Father had already been at the dining room table, reading the newspaper, when I came down to breakfast this morning. He'd looked over his wire-rimmed reading glasses at me as I entered and smiled a firm smile as he folded his paper. "Good morning, Willow." He ran a hand through his thinning blond hair. He was a handsome, ruggedly built man, over six feet tall, with green eyes that twinkled when he was amused. My unease in his presence was constant, and instilled in me as a child. My father was definitely a no-foolishness type of man.

"Good morning, Father," I said out of respect, and took my seat at the opposite end of the table.

"I'm going in to town. I have to go over our shipment with Captain Gillies before it leaves the warehouse for London today. While I'm gone, I need you to handle a situation with the carpenter's boy, Parker. He was caught sneaking eggs from the henhouse this morning, and Jones is too busy overseeing the south field fence repairs to handle it."

"Surely we can spare a few eggs, Father. What harm is there in that?" I avoided his stare, instead looking up at Henrietta, my mammy and the only mother figure I'd ever known, as she filled my cup with piping-hot coffee.

"Willow, don't try my patience today. Do as you're told and be a respectable daughter." He gave me a stern look as he took a bite of his toast.

Knowing better than to question his authority, I took a long sip of my coffee and sighed. Mammy smiled fondly at me as she headed back into the kitchen.

I am the only child of Charles Hendricks. My mother died when I was a few years old. I don't remember her. No portraits of her hang in the mansion, and talk of her is forbidden. Why? I've never been told.

Last fall, in my seventeenth year, when I returned from my studies abroad, Father informed me it was time I took on all responsibilities as the lady of Livingston. I was your typical Southern belle on the surface, which pleased my father, but my wayward opinions gained his disapproval. He often stated that I needed to be an example of perfection, as others were watching, judging him on how he was raising me. I had grown frustrated over the last few years with my lack of control over my own life. What did I care what some old busybodies had to say? Father would remind me that I was a woman and like a child, I was to be seen and not heard. Women in the South are barely above the slaves. The men consider us mere property and often treat us as such.

Slowing my horse to a trot, I guided her to a nearby creek for a drink and wiped the sweat from my brow. How was I going to deal with Parker in a way that would satisfy my father's request for discipline?

"Oh, bother," I complained aloud, annoyed with the whole lot of men.

# CHAPTER *Two*

A SUDDEN CRY JARRED ME FROM MY THOUGHTS.

"Please, Masa! I have my ticket," a man's voice implored.

I turned my mare in the direction of the plea. Rounding a copse of trees, I witnessed three men hovering over a helpless black man on his knees. My eyes narrowed on the captors, and I recognized Rufus, the overseer from the Barry Plantation, along with his two minions, Dave and Yates. They pushed and taunted the kneeling man.

Rufus laughed, jabbing the slave in the ribs with the butt of his whip. "Nigger, I didn't see any ticket. Did you, boys?"

Rufus was a whole five feet tall, a hundred and twenty pounds soaking wet. He walked around with his chest poked out like he was a big man, and he always had a lot to say. Little did he know people laughed behind his back at what a small, weak man he was. I referred to it as small man syndrome; without his two sidekicks he was powerless, and he knew it.

The men looked up in surprise as I edged my horse into the clearing. A burst of adrenaline kicked in and fear removed my inhibitions about—one—being a woman alone, and—two—being outnumbered.

I jumped from my saddle. "What's going on here?" I demanded, eyeing up the situation. Shifting my eyes to the slave, I recognized him to be Gray, the head slave from the Armstrong

Plantation. A nasty gash above his left eye made the eyelid droop; blood oozed from his mouth and soiled the front of his shirt. Gray was a big, strapping slave, but against a white man, he was defenseless.

Gritting my teeth, I turned my attention to the men. "Well, answer me!"

Rufus sneered and turned his scheming blue eyes on me. "What's it to you, woman? You need to learn your place and stay out of men's business."

Laughing, they turned their attention back to Gray, disregarding my existence. I heard the crunch of bone as Rufus ground the slave's hand into the ground with his heel. The injured man let out an agonized cry.

Rage at this injustice welled up in my chest and took over—I flew at Rufus, beating him with my fist. "How dare you! You monster!"

Yates peeled me off of Rufus, securing my arm behind my back and restricting my movement. His face, inches from mine, puckered in an unspoken warning. My nostrils flared at odor seeping from his body, and the overpowering stink of rotten teeth. His lewd eyes trailed over my body, quickening my heartbeat. My breakfast came back up, lodging in my throat as I began to panic. What had I done?

Yates laughed at the panic visible on my face and released my arm. My feet instinctively drew me back, and I scrambled to put distance between us. Tripping over my own feet, I landed in a heap on the ground. Rufus's evil eyes ate through my flesh, and I cringed at the repulsiveness of him. Dave licked his lips as he adjusted his belt on his too-small trousers. The belt disappeared under the massive mound of his stomach. "Boss, what do you say we have some fun?"

I started to shake. Had my acting without regard for my

own safety caught up with me? I tried to stagger to my feet, looking around for an escape route.

Gray rose up behind them and lifted his good hand to send a blow against the side of Rufus's skull, sending him sailing through the air.

In my daze, I was oblivious to the arrival of help until Bowden Armstrong and his friend Knox rode into the middle of the chaos. Quickly sliding from their horses, they took over.

Everything happened in a blur. Punches met their mark. Cries of pain rose from the victims. When things slowed down, Rufus lay in a heap where Bowden had sent him with a hard kick to his scrawny backside. Knox had the fat one, Dave, in a headlock and sent a blow to his head. Yates circled Bowden, who had always been swift on his feet. He managed to close the distance in a split second and knocked Yates onto his back.

Bowden turned to me, his face full of concern as he offered me a hand up. "You all right, Miss Willow?"

Refusing his help, I rose to my feet, smoothing my skirt. Sending a stony glare at my childhood enemy, I said, "I assure you, I'm fine, Mr. Armstrong."

Rufus and his goons hightailed it out of there as Knox pulled up beside us, grinning at their victory. "You all right, Willow?"

"Yes, Knox, thanks for your help." I reached up to pat his arm.

He towered over me. His shoulders were broad as a house and at first glance he was downright intimidating. But his brandy-brown eyes were warm and kind, with a side of mischievousness.

Bowden rolled his eyes in annoyance at my rudeness but turned his attention to Gray, who stood cradling his broken hand. "Gray, you need to go on home and get that tended to. I will pay the Barry Plantation a visit and speak to Mr. Barry about his overseer."

"Yes, Masa." Gray smiled at me and nodded his gratitude. "Thank you, Miss."

"We helped each other, Gray, so I too owe you a thank-you."

He reclaimed his ruined straw hat from the ground along with his torn ticket, then turned and headed for home.

I nodded at Knox and Bowden. "Thank you."

Bowden was brave enough to stir the angry hornet's nest of emotions whirling inside of me. "Next time you should think of the outcome before you get involved in an outnumbered situation. What if we hadn't shown up?"

*He had to! He can't control himself, can he?* "I can handle myself, Bowden." I glared at him, challenging him to say another word.

Never one to back down, Bowden replied bluntly, "It sure didn't seem that way. From now on, let me handle my property."

I was aware Bowden wasn't a cruel plantation owner, but simply a businessman who followed the ways of the South, the way things had been done for hundreds of years.

Grabbing my horse's reins, I swung myself up in one fluid movement. Having to have the last word, I smugly let one last statement fly over my shoulder before I rode off. "Horses are property, Mr. Armstrong. Humans aren't!"

I felt eyes upon me and smiled smugly, imagining Bowden glowering at my back.

# CHAPTER *Three*

## Bowden

Bowden fumed as she rode off. Willow Hendricks had a way of getting under his skin. She was fiery and stubborn as an old mule. She'd turned into a real beauty, claiming the attention of most men who laid eyes on her. He couldn't help but admire her curves as she bounced up and down in the saddle, her back straight and her head held high.

With her hasty departures over the years, he'd come to memorize the back side of her silhouette. He'd tried to no end to right his mistakes of the past, but she would barely let him get two words in before she stormed off with a cloud over her head. She'd looked right past Knox's involvement in the childhood prank they'd played on her and settled all her resentment on him. Knox seemed to have that way with people. Bowden knew it was his secret weapon for getting himself out of tight situations.

Shaking his head, Bowden turned to Knox. "That woman is something else. Makes me want to smile and spit fire, all at the same time." He frowned at the raised eyebrow Knox gave him, followed by a teasing grin. "What is that look for?" he demanded, settling his hat over his loose dark curls.

Knox gave him a friendly jab in the shoulder. "Maybe what bothers you the most is that she holds you at arm's length when you daydream of holding her closer." He hugged himself and swayed side to side.

Bowden chuckled, his blue-green eyes twinkling with mirth. "Oh, I admire her beauty as much as any man, but holding that girl in your arms would be like stepping into a pit of vipers."

Knox laughed and gave him a look that said *if you say so.* "Well, buddy, we better head back and get an honest day of work in." He clapped Bowden on the back.

"When have you ever done an honest day's work?" Bowden laughed, admiring the man who had become a brother to him.

"I don't need to. Do you see this physique? It will get me far in life." He widened his stance and rubbed his chest, posing like a Greek god sent to earth.

Bowden cracked up. "Well, Zeus, I'd say you better get back to your docks before they find you skipped out again."

Bowden mounted his horse and Knox followed suit.

"You'll see, Bowden. I will win the heart of the fairest maiden in the land," he said in all seriousness, sitting taller as he adjusted himself in his saddle.

Bowden recognized the jokester beneath the solemn surface. "Sure—more like a mail-order bride," he shot back lightheartedly. "Race you to the road!" he yelled as he kicked his horse into a head start.

Knox let out a whoop and took off right on his heels.

# CHAPTER *Four*

My resentment of Bowden Armstrong went back for a decade. As young boys, Bowden and Knox were little devils, constantly up to no good. They found it hilarious to torment the younger children at the schoolhouse.

That dreadful day when my torment began, I passed Bowden and Knox resting against the old oak tree in the schoolyard, eating their lunch, as I headed to the outhouse. Bowden was so dreamy, with long eyelashes that brushed his cheeks. All the girls had a crush on him.

He'd come to Charleston the year before with his grandpa and his little brother, Stone. Father said his parents had died in a shipwreck off the coast of Georgia a few years ago. My heart went out to him; he was barely thirteen and his little brother was younger than me. I could relate to the pain of not having a mother, but being orphaned, with no parents at all, I couldn't imagine. When he'd started school the previous year he'd became inseparable friends with Knox. Everyone liked Knox; he was easy and laid back.

I sat down in the outhouse still dreaming of Bowden's smile and his eyes, which looked like jewels swept up from the bottom of the ocean. They sparkled when he laughed and changed color when he was mad. As I sat there with my undergarments around my ankles, I thought, *I'm going to marry that boy someday.*

Suddenly the outhouse began to rock back and forth, and I

gripped the rickety old seat to steady myself. Then with a snap, the seat gave way, and I squealed as I went bottom first into the pungent sewage below. I found myself wedged down in the hole with only my feet dangling out. I quickly tried to dislodge myself but it was too late; the outhouse went over sideways and I was rolling. I felt the wetness and slime of the contents of the hole splashing over me as I tumbled out.

Wiping watering eyes, I looked up to see Bowden and Knox holding their stomachs, roaring with laughter. The other children gathered around, pointing and laughing. Some held their noses against the smell while others looked on in shock and bewilderment. I collected myself from the ground, rage rising up in me as I fought back tears. I swore to myself, *I hate that boy with everything in me.*

"I hate you, Bowden Armstrong. I'll never forgive you. Ever!" I screamed, and stomped my foot.

Ms. Ellen, the schoolteacher, arrived on the scene. She looked at me in horror and turned her gaze on those two boys. Their laughter ceased. Ms. Ellen took them both by the ears and escorted them to the side of the school, where she ordered them not to move. She shouted to the other children to get into the school and wait.

She smiled down at me, her expression full of pity. "I think those boys must have taken a liking to you, Willow. Boys do things like this when they like a pretty girl."

I remember frowning at her as I angrily wiped away my tears. That wasn't the first time I'd been told that kind of explanation, about boys teasing girls because they liked them. I called it a bogus statement and an adult's way of trying to make you feel better.

I stood in sheer humiliation with the whole school's waste covering me. Ms. Ellen's voice was but a mumble as I turned my eyes on Bowden and Knox. The boys were looking at the ground. Bowden shifted his feet back and forth in the dirt, and Knox's face was shadowed with regret. I looked at Bowden, from his feet right up to his head, and said over and over in my mind, *I hate you, Bowden Armstrong, with every ounce of my body.* From that day on I fought to suppress the humiliation I relived every time I heard the mention of his name or saw his face.

# CHAPTER Five

I STEWED OVER THE ENCOUNTER WITH KNOX AND BOWDEN MOST OF the afternoon. I'd been careless in aiding Gray, but I couldn't stand by and do nothing because that made me no better than Rufus and his men. I had to intercede. I'd done the right thing.

Life forced me to grow up fast without a mother, and with a father who was gone more than he was home. I was a dreamer and a thinker, often involving myself in the rights and the wrongs of the world around me. I questioned life as a whole. Only in recent years did I question the ways of the South. How did slavery begin? Talk about groups in the North calling themselves *abolitionist* was becoming more frequent. The changes these people were speaking of made the plantation owners nervous and angry. What if slavery was abolished? How would the plantations and farmers in the South make a living? It would affect their way of life. I developed a maturity beyond my years and a voice Father often tried to silence. I believe he thought of me as the bane of his existence.

"Come on, old boy." I patted our cocker spaniel Beau's head. Knowing I had avoided the situation with Parker, the boy caught stealing eggs, for long enough, I set out to deal with that task.

I found Parker's father busy sanding the shelves of a pantry Mammy requested he make. "Good afternoon, Owen." I offered a weary smile.

The white-haired man looked up from his work then straightened, rolling his shoulder to ease the ache from being hunched over too long. He craned his neck and called over his shoulder, "Parker, get on out here, boy. Miss Willow is here to deal wid your thievin'."

I couldn't contain the feeling of doom that settled over me.

Owen smiled softly. "Et be all right. Parker needs to larn dat stealin' ain't right, no matter who he is takin' from."

Parker appeared from the back of the woodshed, worry knitting his young brow at what was in store for him. His unruly hair stood up on end. He was slight for his ten years. He used a walking cane to support the slack in his left leg.

"Parker, Mr. Hendricks says you were caught taking eggs from the henhouse. Is this so?" I gave him the sternest expression I could muster.

"I reckon so, Miss Willow." He hung his head in shame, not daring to look up at me.

"What do you suppose I should do about this? You could get yourself in heaps of trouble with Mr. Hendricks, or any other master, for that matter. They could starve you, whip you, cut off your hand, or even cut off your good leg...maybe even sell you to a new master."

Parker's head whipped up as terror transformed his face. I knew my message had struck a chord.

"Father is going to be asking me what punishment I dealt you, and I need to have an answer or we will both be in trouble. Come on; we may as well get this over with."

He hobbled over to me, his brown eyes huge with worry.

"Hand me your walking cane and bend over that log." I pointed to the makeshift sawhorse behind him.

He hesitantly bent over and his butt cheeks tightened in

anticipation of what was coming next. He let out a howl as the cane made contact. In two sharp, quick strikes I administered his punishment.

"Now, young man, what will you not do again?"

He looked up at me, tears pooling in his dark eyes. I gulped back the tears welling in my throat. I hated this; it broke my heart.

"I'll never take eggs again."

"And?" I elevated my quavering voice, awaiting the correct answer.

"I ain't gonna steal anything again," he wailed.

"Good boy, now run along."

His eyes widened and he ceased his pitiful wail. "Dat's et?"

Relief washed through me as he flung himself at me, squeezing me around the waist.

"Parker!" Owen strode over and removed his son's arms from me. "Forgive da boy, Miss Willow. In his happiness, he has done gone and forgot his place." Thinking he'd done it for sure now, dread filled Parker's face.

"Pay it no mind," I assured him, and turned to Parker. "Will you do me a favor, Parker?"

"Yessum." His sweet face relaxed.

"Let's keep this our secret. What do you say?"

"Yessum. I ain't goin' be tellin' a soul. No sirree, I be takin' dat up to de big man in de sky." He jabbed his cane at the sky.

"Good." I held out my hand for him to shake.

His jaw dropped, then he pushed a small hand out and vigorously returned my handshake.

I bade them a good day and left. I overheard the exchange between father and son as I walked away.

"She could have you tied to de post and whipped for dat. Boy, you got to 'member your place. You never touch a white 'oman! Ever!"

"Yes, Pappy, but I'm jus' so happy."

"I know, son, I know." Owen's voice carried an undertone of relief and happiness of his own.

# CHAPTER

# *Six*

FATHER HAD BOUGHT OWEN AT THE AUCTION A FEW YEARS BACK at top price for a skilled slave. They threw in Parker for a few measly coins. The auctioneer figured he wouldn't hold any value as he grew into a man, with his below-average stature and his distinct limp that made him drag his left leg as he walked.

Father had compelled me to attend these auctions on a few occasions. He'd said, "You will have to run this plantation someday. That's if we can't find a respectable gentleman to marry you, with all your outspoken views."

The first time I went to an auction I was appalled at what I witnessed. The women, men, and children were chained together and herded in like cattle. Like polished apples on a merchant's cart, they'd been rubbed clean. The sellers looking to fetch the best price had their merchandise oiled, giving their skin the illusion of youthfulness. The men wore trousers made of cream-colored Negro cloth; they were shirtless, exposing their unmarked backs. The women's hair was braided into a single braid or tucked up under a colorful head rag, their simple dresses covered with aprons. The children wore shifts made of the same Negro cloth as the adults. The slaves with trades or skills were marked by the signs hanging from their necks. Only the wealthiest in Charleston could afford the prices assigned to them. Young children clung to their mamas' legs, their faces tear-stained, some hiccupping from hours of crying and exhaustion. Fear was engraved upon the adults' faces at what would come next.

The auctioneer stepped up and the auction began. I watched in disbelief as the first slave was brought forward. She was a pregnant woman with a girl about four years old, her small fist clasping tight the skirt of her mother's dress. The father was pulled away from them and shoved back into line. The mother trembled as her man let go of her, as if his strength was the only thing keeping her together, and the woman and child began to weep.

Nausea roiled through me and I snuck a peek at Father. His face was a blank, his expression controlled and all business. I glanced back at the young family. My focus rested on the mother, the worry she must be feeling, and the sheer panic over what was about to happen to her family.

The auctioneer's voice cut through the murmur of the crowd. "Young mother not but eighteen years old, in the prime of her life. A real breeder, as you can see." He roughly rubbed her rounded belly. "Take the mother with the child or take only the mother, it's up to you," he shouted. A sob escaped the mother's lips.

I pulled on Father's arm in desperation. "Father, can't we purchase the family?" He ignored me. "Please, Father!" I begged with more intensity.

"Hush, Willow!" He tried to silence me with his harsh tone and a look that said *if you know what's good for you, you will stop this behavior now!*

I didn't let worry over his wrath when we got home hold me back. "But Father, it isn't right to break up a family." I grabbed his arm and tugged firmly, letting him know I wasn't backing down.

"Sold! The mother goes to this fine gentleman here," the auctioneer shouted, pointing to a short, stout man in the crowd who looked to be wearing his Sunday best.

The auctioneer forcefully separated the child from her mother. The child's gut-wrenching screams pierced my heart. Her small hand managed to grab her mother as they were plucked apart.

"Mama, I need you!" she'd cried, clutching the lifeline of her mother's hand.

The wail out of the mother came from deep in her soul, a sound that would stay with me for the rest of my life. The child's father reached for the mother and child to comfort them and suffered a blow to the back of the head—only a warning to keep him in line without damaging him, as no one would pay for a battered slave. The man straightened and the agony dropped from his face, replaced by a stone-cold mask. His child wrapped her arms around his knee and let out a soft purr, which carried like the sound of a newborn kitten. "Mama…"

I turned and pushed my way through the crowd, unable to bear the horrible shame and guilt I carried at being the daughter of a plantation owner. I ran as fast as my legs could carry me under the weight of my gown until I got to the ship dock. Hot tears stung my eyes as I looked out over the crowded harbor. Despair and helplessness swept me away, and I crumpled to the ground, sobbing.

Father never followed to comfort me, but stayed to look for the property he had come to purchase. This was the day Owen and Parker came to Livingston.

# CHAPTER *Seven*

I MADE MY WAY BACK TO THE HOUSE AS FATHER DOCKED HIS schooner at the wharf. My chest tightened, as his presence stirred anxiety in me. I rolled my neck, trying to ease the building tension as I waited for his approach.

"How did you manage here today while I was away?"

"Fine, Father."

"Parker?"

"I've dealt with him," I said, eyes downcast so he'd know I hadn't liked it much. I was hoping to give him the impression that I'd handed out a harsh punishment.

"Very well." Appearing satisfied, he turned and went up the steps.

Our manservant, Thaddeus, greeted him with a glass of ice water and a cool, damp cloth to wipe the sweat from his brow.

"Thaddeus, have James come see me in my study."

"Yes, Masa, right away." Thaddeus hurried off to fetch the blacksmith.

I bravely followed Father into his study, hoping to grab a few minutes of his time. He started flipping through the mail on his desk without acknowledging me. I swallowed hard, trying to summon the nerve to ask him something I'd been wanting to ask for weeks, but my nerves always got the best of me. Everything I did, he somehow found flawed. Did he wish I'd been born a son? Would I ever receive his love and approval?

*Well, here goes nothing.*

"Father, there is going to be a picnic this Sunday for the young folk, and I want to attend."

Then came the long pause before he addressed me. "The sort of thing a lady can be up to no good at," he stated bluntly.

I sighed to relieve the anxiety that came with these encounters. This was the way it was between Father and me.

Taking my sigh as a sign of disrespect, he looked at me sharply. "I would suggest you watch your tone, Willow."

Defending myself was not worth the effort. It would turn into an argument and I would end up getting punished for having done nothing wrong. What was good for Charles Hendricks, I was still trying to understand. He would have preferred a meek and mild daughter, I knew. Conversations between us often left me thinking I wasn't good enough. Why did I always have to be a leading example for everyone around me? What did it matter, what people thought? The pressure Father put on me to be an ideal daughter was frustrating and overwhelming. I found myself longing for the days when he would leave on his ships.

As an importer and exporter, Father would often be gone for long periods of time. I had recently finished my studies and would be spending most of my time at Livingston. Father was a successful and wealthy businessman in Charleston. In his success, he'd made Livingston a thriving plantation. For as long as I could remember, we spent our summers at our home in Rhode Island. More frequently, hoping I would learn more about managing a plantation, he would leave me in charge of operations—under the guidance of Jones the overseer, of course. When Father was away was the only time I felt truly free. Was our home a haven? Not in my case; it was more like a prison, and me its captive.

# CHAPTER Eight

JAMES, OUR MOST SKILLED BLACKSMITH, ENTERED, REMOVING HIS worn hat from his graying head. Holding it in his hands, he bowed his head respectfully. Our eyes met from my position at my father's side, and I smiled affectionately at the man who in my heart had become a father to me.

Careful to avoid my open attention, he addressed my father. "Yes, Masa?"

"James, I need you to head over to the Widow Jenson's farm across the way and check out her mule. She says it has been having a problem with its hind leg."

James was handy at most things he put his mind to, but he was especially good with horses. As good as any schooled vet, I'd bet.

"Sho' thing, Masa! Anything else?"

"That will be all." Times like these were when I allowed myself to see the good in Father, with his thoughtfulness toward his neighbors. He'd become a well-respected gentleman in Charleston, acquiring many admirers among the spinsters and the younger ladies of Charleston. Once I asked him why he'd never remarried, and he simply said, "One woman was enough for me." I did not miss how his shoulders drooped and his chin quivered ever so slightly. The pain of losing my mother was apparent on his handsome face.

"Can I go?" I said, in one last attempt to have some kind of life outside of the plantation.

"We will see." With a wave of his hand, he dismissed me like he would a slave.

I dashed out of the room to catch up with James. Father called after me as if he were scolding a child, "No running!"

Out of his sight, I was brave enough to roll my eyes, but I did slow my pace to a fast walk. Once outside I sped up. "Jimmy!"

James turned to wait for me, beaming. "Miss Willie!" he said cheerfully, using the name that had become an endearment from him. He was always happy and I wasn't sure why. It was as if the life he'd been dealt didn't faze him. He had sharp facial features with beady eyes, yet he was attractive in his own way, and was well liked around the plantation, despite being a shy man. He kept to himself except for a few trusted friends, and he'd never mentioned family. His loud and infectious laugh often came out as a roar. It would leave me feeling amazed that a man as shy as him could have a laugh that started from his toes and worked its way all the way up until it filled the air around you with an inexplicable happiness. When I needed advice, I found myself searching him out, and he seemed eager to oblige. If people knew how close I had become to Jimmy, we would both be in hot water. I found comfort in his presence, an acceptance I never had with my own father. Jimmy admired my spunky personality.

"I ran into that awful Bowden Armstrong again today." I folded my arms across my chest.

"Uh-huh." He waited.

"Well, he is as dreadful and smug as ever," I said with a huff as we continued on to the barn. The mere mention of his name annoyed me all over again.

Jimmy remained a willing ear.

"I happened upon Rufus and his men terrorizing Gray, from the Armstrong Plantation, and I kind of got myself involved."

I dared a peek at him. Jimmy stopped, now looking alarmed. I rushed on. "I know it was dangerous and I didn't think it through." I waved my hands as I tried to express myself. I was exasperated with this whole day and wished for it to be over. "I saw red. I couldn't help myself. Rufus is malicious and merciless, and as bad as any slave catcher. I needed to do something."

"Miss Willie, you gwine git yourself hurt or worst—daid!" he said, distress lifting his voice.

I sighed, knowing he cared not out of an obligation to the lady of the plantation, but from the special place he allowed me in his life. "You're right, Jimmy. I will try to use my head and not get so fired up."

His laugh was a deep rumble. "Dat's what makes you so special, Miss Willie, is your love for people of all kinds."

I grinned at his praise. "It is a good thing Bowden and Knox came along. They did help me out of the mess I got myself into."

"Dis time," Jimmy said ominously.

"Miss Willow!"

I turned to see Mammy waddling up. Mammy was short and thick around the middle, but someone who wasn't to be underestimated by her height. She could put the fear of God into you. She had sent many slaves hollering and screaming out of her kitchen, chasing after them with her heavy wooden spoon. She didn't allow anyone to mess around in her kitchen or with her food.

"Yes, Mammy?"

"You need to be lettin' Jim run along before your pappy catches you chattin' up a slave and you find yourself grounded for a month of Sundays."

"Miss Rita speaks de truth. I bes' git gwine." With his usual polite manners, he tipped his hat. "Good day, Miss Willie, Miss Rita." He strolled off toward the barn.

Disheartened at his departure, I stared after him before turning back to Mammy to find her studying me.

"What?"

"Chile, you need to be careful. Dere's no hidin' how much you care about that nigra."

"I am careful, Mammy…for both our sakes."

"You may think you watchful of who be seeing you. But dere ain't no hidin' dat look on your face of de love you hold for dat slave."

"How's it any different than the love I show for you?"

"'Cause I your mammy. I raised you, and Masa and anyone else 'spect dat. But a field slave, dat's a whole 'nother thing."

I followed Mammy back to the house. "I'm going to rest in my room for a bit before I get washed up for supper. Could you please send up Mary Grace to attend me?"

"I will, Miss Willow."

# CHAPTER *Nine*

I DREW THE VELVET CURTAINS CLOSED TO BLOCK OUT THE UNGODLY heat and lay down on my four-poster to await Mary Grace.

"Come in, Mary Grace," I called when I heard the knock on the door. I sat up, adjusting the pillows behind me.

Mary Grace bounced into the room with the usual skip in her step. She'd been born a year before me and had always been a house slave. The other slaves on the plantation considered her spoiled, as she'd never spent a day in the fields. Her fingers weren't marked and bloody from the cotton bushes. Her soul wasn't burdened or scarred by the slave life.

Mammy Henrietta was her mother, and her father was Mammy's previous master. Her skin was a flawless light caramel. Her long dark hair, covered as it always was by a scarf, wasn't wooly like most of the Negroes'. She was tall and slender—willowy, I thought; and I, curvy and of average height, was the one named Willow. Mary Grace was naïve to the ways of the world, Mammy would often say. Riddled by fear that her daughter would suffer the rapes she'd been subjected to with her last master, Mammy tried her best to protect Mary Grace from the same fate. It did not pay to be a pretty slave. When Father would receive male visitors to the house she would make Mary Grace stay out of sight, away from men's wandering eyes.

Father assigned Mary Grace as my handmaid when we were small children. With no other siblings, we formed an unbreakable bond. She'd slept on a pallet on my floor for as far back as I could remember. On my return home from my studies, I was surprised to find that she now permanently shared the room at the back staircase with Mammy. I missed the sound of her breathing as she slept, which had lulled me to sleep many nights.

The first time I realized Mary Grace was different from me, we were around five years old. Father had invited a few of his gentlemen friends over for our evening meal. I'd finished my dinner and eyed Mary Grace in the hallway. She peeked around the corner and waved eagerly for me to come to her.

I turned to Father. "May I be excused, Father, to go play with my friend?"

Wrinkling his brow in confusion, he asked, "What friend?"

"Mary Grace," I said with my own frown at his silliness.

"Willow, no slave can be a friend to a proper Southern belle."

Why not? My confusion deepened. Father then summoned Mammy to take me away before I humiliated him further. Mammy whisked me off to my room with Mary Grace hot on her heels. I sat on the edge of my bed, my arms crossed tight across my chest, swinging my feet angrily.

"You all right, Miss Willow?" little Mary Grace asked me.

I didn't want to tell her what Father said because I was so mad at him. He never found time for me. He was always running off on his big ships sailing the world without me. He would bring me back countless toys and pretty things, but I was still *alone.* Now when I had a friend who made me not feel so alone, he was trying to take her away. *I don't care what Father says, I am not going to let him say she isn't my friend.* I looked at Mary Grace, who sat there beaming, always happy and aiming to please.

"You will always be my friend and I will protect you. No matter what big people say, you're my sister. When I'm the owner of this plantation, I'm going to set you free. Would you like that, Mary Grace?" She nodded earnestly. "It's settled, then. He isn't the boss of me," I insisted with authority beyond my power, placing my hands on my tiny hips.

Mary Grace and I giggled and danced around the room, singing quietly, "Ring around the rosie, pocket full of posies."

In my room that day I made a promise I intended to keep, no matter the price.

Today Mary Grace seated herself on the bed beside me and revealed a bar of bath soap she was holding in her hands. "I made this for you today." Her eyes glowed as she held it up to my nose.

It smelled of lavender, chamomile, and honey; for exfoliation purposes she had added a touch of oats. I inhaled and sighed with gleeful bliss. It was my favorite of the soap concoctions she made.

Mary Grace loved nature. When her daily tasks were done, she could usually be found wandering in the forest and gardens, looking for flowers to make her soaps and oils. These disappearing acts would send Mammy into a frenzy. She would scurry around in search of her daughter, grumbling what a fool girl she was.

"You managed to sneak out on Mammy again? You wicked, wicked girl."

"Mama says I have my head in the clouds and don't pay no mind to the danger around me."

"A handsome slave by the name of Gray wouldn't have anything to do with you being high in the clouds, would he?"

She reddened, but I recognized the dreamy look girls get when they have fallen head over heels in love. "He makes me feel special."

When the slaves got a pass or a ticket to visit other plantations every few weeks, Gray would visit Livingston, as Mammy flat-out refused to let Mary Grace use a ticket to go off the plantation.

"Gray is a good man. And in his eyes, I see a pure soul."

Mary Grace cocked her head, perplexed. "How have you come to this idea?"

"I may be white, Mary Grace, but I'm not blind to a handsome man, no matter his skin tone."

"I mean, how or when have you talked to Gray?"

"Oh!" I decided against filling Mary Grace in on what had occurred with Gray, as it would make her worry for weeks until she saw him. "I've spoken to him in passing."

I rose and went to my closet and picked out an emerald-green taffeta dress with a modest neckline that scooped below my collar bone and tucked in at the waist with an ivory sash. Father had purchased it for me on one of his recent trips. I liked how the dress made my eyes stand out. Mary Grace came to help me out of what I was wearing and I slipped into the green dress, turning for Mary Grace's assistance with the pearl buttons trailing down the back.

I sat down at the vanity, and Mary Grace combed my hair, then swept it to the side and pinned it, leaving the length to cascade down over my right shoulder in soft curls. I studied my reflection in the mirror for a moment before I rose to head down for dinner. I paused and lightly kissed Mary Grace's cheek. "Thank you for my gift and for your help." Then I swept gracefully out of the room, my dress swishing as I went.

# CHAPTER *Ten*

## Jimmy's Story

SLAVERY WAS THE ONLY WAY OF LIFE HE HAD KNOWN IN HIS SIXTY years. As a young man, Jimmy lived on a smaller plantation in Wilmington, North Carolina. His masa was vicious and cold-blooded, showing no mercy to any slave.

His wife was barren and he pressured her for years to bear him a son to carry on the family name. Nightly, it seemed, he freed the evil living in him upon the missus in various forms of mental and physical abuse. The slaves could hear her cries from the house in the slave quarters. She wasn't kind or friendly to her slaves and turned a blind eye to their suffering at the hands of her husband, in the hope he would leave her alone.

Even though she never bore him children, he'd fathered a few with the young slave girls he took to the overseer's cabin. Jimmy saw many young girls, barely twelve years old, enter that cabin with the masa. Masa liked them pure and innocent, just on the threshold of womanhood. Jimmy watched them leave battered, traumatized, and holding themselves, as if to shelter their bodies from the sick, twisted things he'd done to them. The masa would light a cigar and watch them walk away, smirking as if he'd scored another trophy for his wall.

When Jimmy's wife, Nellie, told him one night as they lay in bed that he was going to be a father, he'd been happy but scared at the same time. He prayed for a boy, never wanting to bring a daughter into this world. Nellie shared the same worry. Eight months later when their daughter, Magnolia, was born, he swore as he looked down at her. She was so tiny in his arms, sleeping so soundly, not knowing what life had in store for her. He loved her within those first precious moments even as he assumed the burden of hardship they would face as parents. They knew as slaves they were powerless. Jimmy secretly wished Mag would grow up to be an ugly woman; at least then she might avoid being forced to satisfy the whims of men.

The first year of Mag's life brought Nellie and Jimmy much happiness as she learned to crawl and then walk. She began to say "Mama" and "Papa," and Jimmy adored her. Every morning he would sit on the edge of their bed, rocking Mag in the cradle he'd handcrafted for her. In the dainty headboard, he'd carved angel wings. He couldn't sing a note, but he cooed out the same tune to her every day.

*Fly, my little angel,*
*spread your wings and soar*
*Above the trees may you find freedom,*
*A slave no more.*

In the fourth year of Mag's life she became very sick with influenza. Nellie, sick with worry for her daughter, stole some medicine from the big house. She didn't make it out with the medicine. A servant of the house, known amongst the slaves as "the black rat," caught her and reported back to the masa.

The masa chained Nellie to the post and whipped her until the skin on her back lay open like pages in a book. As a standing example of what happens to all thieves, she was to remain tied to the post for the next two days. They were told the slave caught giving her food or water would suffer the same fate. Jimmy couldn't leave her like that, no matter the risk. That night, after her skin had baked and sizzled in the hot sun all day, he crawled over to her on his hands and knees, using the darkness to shield him. He lifted her head and poured some water on her blistering lips.

She moaned and half opened her eyes, readily sipping back some water before turning her head away. "Go before you git caught," she whispered faintly.

"I can't leave you lak dis." He cupped her face in his hands and brushed away her few unspent tears with his thumbs.

"Mag needs you to stay alive. Now go!" She winced.

After the two days passed, Jimmy carried her limp body back to the shack they shared with another family. An old widow woman sewed her up. Every night after long days spent in the fields, he sat by her side. He laid a cool, damp cloth on her forehead as she lay burning up. Her wounds became infected; she moaned and cried as the fever unleashed havoc on her body. Jimmy worried for Mag and his wife.

A few weeks passed. Mag recovered and was running around, turning the shack upside down. Nellie never fully recovered and developed the cough that seemed to be spreading through the plantation. The epidemic took Jimmy's wife and over half of the slaves on the plantation. The missus had gotten sick too; she recovered, but it left her weaker than before.

Times got hard after the loss of half the masa's property. Businessmen came to the big house trying to collect the outstanding debt the masa owed. As the weeks turned into months, they showed up more often and the conversations turned into threats. The masa would go into fits of rage and have them thrown off his property.

The young slaves with families, including the mothers of the masa's children, took advantage of his growing weakness and ran. Some never returned; others, he hunted down and killed.

One evening Jimmy and the others were sitting by the fire when a fight broke out between the missus and the masa. The missus was asking to go home to her family and the masa, being the usual tyrant, said that she would never leave the plantation as long as he lived. Some slaves whispered, "Serves her right." Their hearts were filled with hatred after years of being tortured and beaten by the masa. Jimmy knew she was an uncaring woman, but no one deserved this. There was a scuffle, and the slaves sat by as her screams haunted the night. Then there was silence.

Days passed. No one ever saw the missus come out of the house. Then Jimmy was summoned from the fields to the big house by the masa. Jimmy found him treading back and forth in the front entry, studying a book he held.

He glanced up as Jimmy entered. "Nigger." The masa never bothered to learn any of the slaves' names. "Can you make one of these?" He shoved the book at Jimmy.

Jimmy had never seen anything like the picture in that book before. It was a chair with wheels. There were words on the page, but he couldn't read them. He looked up at the masa. "I'll try, Masa."

"You'd best do better than try, nigger. Now get your revolting self out of my house."

A few days later, Jimmy delivered the chair to the masa. After a quick inspection of Jimmy's craftsmanship, he turned and disappeared down the hallway. Minutes later he reappeared carrying the missus. Her body was limp from the waist down; bruises on her face were yellowing as they healed. Her body would never heal from the damage Masa had done to her. She was now a cripple and the chair he'd made would be her prison. As the masa dropped her into the chair, she looked up at Jimmy with a broken emptiness in her eyes. Compassion for her surged through him.

"Take this sorry excuse of a wife outside. I grow tired of her whining," Masa ordered before storming off.

They were left alone and Jimmy was forced to speak. "It's mighty breezy outside, Missus. Let me git you a cover." He hurried down the hall in search of a blanket. As he drew close to one door, the smell of urine and feces overpowered his senses. Pausing in the doorway, he looked inside. The shutters were sealed closed, and the room was empty except for a bed on the floor made from a few blankets. Jimmy glanced back down the hall to where he had left the missus, his soul heavy with understanding. The masa broke her body and discarded her as damaged goods. She had not been helped to the outhouse to relieve herself, forcing her to spend almost a week lying in her own waste.

Jimmy found an afghan in another room and returned to the missus. As he pushed the chair with wheels toward the porch, he lifted a shawl hanging from a hook by the door.

Outside, Masa was saddling his horse to go into town, probably to hit the bottle and be entertained by ladies of the night. "You niggers better be here when I get back," he growled. "Don't go getting any fool ideas because the overseer left. I'll find you and wear your black skin for a coat if you even think of running away." His eyes gleamed dangerously as he circled the yard, driving home his threat; satisfied, he turned his horse and rode off.

Jimmy sprang into action. "Harry, I want you to heat some water so de missus can have a bath," he told his friend. Harry left to do his bidding.

"Lucy, I need you to bathe de missus when we git her in de bath," he said to a house slave.

"Why should we help dat waste of human flesh?" She eyed the missus, loathing curling her lip.

He—all too well—understood her hate, and the suffering

they'd all suffered here on this plantation from these masters. "'Cause what good are we, if we become dem?" he said.

"If you want to show her mussy, you on your own." Her scowling eyes locked on the missus. She spat on the ground in disgust before turning and walking away.

On the porch with the missus, he spoke softly. "Et be all right, Missus. I git you cleaned up."

Upstairs he wandered around until he found her rightful room and found a nightgown in her clothing drawer. He lifted a brush for her hair from her vanity. He carried both back downstairs with him and found the bath room at the rear of the house, next to the kitchen.

Harry was tipping enough water to fill a few inches of the tub. More water was heating in the fireplace. "I will do de res' myself, Harry. No need in two of us being punished."

Harry scurried away.

When the tub was ready, Jimmy wheeled the missus inside. She never said a word, even when a male slave removed her clothes. When he lifted her naked body to place her in the tub, she wrapped her arms around his neck. He saw sadness and a lifetime of regret in her pain-filled blue eyes. Jimmy lowered her into the tub and gently bathed her crushed body. He washed her hair. Then, lifting her to him, he wrapped her in a cloth, drying her body. After slipping her into the nightgown he sat her in her chair and wrapped the shawl around her frail shoulders. He tucked the afghan around her legs, then wheeled her out into the sunshine and set to tenderly brushing her graying blonde hair.

That day he found it within himself to show empathy for the wife of the masa, who never showed him anything but hatred and resentment.

The sun had dipped behind the clouds when the masa returned home drunk. Jimmy had retired to the shack for the evening and was telling Mag a story when an irritated masa barged through the door.

"Which one of you animals dared bathe my wife?"

No one spoke up. He rolled out his whip and snapped it through the air. At the loud cracking sound, Mag began to cry.

"Speak up, you bastards, or I'll have you whipped, the whole lot of you."

Jimmy stepped forward. "It was me, Masa."

Masa circled him. "You! A slave! And a male slave, at that. You touched my wife's body?"

"She was soiled wid her own waste and I thought—"

"You thought?" he screamed, his eyes bulging. "What gives you the right to think for yourself, you savage dog?"

Masa did not whip him that night, leaving Jimmy unsettled. The next morning came too soon, as all mornings did on the plantation. Slaves were up and going about their daily work when the masa left, returning to town.

The missus was sitting on the porch in her chair. As Jimmy passed by on his way to the field, she called out, "Stop."

Jimmy stopped. Turning to her, he asked, "Yessum?"

"Come here, please." She beckoned him with a feeble hand.

He went to her, his eyes lowered. "Yessum."

"What is your name?"

"James, Missus."

"Look at me, James."

"Masa wouldn't like dat, Missus."

"He is not here, which makes me the master, and I asked you to look at me," she said.

Jimmy raised his head and respectfully returned her gaze. Annoyance gleamed in her eyes at the mention of the masa. Her eyes softened. "You are a brave man, James, to have done what you did for me. In my shame, you showed me humanity. The kindness you showed me I do not deserve, after the treatment you've endured here."

"Et be de right thing to do, Missus."

"Why did you show me mercy?"

"'Cause what de masa did to you ain't right. We've all been victims of his darkness."

She scanned his face for a moment. "James, will you help me end my life?"

He fell back as if the earth trembled under him, disturbed by her request. "What?"

Tears brimmed in her eyes. "My husband is the devil himself and we all know what he is capable of. I cannot spend the rest of my life forgotten, lying in my own waste. I ask you to show me mercy one more time." She ended on a sob.

"Missus, I could never do dat."

"Why? You could have your revenge. Isn't it what you all have always wanted?"

"No, Missus. Some may see it dat way, but not me. All I ever wanted is to be free. Free to plant my own garden. Sit on my own porch and see my daughter grow widout de fear of what tomorrow holds."

She cocked her head, regarding the man who stood before her. "Very well then, you are dismissed."

"Yes, Missus." He hastily departed without a second glance.

He had been in the field an hour when the shot rang out. Dropping his bag of cotton, he ran at full speed toward the house. The missus no longer sat on the porch. As he approached, Lucy was coming out of the house. A sickening feeling filled him, but Lucy wore a look of satisfaction.

He barreled past her, shouting, "What have you done, you fool?"

He found the missus in her room, sitting in her chair, her

long, slender fingers linked around a gun. Her empty, lifeless eyes stared at him as the blood gushed from a hole in the side of her head.

Terrified, panicking, he dashed from the house and found Lucy sauntering along with a sway of satisfaction in her step. Slaves were gathering, curious about what had happened. He gripped her roughly by the shoulder and swung her around. Her eyes went wide with shock and fright at his sudden aggressiveness.

"Dis is de end of us all when de masa gits here!" he shouted, sending her reeling backward with a hard poke to her shoulder.

His mind was frantic with worry. His thoughts ran to Mag. "We need to leave—now!"

Then he heard the hooves tearing at the ground and whirled. The masa and three other men were galloping up the drive. It was too late. Jimmy knew in the pit of his stomach that life was over for them.

"All you pigs, here now!" the masa bellowed as he swung himself from the saddle to drop heavily to the ground.

The few slaves left on the plantation assembled in the yard. *Mag must be playing somewhere,* Jimmy thought, not seeing her anywhere near. He prayed she would not show her face; maybe the masa wouldn't notice her absence, and she would escape what was coming.

"You have all been sold," the masa said nonchalantly.

A buzz went up amongst the slaves. Jimmy's heart dropped. Dread filled him.

The men stepped forward and started chaining up the slaves.

"Papa?" a little voice called, and Mag's small hand slipped into his.

He stared down into the angelic face of his little girl; she stared back at him with uncertainty. As chains were slapped around his neck Jimmy started to resist, but stopped when Mag started to cry in terror.

Masa stepped up and scowled contemptuously at Jimmy. "The child goes with the other group, to be sold to the plantation in Virginia."

"No!" Jimmy cried.

"I told you you would pay, nigger." A sneer curled the corner of his mouth.

Bound with chains around his ankles, wrists, and neck, Jimmy was unable to stop them. Mag was led to the small group of mangled old slaves to have child-size chains fastened around her delicate neck. The slave traders left her feet and wrists unchained, figuring she was no threat and she would only slow them down.

As the group of slaves was led away, she looked back at her father with tears pouring down her dirty cheeks. "Papa, I want to go with you. Please, Papa, I'll be good!" she begged over and over until her tiny voice faded out.

His legs could no longer hold him. He crumpled to the ground in anguish. He pounded his fist in the dirt, wailing as he rocked back and forth, calling out her name.

# CHAPTER Eleven

## Willow

THE DAY OF THE PICNIC WAS A PERFECT SUMMER DAY. A LIGHT breeze rolled in from the ocean, leaving the waves to splash angrily back and forth against the shoreline. Noisy gulls soared low, scavenging for food. Little crabs scuttled over the sand, building their homes. I let the hypnotic, peaceful sound of the ocean carry me away to the times in my childhood when Father brought me here to play. They were the happy memories between Father and me.

It was only when I grew older and began to question the ways of life that our relationship changed. The playful father of my youth was no more, and with every passing day he drew further away from me while at the same time, his grip had tightened on me. I lost the freedom to venture off, as I had once done. He filled my daily life with responsibilities at the plantation that would keep me busy and isolated. Friends were few and far between. If it wasn't for Mary Grace, Mammy, and Jimmy, I might have gone crazy out of loneliness.

But today—I was determined to make the most of it. There was so much activity around me, and laughter and cheerful voices filled the air. Tables were set up with a bountiful feast prepared by the young ladies and their mothers. Girls sat giggling and socializing as they picked at the plates of food resting on their laps. Others were locked in a friendly though competitive game of croquet. Courting couples stood off to the side, engrossed in each other, shutting out the world around them.

"Willow!" someone called.

I scanned the crowd in search of the caller, and my eyes finally fell on Julia Matthews, who excitedly waved me over to her and her friends, who stood observing me.

"Hello, Julia." I embraced her wholeheartedly, then stepped back to nod politely at the others.

Julia was jolly and inviting, always seeing the best in people, which I appreciated. Eyeing up the two girls with her, Josephine and Lucille, I momentarily speculated about why Julia was friends with them; they were so distinctively different from her. Josephine was stuck up and snooty, with her nose always turned up, giving the appearance she thought she was better than everyone. Lucille was negative, condescending, and one of the town chinwags. If she laid eyes on you when in town, she would be sure to fill you in on the latest gossip. I dreaded it when I saw her coming.

Turning my awareness back to Julia, I admired her strawberry blonde hair, which was neatly pulled back into a French braid, with wisps and tendrils framing her pretty freckled face. "It has been far too long, Julia," I said. "What is new with you?"

"Well..." She paused, then continued. "I'm getting married this year. In a few months, in fact." A sudden gloom fell over her.

"What!" My mouth gaped in astonishment.

"Now that Pa is gone, and with my brother deciding to join the Army without a second thought for Mother and me, we have sold everything here and are moving to Ontario, Canada. My mother has arranged a marriage for me with her friend's son," she declared, though her expression revealed she was disheartened with her new state of affairs.

"Have you even met this man?" My brows narrowed.

"Once, when we were children. He was shy and an awful bore," she moaned, casting a forlorn look at the other girls. They hung on her every word, as if hoping to suck out the bubbly, positive energy Julia usually exuded. They drove me insane!

If I ever married, I would marry for love. No matter what Father said, I would never be forced into a marriage to a man I didn't know or love. I found it impossible to imagine being bound to the same man for a lifetime without love.

"Oh, I'm so sorry," I said, not knowing how to comfort her. Sometimes life took an unexpected turn and you had to roll with the punches. But I would do more of the punching before I would let life lead me down that path.

"Well, enough about my sorrows. Let's enjoy our freedom while it lasts, shall we?" She beamed, revealing the girl I regarded with such esteem.

"Hello, ladies." A tall, slender woman approached us. She wore a pale green silk gown adorned with some of the modern details that were trending in Paris. The gown gathered in at the waistline, showing off her tiny waist.

"Whitney!" Julia squealed, gathering her into a massive hug. The newcomer returned her hug, adding a sincere caress of her own back.

Turning to us, Julia introduced her. "Girls, I'd like you to meet Whitney Barry; she recently moved here from Boston to live with her pa on his plantation. This is Willow, Josephine, and Lucille."

"Welcome," we said together.

"So, why did you move here? If you didn't live with your own father in Boston, whom did you live with?" Lucille, being Lucille, wasted no time and got right down to picking for information. She was probably already forming a list in her head of those she would race off to find first to share her new gossip.

Whitney didn't seem fazed at all by Lucille's blunt questions. "I went to live with my auntie in New York after my mother passed. I was twelve. Then a few years later my pa returned and moved me to Boston again to care for the twins he had with his second wife. After she passed from cholera last year, he moved us here."

"What was it like, having two mothers?" Josephine asked.

The girls were so meddlesome with their questions! I waited apprehensively to see how Whitney would respond.

Lifting long fingers to toss a stray auburn ringlet over her shoulder, she answered disdainfully, "Didn't have any use for the likes of my stepmother. She didn't have a motherly bone in her body." Her lively green eyes flashed.

There was something captivating about this woman, I thought as I watched her conversing, her hands moving wildly to punctuate her points. I laughed to myself; that was a trait we shared. I liked this girl.

As we all continued chatting, Whitney's voice grew louder, excited. Was she starved for female company? At one point, she eagerly reached out and touched my arm. "Father tells me we are neighbors. I'll stop by sometime for tea."

I was taken aback by her boldness. Was this how they did things in Boston? She seemed unaware how impolite it was to ask herself over without a proper invitation. Even so, Whitney Barry intrigued me, despite her rough edges. "Why, yes, we are," I replied. "Your plantation isn't but a thirty minute ride from ours."

"Ladies," a masculine voice interrupted.

Knox and Bowden strolled up, to my dismay and the others' obvious pleasure. We made room in our circle for the men.

"Bowden!" Josephine purred in a saccharine voice, peering up at him, eyelashes fluttering. I cringed, annoyed by such behavior.

Bowden gave her a polite nod and turned his attention to Julia. "News has reached my ears that you are leaving us."

Julia produced an exaggerated pout—giving Knox the perfect opportunity to chime in. Swiping his hat from his sandy-blond head, he dropped to one knee and snatched Julia's hand to his chest. "Don't go! Marry me!" he pleaded. "All the girls want to marry a Southern gentleman like me. I'm a catch. The ladies are lining up at my door. I'm having to beat them off with sticks."

This brought gales of laughter, and I found myself laughing too. He was clever and charismatic and knew how to use both to his advantage

Julia blushed. Always the good sport, she pulled her hand back and held it over her heart, assuming an expression of dismay. "Why, Knox Tucker, I would never marry the likes of you, with all your seducing of the female kind." Acting appalled, she lifted her chin and turned her head away, dismissing him.

Knox chuckled and rose, giving her a wink. "But I had you considering, right?"

Eyebrows raised, Whitney regarded Knox. "Really?"

"What?" he said with a slight smirk. There was a glint in his eyes as he sized up the bold woman before him.

"This is how you aim to court? Are you sure the women aren't knocking you off with a stick?" She let out an unladylike snort. Yet all the while she was challenging him, she was regarding him with interest.

Oh, how I liked this girl! I found myself chuckling.

Julia giggled, linking her arm through Whitney's. "Gentlemen, meet Whitney Barry."

"It's a pleasure to make your acquaintance." Bowden offered his hand, which Whitney accepted with a firm handshake.

I found myself studying Bowden—the tanned face from long

days in the sun, the strawberry birthmark tracing along his jawline, the dark curls that feathered back from his face and tucked behind his ears. Realizing I was gawking, I promptly looked away. "Well, if you all will excuse me," I said abruptly, "I promised Father I would be back soon." Father wasn't expecting me home for hours. Once again, the awkwardness I felt when I was around Bowden sent me running like a coward. Saying my goodbyes, I extended a proper invite to Whitney to stop by Livingston for a visit soon.

I made it a hundred paces before I heard him call, "Willow?"

I grudgingly turned as Bowden jogged up to me. "Yes?"

"I wanted to speak to you, and I hope you will stay long enough to hear me out." He shifted his feet uneasily.

Not finding words to form a reply, I stood in silence.

"I'm sorry. I know, I've said it before, but I mean it. We were foolish children. I've never forgiven myself and, it appears, neither have you. I wish I could take it back. Can you please forgive me so we can somehow move past this and be friends? I would sure hate to spend the next decade with you hating me." His face reflected sincerity and regret, making my heart leap with mixed emotions.

I'd spent so many years reliving that embarrassing day. He was a constant reminder of the humiliation I'd endured. Today he pleaded for forgiveness, and I knew he meant it. *Why, today, do I feel different? Why do I see now how tiring this anger I have chosen to bear has become? Now he stands here asking to be friends, and God knows I am short on friends.* Unsure how to deal with all the sensations welling up inside of me, I remained quiet.

"Please, Willow." His eyes beseeched me.

"Very well then, Mr. Armstrong," I said, turning and walking toward the wagon.

I found our driver, Isaiah, leaning against one of the wagon's wheels, his hat pulled over his face. The wagon was loaded with the supplies Father had requested. I nudged the sleeping man's shoulder. "I'm ready to go home, Isaiah," I said, suddenly drained of all energy.

Instantly wide-awake, he leapt up. "Already, Miss?"

"Yes. I'm feeling fatigued today."

I couldn't refrain from sending one last glance in Bowden's direction. He stood with his hands tucked into his pockets and his eyes latched onto me. The soft smile he gave me activated the butterflies in my stomach.

"Miss." Isaiah offered a hand, which I gladly took. He helped me into the wagon, then scrambled up beside me, and we started our long journey home.

# CHAPTER *Twelve*

I DRANK IN THE WELCOMING BEAUTY OF LIVINGSTON AS WE TURNED the bend. It briefly took my mind from the swaying and rocking of the wagon as we drove down the lane. My body ached from the ride. I wished we'd been permitted to take a carriage, as it was a swifter and more comfortable ride. But Father had allowed me to attend the picnic on one condition: that I save him a trip and pick up the needed supplies.

"Isaiah, I'll get off here. I'd like to walk."

"Yessum." He pulled the wagon to a stop, and I thanked him and climbed down. Isaiah clicked his tongue and the horses carried on.

I cut through the trees and across the fields lying fallow, heading toward the forge in search of Jimmy. I found him bent over, examining a horse's hoof, muttering and cursing under his breath.

"Good afternoon, Jimmy."

"Ah...Miss Willie." He straightened. The wrinkles mapping his face showed years of hardship; the emptiness I sometimes saw in his eyes held the secrets to his past. But now his face glowed with delight at the sight of me. "What can I help you wid today, young lady?" He set the tools he held down on his work station.

I laughed lightly. "Besides wanting to be in your easy company?"

"I allus happy to see you, Miss Willie."

Leaning against his work bench, I picked up a hammer and twirled it around in my hands before moving forward with what I came to discuss. "Today, Bowden Armstrong apologized again for when we were children." I heaved a sigh.

"And?" He wiped his hands on his apron.

"Well, I feel he means it and maybe it's time I forgave him. I've been carrying this humiliation and anger for too long. The thing is, I'm not sure how to let it go." The animosity I'd carried for so many years had become a protection I hid behind, I realized.

"One day at a time, Miss Willie, dat's all you can do. You gotta live for each mornin' in hopes of a better day." His mind seemed to drift a million miles away, and the face I held so dear grew sullen. What was drawing his attention to another moment in time? What pain had he bottled up and locked away as a way to deal with life?

"You're right, Jimmy. You're always right." I gently took his hand in mine, bringing his focus back to me.

He jerked. He didn't wear his emotions for others to see, and he showed his discomfort at my gesture of affection. I released his hand, smiling softly at him. "Jimmy, you have never told me whether you had a family or not."

The sadness returned and I was certain his thoughts had wandered to someone a moment ago. "I was married once. My Nellie, she passed away soon after our gal was born. Den de masa lost evvything and sold us off. Split me from me gal. Dat was de last time I seed my Mag." Grief shone in his eyes. Picking up his farrier tool, he turned away, wiping a tear from his eye.

"I never knew you had a daughter." He had never mentioned this before! I sensed he wanted to be left alone and gave him the respect he deserved. Leaving him to his thoughts, I said goodbye.

Thoughts of Jimmy's Mag carried my own thoughts away.

The cruelty of the slave world was so unfair. What made men think they could own other men? What right did they have to tear families apart? To rape the women because they were black and their pain meant nothing? The suffering of the Negro race I witnessed in this way of life sickened and angered me. I swore to myself that I'd make a difference in this cruel and unjust world I lived in. I was but one voice, but I would use it to effect changes. Starting with the promise I made to Mary Grace when we were little girls, regarding her freedom.

Entering the house, I found Father in his study going over his financials. Driven by the pain I'd seen in Jimmy's eyes, I found the courage to approach Father with the question I had been planning to ask him for years.

"Hello, Father. We have the supplies you requested."

"I saw the wagon pull up. You are back so soon?" He flipped through the pages of his ledger without glancing up.

"Yes, I was tired."

He frowned and I'm sure he wondered why I'd fought so hard to go, only to cut my day short.

"There is something I wanted to ask you."

"Yes?"

"I want to free Mary Grace." There, I'd said it! I gripped the layers of my skirt to mop my sweaty palms. I stood waiting for his reaction, heart pounding.

Father coughed and sputtered. "Excuse me. Would you please repeat yourself?"

I swallowed hard and my body tensed, but I wouldn't allow him to intimidate me. "I want to give Mary Grace her freedom."

"We don't free slaves, Willow. How do you suppose we would run this plantation without them? What of our livelihood?"

"She's been a trusted servant and I promised her her freedom."

"You *what?*" he shouted. Rising, he leaned on his desk, one fist balled and his face filled with rage.

"I told her I would free her," I whispered.

"I am the master of this plantation. You will quit this talk of freeing slaves, Willow, if you value your life." I saw fear in his eyes, which puzzled me.

"She's been good to me."

"She has to be, or she would find herself hung from one of those oak trees out there!" he bellowed, flinging his hand toward the window.

"It's not right," I said timidly.

He lifted his hand abruptly and struck me across the face with such force, it sent me reeling backward. I cried out then stood stunned, my hand cupped to my stinging face, tears spilling.

I found my legs and flew from the room and up the spiraling staircase, tripping over my skirt in my haste to get as far away from my father as possible.

In the safety of my room, I collapsed onto the bed, horrified at what had happened. Never had he struck me like that before. This time I'd pushed him too far. Burying my face in the silk sheets, I clutched at them with my fist. All the pain, rejection, and abandonment I felt at my father's action flowed out as hopeless sobs.

# CHAPTER *Thirteen*

I HAD DRIFTED OFF IN A SOB-INDUCED SLUMBER WHEN A LIGHT TAP AT the door woke me. My muscles were taut and cramped from the hours of crying. The door opened; I recognized Mammy's heavy tread that made the floorboards creak. The bed moved under Mammy's weight as she sat down.

Her voice came softly. "Mammy's here, chile."

I sat up and looked into the eyes that held deep affection for me. Then I flung myself into her arms as I'd often done as a small girl, and lay my head on her shoulder. Finding the safety I longed for, the tears I thought were spent flowed anew. I felt like a broken child.

"It'll be all right, angel gal." She wrapped me in her embrace.

"How, Mammy? When will this world ever be all right? It's an evil world filled with so much pain and suffering. You know this best of all." Pulling back, I beheld the face of the woman I loved like a mother. Years of hardship had prematurely grayed her hair and etched deep wrinkles in her forehead and around her mouth.

"We can't luk at et dat way, Miss Willow, or we may as well lay down and die. Life ain't worth livin' if you don't have hope and dreams. Et jus' ain't."

Life experiences had made Mammy wise. I trusted her wisdom.

"You and your people have suffered so many wrongs. I love

this place, but how can I when what the South stands for makes my stomach sick? Am I to go about my life turning a blind eye to the horrors I witness? I don't know where I belong anymore."

"Shh, Miss Willow, don't be lettin' your pappy hear you or I'll be hangin' from a rope and you be taken to de woodshed." She nervously cast an eye at the door.

"I hate him."

"Hate is a mighty strong feelin', Miss Willow. And et be eatin' at your soul. Et be a disease dat will eat you up from de inside out. Et will overshadow de good in you. De good you can do in dis world."

"What can I do in this world, Mammy? I'm a useless woman in a man's world. Every time I try to have a voice, Father shuts me down." Misery vanquished me and I slumped in her arms.

"You don't fail until you give up, chile. Your heart be pure and you love human life, no matter de color of deir skin. Be wise and use dat voice wid anyone dat will listen. You got a passion dat runs through your blood like a hot iron. One day dis plantation be yours and den, chile, den you can take your stand. You jus' got to be patient."

"Patient!" I raised my voice. "Your people have been waiting years for freedom. Years for a fair shake at life. Years to be in control of your own lives."

"Hush, chile. Calm down now." She grabbed my hand, trying to quiet me. "You may not change evvy nigra's life. But you changed de lives of slaves on dis plantation right here. You are hope. Hope dat things can change. You are our hope." Tears ran down her plump face.

In all my years, I had never seen Mammy cry. Hope? The slaves at Livingston looked to me for hope for change? Had I been so wrong to think I, merely a woman, was incapable of bringing about change? Yes, I would begin here at my own home and bide my time.

My earlier gloom faded away and I smiled with a renewed faith. "Oh, Mammy, you are so right. My thinking was so foolish and childish. I will start here on Livingston, applying changes wherever I can. My father will be a problem, but I will find a way to outsmart him." I smiled wickedly. Grabbing Mammy's face, I peppered her cheeks with kisses. "You are brilliant."

Mammy swatted me off. "Now, mind your manners," she said, feigning disapproval over all the fuss. She shuffled to the door, where she turned and shot me a toothy smile. As the door closed behind her, I heard her soft chuckle.

As she wandered down the corridor, she began to sing.

*Swing low, sweet chariot*

*Comin' for to carry me home...*

# CHAPTER *Fourteen*

"Mary Grace, you git out and help de womens git de laundry hung out so et be dry before evenin'," Mammy bellowed from the kitchen house as Mary Grace and I tried to slip into the laundry outbuilding undetected by Mammy.

Mary Grace groaned at being caught. Mammy often said she had eyes in the back of her head, and as children we believed her. We would try to catch Mammy with her head rag off, hoping to see the extra pair of eyes.

Mary Grace beckoned me to follow her and we ducked into the kitchen, where Mammy was chopping vegetables for the evening meal. The scent of rosemary, thyme, and garlic-braised meat filled the kitchen with an enticing aroma. Tucked in our aprons were fresh bunches of lemongrass, mint, and bayberries. "I'm sorry, Mama, I lost track of time," Mary Grace said as we placed our collection into jars on a nearby shelf. "I'll get right to the laundry."

"Dat is a good gal. Now git gwine. You have dillydallied long 'nuf. De other womens be back soon and we don't need dem squawking 'bout you."

Mary Grace popped a chunk of carrot into her mouth as she passed the table on her way out the back door. Mammy swiped at her hand. "Go on, gal."

Mary Grace lifted the basket of damp kitchen linens.

Tucking them under her arm, she effortlessly sailed out the door.

I giggled at their playful back and forth and leaned against the kitchen-house door frame, looking out over the yard.

The backyard of the main house was alive with hundreds of slaves performing their daily duties. Stablemen pushed wheelbarrows overflowing with hay toward the stables. Owen and Parker sawed away on wood that was most likely destined to be new furniture for the main house. The coopers were making barrels for father's warehouses. Jimmy and the other blacksmiths had the forge piping out the heat, readying it to form and repair tools. And it was again laundry day at the plantation, so the washerwomen carried baskets of freshly washed clothes into the yard from the river. Infants were strapped to the backs of mothers as they went about their tasks. Children too young to work in the fields darted around everyone as they played. The slaves sang a familiar tune as they worked, which filled the yard and carried on to the fields.

*Deep river, my home is over Jordan,*
*Deep river, Lord, I want to cross over into campground.*
*Don't you want to go to that Gospel feast,*
*That promised land where all is peace.*
*Deep river, Lord, I want to cross over into campground.*

Jones, our overseer, sat upon his horse with a whip in hand. I'd seen him serve out punishments, but never had I seen him use his whip. The man never found any pleasure in cruelty and the slaves respected him for it. There were the rebellious slaves, but overall most performed the tasks set out for them. I'd heard the slaves speaking amongst themselves, and most said Jones was the better of the overseers they'd had. There was no talk of him bedding the slave women or children. Father trusted him more than an employee. I often saw them deep in conversation, falling silent when I came near.

I looked toward the riverbank, where a schooner had docked and its passengers, a colored man and a white man, stepped onto the dock. They started toward the main house and, curious about our unexpected guests, I bid Mammy a good day and hurried to enter the house.

Entering through the French doors off the library, I heard voices in Father's study. I recognized Father's and the other's, as well—Bowden Armstrong.

"Good day, sir," I heard Bowden say. "I was hoping to arrange a marriage joining your household with mine."

Heat flushed through my body. The nerve of this man, that he would think for a second my forgiveness meant I would consider marrying him! I marched to the open door of the study and stepped imperiously inside.

"What are you proposing?" Father asked as he caught sight of me. He raised a hand to stop me from barging in.

I wasn't sure why I obeyed, but I paused as Bowden turned to look at me.

"Good day, Willow." He smiled politely, but it faded quickly as he saw my sour expression.

"Hello, Bowden." I leveled a glare at him as I struggled to restrain my tongue.

"I was going to propose to your father the marriage of Gray and Mary Grace."

What? Mary Grace? "Oh."

Bowden frowned, then realization lifted his brow; flustered, he stumbled over his next words to Father. "Wha-what do you say, Mr. Hendricks?"

"I understand the two have an interest in each other, and with our plantations being so close, I think it would be a good union," Father replied. "You do realize any children born to the two would be the property of Livingston?"

"Yes, sir. I know this union to be the desire of Gray and Mary Grace. Gray is my most trusted right-hand man and I wish to make him happy."

My father tilted his head as he studied the man before him. "We will make the arrangement sooner rather than later, and I will have a cabin prepared for your slave's marital visits."

The men shook on the agreement, and it was as simple as that. Mary Grace was to marry whether she was ready to or not. I left the house through the doors I had used to enter.

Gray had found Mary Grace. I stopped and watched the exchange. Mary Grace squealed and threw her arms around Gray's neck. He had her approval, and I smiled at her happiness.

# CHAPTER *Fifteen*

Whitney Barry was coming for a visit today, and I found myself wishing the morning away in anticipation of her arrival. Days on end spent cooped up on the plantation dulled my mind.

As Whitney's open carriage turned down the lane, I stepped out onto the veranda and descended the front steps. The fragrance of the red climbing roses infused the air, filling my nose with their heady scent as I walked down the path to greet my guest. A bright smile widened my cheeks as her carriage came to a stop at the carriage stone.

"Whitney, it's so nice to see you again!"

"I was counting down the days. Plantation life has made me question my sanity." Whitney waved away the hand her driver offered and step out.

"Mammy has prepared some refreshments and left them in the music room. Afterwards, we can walk the grounds and I will show you around."

"Sounds lovely."

As we entered the house, Whitney let out an unladylike whistle. I turned to find Whitney taking in our home with wide eyes. She stopped and brushed her fingers over the head of one of the gold lion statues that stood in the central passage, which Father had purchased while in India. Her eyes traveled up to the crystal chandelier in the middle of the high ceiling, where it caught the light coming in from the windows and refracted it as bright diamonds across the mahogany ceiling and walls.

"Goodness, Willow. I heard talk of how well off you were, but this is a palace!"

My mouth sagged open and heat surged through me at her impolite reference to our financial status. "Whitney Barry! Where did you ever learn your manners?"

Whitney chuckled, brushing me off with a wave of her hand. "Aunt Em taught me all the proper ways of a lady, and I use etiquette when needed, but honestly, I have no use for the uppity airs of 'ladies and gentlemen.' You need to learn to relax. This is our life to live and I, for one, will be dictated to by no one."

I admired her determination to avoid stereotypes; in her, I found a kindred spirit.

"Your father doesn't breathe down your neck about your untraditional ways?"

She shrugged half-heartedly. "Art Barry is simply a man who conceived me with my mother. His heart is black and his mind is twisted. If it wasn't for the twins, I would get as far away from him as possible." Whitney's shoulders slumped as she spoke of the reality of her situation.

Something else we had in common—our relationship with our fathers.

In the music room, Mammy had neatly arranged bite-size cakes and tea biscuits on a golden platter to accompany our Earl Grey tea, and left it all on the small cherry-wood table in the corner, where we could look through a large window draped with red- and gold-striped curtains at the lush gardens.

Whitney took a long sip of her tea, and then another. "This tea is delightful. Where did you obtain it from?"

"Father imports it from London. You can purchase it from the general store in town. But I will be sure to have some delivered to you."

Whitney smiled her appreciation. "I'm so happy to have met you. I never took much to girls I've met in the past, but you are quite different."

"I assure you, the feeling is mutual."

"I couldn't help but notice there are no pictures of your family hanging on the walls."

"We have but a few," I replied. "One is in the parlor, over the fireplace; it's Father and me when I was a small girl. And there is one of me in the library that Father had painted when I was fifteen."

"Nothing of your mother?"

"No." I'd once asked Father this question, but he had deflected it and I'd never received an answer.

"Doesn't it seem strange to you? I mean, people generally keep portraits of their family and ancestors on their walls."

"I know little of my mother. What little I learned of her came from the slaves who were here when she was alive. Father never speaks of her. When I try to ask about her, he gets agitated. I have learned not to speak her name."

"Do you remember her at all?"

"No, but I do know from Mammy that I was a few years old when she died. Mammy did say I was her joy, and she would carry me on her hip for hours and sing to me. I try not to think of her too much, as the pain becomes unbearable." I lowered my eyes to my cup. "I used to ask God why he took her, a parent who loved me, and left me with one who barely tolerates me." My voice broke with emotion.

"Forgive me for bringing it up." She lightly grasped my hand.

"I'm fine, don't worry about it. We can relate to each other in the yearning for the love of a mother and the ache of being left with fathers who don't know we exist."

"Though I haven't met your father, Willow, I've only heard good about him."

"I witness this good. But why can he not give the same kindness to his own daughter?" I had tried to figure this out most of my life.

"I hope for your sake that he will somehow learn to give you the love you seek. Please find peace in the fact that there is goodness in him somewhere, unlike my father."

A cloud of melancholy settled over us both.

Knowing I needed to turn this visit around, I swept my arms wide in a grand gesture. "All right, let's rid ourselves of these heavy thoughts! Let me show you the grounds."

People loved the peace and beauty Livingston provided, and I wanted my first visit with Whitney to be a success. We spent the rest of the morning and part of the afternoon laughing and covering every inch of the plantation.

Before Whitney stepped into her carriage to head home, she turned to me and said, "Willow, I find that in you, I've found a true friend."

Her words touched my heart.

"Of all the girls I met while away at school half my life, I never felt a connection to anyone until you came into my life with your backward ways. I believe you to be part woman and part man," I said. Whitney shook with laughter.

We promised to visit each other again soon as she climbed into the carriage.

"All of this…" she looked around "…should fill you with pride. Your slaves are happy and, I daresay, almost content. This should make you see the good in your father. Bad men don't run this kind of plantation."

I stood at the end of the path until her carriage was long gone, evaluating her words.

# CHAPTER Sixteen

## Whitney's Story

SHE HAD RECENTLY CELEBRATED HER THIRTEENTH YEAR WHEN HER mother died. After his wife's death, her father disappeared for long periods of time, and Whitney was left to fend for herself. Art Barry had been a drunk from her earliest memories. He would often come home drunk and, like a madman, turn the house upside down, destroying the precious few possessions they had. When his intoxicated eyes fixed on Whitney, her mother would step between them, taking the brunt of his violence.

Bella Barry had been born with a compromised immune system, leaving her weak and feeble. Doctors said Bella wouldn't reach the age of thirty. After the beatings, her already depleted body would leave her bedridden for days.

Bella took a turn for the worse and the doctor ordered strict bed rest, informing Whitney her mother wouldn't recover. They couldn't afford a nurse to care for her mother around the clock, as required, so Whitney dropped out of school to care for her. Art was absent more often, leaving Whitney as the sole caregiver for her mother. Whitney took up permanent residence in a rocker by her mother's bedside, and spent hours reading to her. She savored the few precious hours her mother was alert. Whitney would climb into her mother's bed after she had fallen asleep, snuggling against her and whispering her love. She cried herself to sleep many nights, filled with worry and fear about what life would be like without her mother, the only sure person in her life.

When the day came, her mother opened her eyes and smiled faintly at her. Whitney knew her condition had changed yet again. Her skin was hot to the touch and a gurgling sound was coming from her chest. Bella lifted a trembling hand to motion her daughter closer.

"Yes, Mother?" Whitney said, taking her mother's hand between hers.

"My beautiful Whitney, my time on this earth is almost up," she whispered.

Whitney remembered holding her breath until her chest felt as if it was going to burst. Her head filled with pain from the lack of oxygen.

"You must care for yourself now, darling. You can't stay with your father; he isn't right in the mind." A tear escaped her eye and she closed her eyes as she continued. "I'm sorry for bringing you into a world where he is your father. Never forget my love for you. You're the greatest blessing in my life. I wrote a letter to my sister Emily, and requested she take you in when I'm gone. She will care for you as if you are her own—" She'd stiffened and moaned as pain wracked her body.

Whitney administered the black drops prescribed by the doctor, and soon her mother's body relaxed. The two held each other until her mother fell off into a sleep from which she never awakened.

Whitney was left to contact the coroner to come and take her mother's body. There was no funeral, as her father had isolated her mother from the world. In the weeks that followed, Art Barry never returned. Whitney sent a letter to her Aunt Em in New York, hoping she would arrive quickly, and in the meantime she cared for herself, finding creative ways to make the meager supply of food in the house last; but with the lack of nutrition she became lethargic.

When the knock sounded at the door, she slowly shuffled toward it. Standing on the front steps was a smiling Aunt Em, there to rescue her from this life of loneliness and misery. One glance at the condition of her niece, and her smile faded. Whitney tumbled into her arms and sobbed, letting out all the worry, fear, and pain she felt. Aunt Em had soothed her that day with the promise that she was going to care for her and she would never leave her.

Her aunt was an independent, self-made woman who had never married. In Whitney's younger years, the few times her father had permitted her aunt to visit were happy times, and Whitney remembered her mother's laughter, frequent and light with joy. Emily, unlike her sister, could hold her own. Whitney believed her aunt's strong personality intimidated her father, prompting him to cut off all visits from her.

Whitney thought of her mother and longed for her often, though life with her aunt was better than she could ever dream. Never having children of her own, Emily doted on Whitney. Whitney's new lifestyle involved a grand social life, and her aunt made sure she never wanted for anything. She learned to be a proper lady in every way. She aspired one day to be a woman of worth like her aunt. She promised herself she would never allow a man like her father in her life. No one would control her life or lay a hand on her again. She blocked him from her memories, allowing herself to believe her life before coming to live with her aunt had consisted of only herself and her mother.

Around her sixteenth birthday, her father came back into her life. She was relaxing with a good book in her room when she heard loud voices downstairs. Dread rose in her at the sound of his voice. Pulling on the strength and courage she had developed, she left her room and stopped at the top of the staircase to listen.

At that height and distance, she could push down the desire to flee as her eyes came to rest on her father. He looked like he had aged ten years. He still wore his hair brushed back and tied with a black ribbon, but now it was fully white. His rounded belly protruded over his narrow hips. Aunt Em and he stood in the foyer, engaged in a heated argument.

"I won't allow it!" her aunt shouted at him. She always spoke her mind to her brother-in-law and that day had been no different.

"She is my daughter and you have no rights!" he snapped back, his face flushed red.

"You abandoned her. It was Bella's wish for her to live with me. For Pete's sake, Art, she is almost grown and has thrived under my care. If you have any love in that cruel heart of yours for your daughter, leave her be."

As Whitney made her way down the stairs, they both became aware of her presence. Art looked in awe at his grown daughter as she swept down the staircase, carrying herself with elegance and grace. She was no longer the tall, lanky, fair-skinned kid with freckles. Though her skin remained fair, it now glowed with a creamy peach complexion. Whitney had blossomed into a striking woman and mirrored her mother's looks for the most part, but she did inherit her father's height.

"Whitney, how I've missed you!" His high-pitched voice cracked. He crossed the short distance and forcefully crushed her to him in an embrace. Surprisingly, he did not reek of alcohol, the usual perfume she had become accustomed to near him.

What could he possibly be doing here? She felt the old, familiar panic rising.

"I have come to take you home." He grinned, revealing a half-toothless smile from too many drunken fights. He left his arm around her shoulders and held her next to him.

She questioned her aunt with her eyes. Her aunt's mouth was pursed and her eyes flashed with anger at her brother-in-law.

Turning her from her aunt's visual daggers, he placed his hands on Whitney's shoulders, holding her at arm's length and inspecting every inch of her. She stared blankly back. "I've come to take you home, my dear," he repeated.

Whitney managed to wriggle out of his grasp. As his words sank in, she grew angry. He thought he could waltz back into her life after all these years and lay claim to her! She was sure of one thing: she never wanted to live under the same roof with this man again.

"Aunt Em has given me a life here, and I do not wish to live with you." She moved to stand by her aunt.

Her father's pleasant façade vanished. "I'm not asking, Whitney."

It was the old Art Barry who retrieved a cigar from his high-end waistcoat pocket and bit off the end, spitting it on the floor. He lit the cigar and struck an arrogant pose while taking a few puffs. Blowing out the last cloud of white smoke, he paused for effect, the cigar held several inches from his mouth, before saying, "You have a new stepmother and we have twins together."

Not sure if she'd heard him correctly, she asked, "Twins?"

"You have a three-year-old brother and sister."

Whitney kept her expression blank as she took in the shocking news. A stepmother and siblings? She had always longed for siblings.

"I'll be back tomorrow. Get your things ready so we can be on our way." He headed for the door and without so much as a goodbye, he closed it briskly behind him.

Whitney's head spun with the news. Feeling her knees weaken, she sank onto the bottom step of the staircase.

Defeated, her aunt lowered herself down beside her, glaring at the closed door. When she turned to Whitney, sadness softened her face. "I promised you I'd protect you from that man. I never dreamed he would come back. I thought he would be glad to be rid of the responsibility of a child. I don't understand why he would come looking after all these years."

Whitney had no answer. She'd never wished to have him back in her life and never thought she would have to consider it. "I know this isn't your doing, but it seems to be out of your control. Maybe he has changed?"

Aunt Em scoffed, her expression dark with disapproval. "There is no way Art Barry has changed. A man like him is incapable of change."

It didn't matter what questions they both had. As he'd promised, Art Barry showed up first thing in the morning in a carriage that drew up at their front door. As the driver loaded her trunks, Whitney clung to her aunt as if trying to soak in the love and protection of her embrace.

"I will write to you every week. I want to thank you for picking me up and caring for me when I was all alone in this world. I won't forget your love." Whitney gazed into her aunt's face, memorizing every angle and nuance, for the future held no promise that they would see each other again.

Her aunt's eyes glittered with tears. "Whitney, my love, you filled my life with purpose. Bella would be proud. Don't forget I'm always here for you, and you are loved more than you will ever know," she whispered as she embraced Whitney. "Stay strong. Don't let him break you."

"I love you, Auntie," she said.

"I love you too, my precious girl. Until we meet again."

As they drove away, Whitney waved frantically until her aunt was no more than a speck in the distance. She did not want to look at the man sitting across from her. He ignored her for the whole trip.

When they arrived in Boston, childhood memories of her hometown flooded Whitney's mind, and she longed for her mother, or the security of her life with Aunt Em. She reckoned neither love nor security waited for her here.

The carriage came to a stop in front of a three-story brick townhouse in one of Boston's affluent neighborhoods.

"This is home," her father said proudly.

Whitney studied the striking house before her. She doubted he had acquired a home of this magnitude by honest means.

The front door opened and a servant in his fifties started down the steps to greet them. Her father, impatient at his slow pace, opened the carriage door and jumped out to walk toward the front steps without any consideration for his daughter.

"Joseph, have Whitney's things brought to her room," he ordered as he strode past the man and disappeared into the house.

Whitney remained unmoving in her seat.

"Miss?" Joseph held out a white-gloved hand to her.

She fought the pressing impulse to run and keep running until she was back at the refuge of her aunt's. She reached out, taking the hand he offered, and stepped out of the carriage. "Thank you, Joseph," she said politely.

Surprise crossed his face, swiftly concealed.

Whitney climbed the stairs and paused at the front door before entering her new home. The foyer was empty of life and no one came to greet her. She wandered through the main floor and ended back at the foyer, having seen no sign of her father.

Seeing her standing there, hesitant about where to go or what to do as he lowered her last trunk to the floor, Joseph said, "Follow me, Miss Whitney." He ambled to the rear of the house and opened a set of French doors, which led to a small, enclosed garden.

Squeals of laughter and little voices hit her as she stepped into the garden. Joseph led her along a cobblestone path to where her father sat at a wrought-iron table, speaking to a woman sitting with her back to Whitney. The two small children chasing a ball around the path drew Whitney's attention. The boy had her father's dark hair and a chubby face. The girl, blonde like the woman with her back to her, was petite and dainty, unlike her brother.

"Miss Whitney is here, Mrs. Barry," Joseph said, bowing to the woman, who did not turn to acknowledge them. Joseph, apparently accustomed to this behavior, excused himself and left.

The woman turned to regard her with hard, dark eyes. Her features were harsh, with high cheekbones, a thin, pointed nose, and a stern mouth that, if the deep creases on either side were any indication, was a normal expression. "Well, you're as tall a man and straight as a beanpole. Not much to you, I see," she said. Whitney would later realize that the woman was jealous that her father had had a child with another woman.

Whitney's father sat in his chair with a smug look on his face, indifferent to his wife's rude treatment of his daughter.

Whitney knew she needed to stand up for herself now, or this woman would make a habit of running her over. "Well, I see your parents must have been part raven, with a face like yours!" she retorted angrily.

Her father had taken a sip of his tea; he coughed and leaned forward, sputtering. Whitney noticed he was watching his wife for her reaction. Could it be her father was intimidated by his wife?

She rose and stood erect, which left her a few inches shorter than Whitney. Reaching out, she struck Whitney across the face.

The sudden attack took Whitney by surprise, but she recovered quickly. Never again would she be mistreated by anyone. As her stepmother raised her hand to strike her a second time, Whitney grabbed her arm and pinned it to her side.

"Don't you ever lay a hand on me again, you little witch!"

Sophie Barry stumbled back, surprised at Whitney's boldness, and shot a look at her husband.

Her father barked at her, "That's enough, Whitney. Go to your room and unpack. Joseph will show you the way. Now leave us."

Whitney dropped an exaggerated curtsy and walked away. Behind her, her stepmother yelled at her father, "Why did you insist on bringing that ill-mannered girl here?"

"You know why. The twins exhaust you and with her here, you will get your freedom."

Ah, his reason for bringing her here had become clear. He hadn't missed her or even wanted her. She was brought there to mother the twins, who had dared burden the two of them with being born.

Over the next four years, the two were rarely home. They traveled the world on business, they claimed. The full responsibility of raising the twins fell to Whitney. The twins were still young enough not to be tainted by their parents' ways. She loved them like her own and they began to depend on her. When their parents were home, it was Whitney they came to for comfort when they woke from bad dreams. It was Whitney they sought out when they were hurt.

Her time spent with Aunt Em had taught her courage and allowed her to discover her own strength. Art and Sophie Barry learned to tread lightly around her, for they needed her. As long as she cared for the children and their absent parents provided money, the arrangement worked for all of them.

Their adventures were cut short when Sophie became gravely ill and had to return home. The doctor visited the house and diagnosed her with cholera; he told Art Barry it was best to send Whitney and the twins away immediately, and ordered Sophie quarantined. Whitney and the children took the next train to New York, where they were to stay with her aunt. No word was sent ahead of them, and Whitney was unsure how Aunt Em would feel about caring for the twins.

Aunt Em was not home when they arrived, but the housemaid appeared more than happy to see Whitney, and let them in. Her aunt was expected in a few days, the maid told her. Whitney longed to stay in New York, but she knew she could never leave her brother and sister.

She was curled up in the library in front of the fireplace reading when the front door opened. Whitney heard the maid greet her aunt and leapt up to run out and see her.

"Aunt Em!" Whitney flew into her arms, kissing her face over and over in her excitement.

Though stunned to find her there, Aunt Em laughed under Whitney's affectionate attack. "Dear girl, what are you doing here?"

"Sophie has cholera and the doctor told Father to send us away." She released her aunt and stepped back to regard her. She hadn't aged a day in the last four years.

"Us?"

Whitney shifted uncomfortably and looked at her aunt with beseeching eyes. "The twins have come with me. They have no one but me."

"It's all right, dear. I know how much you have grown to love those children." She removed her hat and, taking Whitney's arm, retired to the sitting room.

The months spent with her aunt were glorious, and the

twins came to adore her. The happiness they found together ended when their father sent word that Sophie had died, and he had sold the townhouse; the family would be moving to Charleston, South Carolina, where he had purchased a plantation. Whitney was not sure how her father had moved from rags to riches, but she was certain it wasn't through legal methods.

Whitney and her aunt once again exchanged goodbyes, and the three siblings made the long journey south, leaving the city life behind. The twins cuddled against Whitney as the train left New York, en route to a new and uncertain life with an unpredictable father.

# CHAPTER *Seventeen*

THE FOLLOWING SUNDAY, THE SLAVES' ONE DAY OFF, MARY GRACE and Gray jumped the broom. Mary Grace wore a simple, white cotton dress and a lace veil held in place with a crown of daisies. Earlier that morning I'd applied shea butter to her long, raven-black hair and brushed it until it was smooth and shiny. She'd pulled it back from her heart-shaped face and held it with a simple pin. She was the image of a beautiful, glowing bride.

Father forbade me from attending the wedding, as it was a slave celebration, he said. I spent the afternoon in my room, where my window provided the best view of the slave quarters.

On an old wooden table stood the five-tier wedding cake that I'd insisted Mammy let me help her make. It was white to honor the purity of the day, with each tier decorated with edible flowers in shades of pink and mauve. People danced and clapped to the fiddler's songs, celebrating in genuine happiness for the couple. Their joyous laughter filled the evening air.

I watched as Mary Grace lovingly kissed her groom, then let the curtain fall and leaned back on the window seat, feeling a little sad at how things would change between us, now that Mary Grace was a wife. How time had flown! We were no longer children, and with age came expectations. I was concerned about what Father would try to do about my unwed situation.

With the nightgown I'd purchased for Mary Grace for her wedding night tucked under my arm, I headed downstairs.

Mammy entered the house from the celebration, her face aglow with happiness. "Et's a blessed day, angel gal, a blessed day!" she sang.

"That it is."

"Dat Gray will make my gal happy."

"He is a good man, and dashingly handsome," I said with a smile.

"Dat he is, chile!" Mammy chuckled, her large body shaking. Noticing the package I held under my arm, she asked, "What do you have dere?"

"It's a new nightgown for Mary Grace."

"You're a good gal, Miss Willow. A real fine gal. You best git movin' if you are wantin' to catch her 'fore she leaves. Your pappy done gave her a pass. She gwine to Gray's cabin on de Armstrong Plantation for de night."

I scooted out the door, hoping to catch Mary Grace before they left.

Finding Mary Grace seated upon Gray's horse and Gray about to swing himself up, I called out, "Mary Grace!" and waved, trying to grab their attention. Gathering my dress, I ran toward them.

Breathless, I stopped and just soaked in the joy radiating from their faces. I smiled as I gazed into Mary Grace's dancing eyes and held up the package. "A gift for you." She held the gift to her chest and thanked me.

I smiled fondly at Gray. "Congratulations on marrying the most beautiful woman in all of Charleston."

"Don't I know et." He grinned.

"You'd best run along." I gave Mary Grace's hand a squeeze and stepped back.

Gray mounted up and the cloudless, moonlit night swirled them away.

# CHAPTER Eighteen

## Mary Grace's Story

Mary Grace couldn't remember a time when Willow wasn't in her life.

When they were small girls, she'd found Willow hiding in the closet of her room, sobbing. Concerned, she knelt beside her and asked her what was wrong. Wiping her tears with the back of her hand, Willow told her what devastated her so. Willow had asked her father if Mary Grace could have a bed like hers in her room. Her father had grabbed her roughly by the arm and shook her, saying Mary Grace was simply a toy to keep her out of his hair, and not to forget that.

Mary Grace's thoughts ran forward to a time when they were ten years old or so; they were having a tea party in the sitting room. Mammy had made them little sandwiches and cakes to eat with their hot lemon and honey water.

Willow held her teacup with her pinkie finger pointed out and said in a grown-up tone, "Miss Mary Grace, I do suggest we do this more often."

"Why, yes, Miss Willow, I believe that is a splendid idea." Mary Grace lifted her chin slightly. Taking her cue, Willow straightened her posture to make herself appear taller.

"It's been a delightful afternoon, if I must say so myself." Willow dabbed the corners of her mouth with her napkin.

"That it has, my dear," Mary Grace said.

They looked at each other, not sure what to say next or which words would make them seem like sophisticated ladies. After a few moments of stale silence, Willow sighed and dramatically slid down on the sofa, flipping her head against the back of it. "This adult playing is exhausting."

Mary Grace sighed with relief as she let her shoulders relax. "Yes, it's boring. What should we play now?"

"Let's go to my room and I will read to you," Willow suggested.

Willow loved to read; she said it helped her escape to a different world. Mary Grace cherished the times when they were in Willow's room; they would lay on Willow's luxurious bed and she would read to Mary Grace for hours. In Willow's books, they would travel the world, face many obstacles, and enjoy many adventures.

That afternoon Willow sat on her window seat. Mary Grace stretched out on the floor on her stomach, her ankles crossed in the air and her mind whirling with excitement as Willow's smooth voice poured out the words of *The Three Musketeers.*

She hadn't noticed that Willow had stopped reading until she said, "I have a brilliant idea, Mary Grace. Why don't I teach you to read?" She bounced up with enthusiasm.

Mary Grace was astounded by her sudden suggestion, and apprehensive, as she knew it was strictly forbidden; a slave would be put to death if anyone found out. "I don't know, Miss Willow, your father won't like that. He already thinks we be joined at the hip."

"Not 'we be,' Mary Grace, you must say 'we are.' If you are going to be an educated black woman, you must speak with proper grammar so people learn to respect you," Willow said, conviction shining in her dark green eyes.

"Your father would be angry if he found out," Mary Grace said again, but she knew her expression betrayed her anticipation.

"Well, we will keep it our secret, then." The headstrong Willow had made up her mind.

Every day afterward, she dedicated herself to teaching Mary Grace to read. Willow said she was a brilliant student and caught on fast.

For a slave girl, Mary Grace was happy and had never known what fear truly was in her life on the Livingston Plantation. Besides a few trips into town with Willow, she had never been off the plantation. Mammy prohibited her from getting a pass to visit friends on the surrounding plantations. Mammy had been the best mama a girl could ever ask for, and Mary Grace didn't want to cause her extra worry or stress, so she abided by her wishes.

In her teenage years, though, Mary Grace became frustrated at the restrictions Mammy placed on her life. In her mind, she believed Mammy wanted to make her miserable. One day, after Mammy's refusal to let her go with her friends, she cried until her eyes were empty of tears, but Mammy stood firm.

"You don't want me to be happy!" Mary Grace wailed.

"Yes, chile, dat is what I do. I set out every morn to ruin your life," she said sarcastically, and threw her hands in the air with as much drama as her daughter.

"Mama, please, I must go. All the others say I'm a spoiled black princess and you keep me tied to your apron strings. I'm the laughing stock of the whole plantation." She repeated what she'd heard the old gossipy hags say on washing days. "'Oh, look at Miss Fancy Pants, too good for the laks of us. All kept up in dat big house, hidden away lak she is a china doll.'" Mary Grace would snatch the laundry from them to hang on the line and stick out her tongue as she left. She knew it wasn't polite or right, but neither were their mean words.

"Mama, how do you suppose I'll ever marry or give you grandbabies if you don't allow me to go to these dances and gatherings?"

"Chile, de folkses over on de Armstrong Plantation shows up here at leas' once a month. You will not go unwed." Mammy turned the dough with a little extra force; the kitchen house echoed the loud smack. Her daughter's whining had started to wear on her.

Mary Grace felt remorse as she saw Mammy's shoulders sag. She was a good mother, and Mary Grace couldn't imagine having any other. "I'm sorry, Mama. I don't understand why you hold me so close. Why do you fear so, Mama?"

Her mama started to knead the dough harder. "I jus'..." She stopped kneading and turned to Mary Grace, her shoulders curled forward and her head lowered. "I guess et be time to have de talk wid you. I knowed one day it would come." She sat down with a thud on the wooden bench at the end of the small table.

Mary Grace sucked in her breath as dread filled her; her intuition told her what Mammy was about to say was going to be life-changing.

"I was taken from what was left of my family jus' 'fore I had my fust bleed, and sold at auction. De man who bought me had eyes full of lust. His eyes et up my body as he luked me over from head to toe. I 'member holding myself real tight-lak, tryin' to cover my new buddin' breasts. I seed what mens wid dat luk in deir eyes done to young gals 'fore.

"I walked de five miles to my new home wid de other slaves purchased dat day, tied to de back of his horse. A home dat would become my nightmare." She hung her head as she twisted her floured hands in her lap. "Masa Adams made advances toward me over de next few years, but I allus managed to escape.

"Happiness entered my life when de masa brought a slave

home dat catch me eye. Dere be somepin' 'bout this black as coal man dat drew me in. He be an African prince dey called Big John. He was a gentle giant. My walls came down and I was able to love again. We came to love each other and as de masa became more desperate to have me, I know I don't want my fust time to be lak dat. I begged Big John to marry me and make my fust time wid a man be one of love. I married me my African prince, under de stars before God.

"Den came de night I wasn't so lucky—de masa catch me alone. He took me with force. De pain I felt as he drove his manhood into my body parts was de worst thing you can ever imagine. I bled for days and my insides were torn and damaged. Big John feared I may never have chillun." She lifted her face, which was filled with an unimaginable agony, and the tears poured down her cheeks as she relived the rape. "I begged God to save me from dis torture. When no savin' came over de next few years, my prayers turned to axin' de Lord Almighty to take my life. 'Most nightly he tuk me in whatever way he could. I larned to never 'low my mind to go to de pain of what was being done to me, I larned not to fight back, 'cause et be de fight dat drove him wild wid lust.

"Den I became pregnant wid you, seeded by de masa. I was eaten up wid anger and bitterness but John helped me wuk through dat. We decided if you be born a girl, you would be called Mary Grace. And if you be a boy, we would call you Matthew, meaning gift from God. As you grew inside me a love I never felt 'fore stirred in me. I swore to protect you, to die before I ever let de sins forced on my body be done to you. You and John give me hope and somepin' to live for.

"Big John and I prayed you come out real dark, but you come out a white babe for sho'. We knowed what would come next and sho' 'nuf, de missus had you and me sold as quick as nothin'." She peered up at her daughter while wiping her eyes with the corner of her apron.

Mary Grace stood with her soapy hands hanging in fists at her sides. A rage she'd never experienced before awakened in her.

Mammy continued. "Not a day goes by dat I don't long for my John. But den evvyday I thank de good Lord dat de missus sold us, 'cause dis here life at Livingston be a good one. Et's as good a life a slave can ever have. Masa Hendricks don't use his slave womens in de ways of other masas and he sho' mussy."

Mary Grace felt ashamed for testing Mammy's rules and the fears guiding them. She closed the distance between them and threw her arms around her mama, and her tears trickled into the warmth of her thick neck. "Please forgive me, Mama. I've been such a selfish and horrible daughter. I never stopped to wonder why you were so strict with me. I thought you wanted to confine me, to keep me a child."

"No, gal, I want you to have a full life. I want dat purty face of yours to not be hung low wid worry or dose beautiful eyes filled wid pain."

"I see that now, Mama. I will not test you so."

"You're a good gal, but your free spirit will be de death of me." Mama chuckled, brushing a stray hair back out of Mary Grace's face.

"I love you, Mama," she whispered. "Thank you for giving your life to protect me."

That hard conversation changed Mary Grace's outlook on the world. She now viewed it without the sense of safety she once had. It gave her a new understanding of Mammy's reaction when Masa's friends visited the plantation. Now she knew why Mammy shut her up in her room until they left.

Then love came into her life in the form of a handsome slave. She first met Gray when he attended a gathering of the slaves at the Livingston Plantation.

At the end of the night she ran to Willow's room and collapsed on her bed, breathless and flushed with excitement. She lay staring at the ceiling for several seconds, then squealed and kicked her legs in the air in an unladylike manner.

"Good Lord, Mary Grace, what has gotten into you?" Willow asked, appalled at her odd behavior.

Mary Grace couldn't contain herself. She giggled, bubbling over with joy. "I met a young man tonight."

Willow's shock turned to pure delight. She demanded that Mary Grace share every detail of the evening with her—especially a full description of Gray.

Over the next few years, her and Gray's relationship blossomed—and now she was his wife. She dreamed of having many babies with him. She longed for a time when they could see each other every day and spend their nights together in the same bed as a married couple, but until then she would savor the nights they got to lie in each other's arms.

Gray said someday he hoped to buy his freedom from Masa Bowden. Mary Grace questioned why he would ever dream of the impossible. He told her it was no more impossible than them staying in the same shack at night. They could dream, he said. Masa Bowden wasn't the same as other masas. Gray had become his most trusted slave. He'd been saving every coin he earned. And someday hoped to buy her freedom, too.

Freedom was what every slave longed for, but she knew she could never leave Willow and Mammy behind…not even if the price was her freedom.

# CHAPTER *Nineteen*

## Gray's Story

GRAY HADN'T REALIZED HIS HANDS HAD STOPPED WORKING ON the butter churn he was carving until his pappy called to him, "Son, dat dere churn ain't gwine make itself." He chuckled, shaking his balding head.

"You be right about dat, Pappy." Gray grinned back, pushing his thoughts of Mary Grace aside.

His pappy had taught him the trade of coopering from the time he was a small boy. Like his pappy, he'd mastered it, and now their work was highly sought after at the shipping docks. Gray was fast and efficient and for this reason, he finished the daily orders set out for him in a timely manner. When he exceeded the number of products required, Masa Bowden allowed him to sell the extra items and pocket the return for himself. When Masa Bowden's grandfather was alive and running Armstrong Plantation he was good to the slaves, but he never allowed his skilled slaves to earn coin. He was a businessman first and a human being second, and didn't show the same respect for his slaves as Masa Bowden. Ol' Masa Armstrong saw them as investments.

Sure, Masa Bowden still owned slaves, and for any man to own another man warn't right. But Masa Bowden enforced his rule that no slaves on his plantation were to be mistreated, and the first hired man on his plantation who touched a slave in any way would answer to him. He treated Gray as he would another white man, and he admired Masa Bowden for it. Masa asked his opinion on matters to do with his plantation. The masa respected him and his wisdom, and this made Gray feel like he valued him as an equal.

No matter how good they had it, some slaves would still grumble and stir up trouble. Some of the slaves came to Gray suggesting he may as well be white, with how the masa treated him like he was his right-hand man. Some said the masa might go as far as to make Gray an overseer. Gray didn't think the masa would go that far, but if he did, Gray would turn him down. He would not be an overseer of slaves.

Given the mercurial nature of slave chatter, his pappy thought it best for Gray to keep the fact of the coin masa paid him on the down-low. Pappy said many times, "Life be hard. No one's gwine look out for you but you." His pappy was a good and wise man.

Over the years he'd seen his pappy yearn for his mama, who was left behind when their masa sold them to pay his debts. As age started to creep into his old, tired bones, Pappy longed for Gray's mama even more. Gray could only imagine the sadness of growing old without the one you love by your side.

His mama had been a devoted and loving woman. She took pride in being a wife and raising her children in the few hours a day they got to spend together as a family, when their work was finished.

Gray's younger sister, Millie, had been born with a simple mind, and Gray loved and protected her. When the slave children taunted her and called her "retarded," she would run to her big brother, crying over their cruel words. Gray would find the children and lay a beating on them that ended up getting him in trouble with his mama. The parents of the children would show up at their shack to demand he be dealt with. He never told his parents why he had done it. When his parents dealt out his punishments, he took them with no objection. Millie would sit rocking herself on her bed, crying, "No, no, no." Telling them why he had been fighting would cause them unnecessary pain.

One day he happened upon two slave boys who had Millie cornered and were saying, "You so ugly your own mama should have drowned you when you were born. Dis here world don't need nobody lak you." Gray laid a beating so bad on those two boys that one had a broken nose and the other was unable to see out of both eyes for a week.

Millie never cried that day as he held her in his arms. She looked up at the brother she trusted and adored and said, "Dey be right, dem boys. Mama should've had a beautiful gal. She would be smart like her." There was no self-pity in her eyes, only a new understanding of herself, and it scared Gray.

"Hush now, Millie. Don't you be talkin' lak dat."

Her words played over and over in his head every day after that. What if he'd told his parents about the teasing and bullying Millie suffered from the children? Maybe she would still be alive.

The day of her death was burned into Gray's mind forever. At the end of their day in the fields the slaves were heading back to their quarters, chanting a song of their people, when an ear-piercing cry went up at the front of the line. People started pointing toward the creek they passed every day on their way to and from the fields.

Gray and his parents moved forward, threading through the crowd to see what was going on. His mama reached the scene first. She let out a primal scream and bolted into the creek. Gray felt a pain so great in his chest, he knew what he was going to see as he pushed against the slaves in front of him, trying to get to his mama.

The body floating face down in the creek was his little sister.

The water splashed about like ocean waves as his pappy raced to his wife and daughter. His mama turned over the body and gathered his sister to her breast. Sobbing, she smoothed Millie's wet hair away from her peaceful face. His pappy embraced them both in his strong arms. Gray's feet seemed rooted to the creek bank.

Soon after, he and his pappy were sold. The expression on his mama's face as the last of her family was chained and led away was that of a broken woman. She'd tragically lost her daughter, and now her husband and son. He didn't know what would become of her. He memorized every detail of her as they took him away so he wouldn't forget her.

He began to sand the round edges of the churn as he thought of his mama. After fifteen years, her face had become a faded image and the warmth of her touch was a distant memory.

His thoughts turned once again to Mary Grace. She was hope. She made him feel alive! She gave him purpose! He would earn his and her freedom. He'd heard tell of slaves who'd managed to buy their freedom. Though he never saw a free slave, he dreamed of the day they would be free.

# CHAPTER Twenty

"YOUR FATHER WANTS YOU IN THE PARLOR, MISS." THADDEUS stood in the doorway of my room.

"Thank you, Thaddeus. Let him know I will be right down," I said, putting aside my needlework.

*What did I do now?*

Mary Grace looked up from changing the bed linens. Knowing me best, she picked up on my worries. Smiling reassuringly, she said, "It will be all right."

"I guess we shall see, won't we?"

In the parlor, Father stood chatting with a young gentleman in his twenties who stood casually, his arm resting on the marble mantel of the fireplace. They turned as I entered the room.

"Hello, my darling. I would like you to meet Kipling Reed from Virginia. Kipling, I would like you to meet my daughter, Willow," Father announced with pride.

My darling? What was Father up to?

Kipling moved forward and took my hand in his with a firm friendliness. His eyes met mine. I curtsied and Father nodded his approval.

"Very pleased to make your acquaintance," we both said at the same time, and we laughed awkwardly.

He was tall and lean. His short, dark hair was neatly combed to one side. He had a pleasant face with a nice smile that reached his whiskey-colored brown eyes.

"Kipling is in town for a week on political business and will be staying with us," Father informed me.

"How do you and Father know each other?" I said, noticing his nicely tailored clothes.

"His father and I have been business associates in the past," Father answered for him before taking a sip of his brandy.

"To what do we owe the honor of your visit, Mr. Reed?"

He looked nervously from me to Father. I saw the question in his eyes. "My understanding was you knew—" he began, eyes still on Father.

Father cut him off, taking control of the conversation in true Charles Hendricks fashion. "Please sit down, my dear."

"Honestly, Father, enough with the dear and darling. You never speak to me this way, so please do not patronize me because we have company," I retorted, growing tired of him pretending to have a fondness for me.

"Willow, I would suggest you mind your manners for the sake of our company." He adjusted his collar.

For Kipling's benefit I held my tongue and sat down, waiting for him to explain the real reason behind this meeting.

"Kipling's father and I have agreed on an arranged marriage between the two of you."

"What!" I yelped. I gaped from one man to the other.

Father's jaw locked and his face settled into its usual firm, unapproachable expression.

Kipling's body language practically screamed that he was extremely uncomfortable and desired to be anywhere but in this room.

I felt sorry that he had to endure this conversation. The tension between Father and me was unmistakable, but I couldn't spin my mind off what Father was proposing.

"Willow." Father's voice softened, and he lifted a hand,

signaling me to relax. "Hear me out before you embarrass us both."

Trying to calm my anger, I waited.

"You are of age to be a wife and it's time you caged those wild ideas of yours. I won't always be around and I want to see you taken care of." A gentleness flickered briefly in his eyes as he explained his reasoning.

"But Father, when I marry, I want to marry for love." I looked to Kipling. "I'm sure you are a fine catch, sir. I never gave much thought to a day when I'd marry, let alone have it arranged for me." Turning my attention back to Father, I said with more conviction, "Please, Father, I beg of you to let me choose my own husband when the time is right."

"Willow!" he declared, shaking his head in disappointment.

"Did you love my mother?" My fist knotted in the pleats of my gown.

"Yes, I loved your mother."

"Well, could you imagine marrying someone else?" I stood, baffled by the whole idea. Concealed by the skirt of my gown, my foot tapped repeatedly as I grasped for a plan in my head.

Kipling stood looking like he wanted the floor to open up and swallow him. "Miss Willow, I didn't know you were unaware of this arrangement and hadn't given your own approval." Looking at Father with disapproval, he said, "Sir, I respect you as a friend, but you have humiliated me and your daughter by not discussing this with her in private. Will you both please excuse me?" With a gentleman's grace, he bowed and left the room.

Father and I stared after him. I felt my cheeks flush in humiliation.

Father's voice deepened as he said, "You will court Kipling for six months, then you will marry him, Willow. I won't listen to another word from you." He rose to his full height.

I trembled under his gaze but stood my ground. "Why are you

so controlling, Father? What makes you feel you have to control me and everyone in your life?"

He clenched his fists. "Why weren't you born a boy! You selfish, sinful abomination!"

All common sense left me as resentment replaced my fear. "What, Father? Are you going to hit me? Go ahead—the only way you seem able to control me is to cause me physical pain." I braced for the blow.

Father lost control and unleashed his anger on me. Grabbing me by the hair, he yanked my head back. His eyes flashed. Through clenched teeth, he hissed, "How dare you. I'm your father and you will do as you're told. As long as you live under this roof, I am your master. Don't ever forget that!" His voice rose to a shout as his hand made contact with my face.

I screamed in pain as my head snapped back with the blow.

"Masa!" Mammy rushed in. "Please, Masa, let de chile go," she begged.

Father released me and snapped out of his rage. He stared at us in shock. "Oh, God, what have I done?" he cried. Guilt and shame cloaked his face and he turned away.

I glared at the man who had fathered me. He was big, strong, and powerful. This man was supposed to love me and protect me, but he inflicted this pain on me. The words from his own mouth justified what I had always felt—words he could never take back.

A rage much like Father's enveloped me, and tumbled from my lips. "I hate you, Father," I said in a voice trembling with raw emotion. "I spit on the day I was born as your daughter."

I turned and saw Mammy and Kipling standing behind me. Their expressions reflected a mixture of distress and astonishment.

Shaking uncontrollably, I moved in a daze, pushing through the French doors to run outside. I had to get out of there and put as much distance between him and me as possible.

# CHAPTER Twenty-One

I SHUT OUT THE WORLD AROUND ME. LOST IN MY OWN MISERY, TIME escaped me. I wandered aimlessly in the cypress forest surrounding the plantation. I cried for the mother I never knew and for the father I wanted to love me.

Why was he so harsh? Why did he hate me so? Was it as simple as me becoming the meek and mild daughter he wanted? I would not be controlled by him or his views. My life had become a tug-of-war between my individuality and Father's will to break my spirit. I cried for myself until I had no tears left to cry.

Finally, spent of all energy, I used my skirt hem to dry my tears and drew a deep, shuddering breath that turned into a hiccup.

A twig snapped behind me. Startled, I spun around.

Kipling! What did he want?

"Sorry, Miss Willow. I couldn't leave with you like this," he explained, fumbling with a blade of grass he held between his fingers.

I muffled the sigh that came up after a good cry and pulled myself up.

"You all right?" he asked with concern.

"I will be. And I'm sorry you had to play witness to that." I dropped my gaze to my hands, clasped firmly in front of me.

"It was my understanding that you knew what our fathers had discussed, and you were open to it." He leaned against the tree beside him.

"No, but it doesn't surprise me. My father tries to project an image of superiority; perfection, even. He would like me to be everything I am not and say *yes, Father* and *no, Father*—but mainly the *yes, Father*." I scowled in annoyance.

He listened without interrupting as I grumbled about the ways of my father. Realizing I was rambling to a stranger, I stopped in mid-sentence and assessed the man before me. His face was kind and sincere, not guarded. His skin was not kissed by the sun, probably from too many days behind a desk. He appeared well put together and a gentleman of quality, and it was obvious why Father had chosen him. I had to allow my father credit for picking a man who possessed all of these great qualities.

"Mr. Reed?"

"Kip, please." He smiled, showing off dimples.

"Very well. Kip, you are comfortable with this arrangement between our fathers?"

"Before I met you, Miss Willow, yes, I was. After meeting you, how could I be?"

I stepped back defensively.

He raised a hand for me to hear him out. "Not that you aren't beautiful, and you do have a certainty about yourself, which is admirable. You are a woman with her own mind, and I can appreciate that. I am not looking to force you into a marriage you don't want. A marriage starting out on those grounds is bound for failure."

Softening my manner, I nodded. There was an honesty and a trustworthiness about him that drew me to him. He did not seem to be ignorant or mean-spirited. I relaxed and offered my arm. "Would you care to join me for a walk by the creek?"

Obviously glad to move past the events of the past hour, he

linked his arm through mine.

Later, in the privacy of my room, while my father and Kip sat in the parlor drinking port and visiting, I thought of the young man my father had dumped into my lap today. In the hour I spent with him, I thoroughly enjoyed his company. He was easy to talk with and we had laughed a lot. I could never see myself married to him, but we agreed to be friends. He promised he would speak to Father and refuse the arrangement between our fathers.

Even though I would be freed from marrying Kip, how long would it be before my father found the next suitor who would try dragging me kicking and screaming to the altar?

# CHAPTER Twenty-Two

A FEW MONTHS AFTER KIP'S VISIT, ON A COOL FALL MORNING, I sat in a rocker on the front veranda, a fresh cup of brewed coffee nestled in my hands as I listened to the chickadees singing high up in the sweet bay trees. A light wind ruffled the leaves and sent a chill through me, and I pulled my red crocheted shawl closer.

This morning as I'd arrived at the breakfast table, Mammy informed me I would be eating alone; Father had gone on a sudden business trip and would be gone for a few weeks. *Perfect,* I thought, unable to hide my smile. But I found myself speculating where he was off to now.

"Probably gone off to hog-tie another husband for me," I said sardonically.

Mammy chuckled. "Now chile, you're gwine have to marry someday. So I figure you better start lukin' for a man you could see yourself jumping de broom wid 'fore your father does jus' dat. Speaking of mens, you received a letter from young Mr. Reed today."

"Truthfully, Mammy?" When he left, he'd promised to keep in touch, and I was delighted he'd followed through.

Mammy took an envelope out of her apron pocket and laid it on the table beside my plate. Picking it up, I turned it over and traced my fingertips over the Reed family crest.

"Well, are you gwine jus' sit dere or are you gwine open et?"

Mammy asked as she filled my glass with milk.

I laughed at her impatience and opened the letter to read:

*My Dearest Willow,*

*I hope this letter finds you well and happy. I know it's a little late coming, but I wanted to thank you for the enjoyment of your company during my week at Livingston Plantation. I've been chained to my desk with an overload of work since I've returned, due to new developments. I am thinking of a change in my career, so I'm unsure of where I will end up. Please, know that I think of you often and look forward to the day that we can meet again.*

*Sincerely, your friend,*

*Kip*

A friendship with no strings attached, he'd promised, and he'd stayed true to his word. I reflected on the letter. When would we see each other again? Next time Father went on business to Virginia, I would ask to go along.

# CHAPTER Twenty-Three

THE SHINY BLACK OPEN CARRIAGE COMING UP THE DRIVE CAUGHT my attention. I shielded my eyes from the sun to see who had come calling. I recognized the auburn ringlets bouncing up and down in time with the movements of the carriage, and ran to meet it.

"Welcome, Whitney! What a surprise!"

"Hello, Willow." She smiled and waved as the driver pulled the horses to a stop. "I was heading into town and was wondering if you would like to come along. I know I would enjoy your company."

"That sounds like a lovely idea. Let me fetch my bonnet and a shawl against the breeze."

Whitney had come to visit a handful of times over the past months, and I found myself looking forward to her visits. I quite liked having a woman my age as a neighbor, as it made the long months on the rather isolated plantation bearable. When Father was gone I freely mingled with the slaves, which helped subdue some of my gnawing loneliness.

A few minutes later, with me aboard, the carriage was trundling back down the lane and through the heavy iron gates to turn in the direction of town.

"So, how have you been?" I asked, keen for company and anticipating a change of scenery.

"Bored stiff, to be honest. It's a whole new world for me. I'm still getting used to the quietness of country life," she said, languidly waving her hand at the open countryside surrounding us.

"We will adapt to all of this together," I told her. "Now that I've finished my studies and won't be returning to school this year, I suppose I will also have to adjust to this lifestyle again."

"If it wasn't for the twins keeping me busy, I'd damn well go stir-crazy."

My mouth dropped open at her profanity. This type of language did not sit well with certain people of society, especially coming from a lady.

Whitney frowned at my gaping mouth. "You all right, there?" she asked, cracking her ungloved knuckles.

I couldn't help but giggle at her directness and her indifference to what others thought of her. I had grown fond of her and we had developed a solid friendship, but we were as different as night and day—and yet her ways entertained me.

"I am." I tried to mask the smirk that played at the corners of my mouth.

We continued our lighthearted chatter, Whitney barely pausing for breath.

What had started as a peaceful morning changed when the horses became nervous and agitated, squealing and rearing back and stomping their hooves in the dirt. They'd nearly come to a standstill.

Whitney leaned forward and asked in exasperation, "Thomas, what in the world is the issue?" I'd learned one thing about Whitney: she disliked being inconvenienced. Feeling out of control rattled her.

"Somepin's done spooked de horses, Miss Whitney." He tried to regain control.

Then we heard the strident baying of bloodhounds on the scent. A dull ache throbbed at the back of my throat as I realized what was happening.

The bushes to the right of the carriage rustled and two panting, sweat-drenched slaves emerged. One was a middle-aged man with a sack over his shoulder, the other a boy around twelve years old. The whites of their wide eyes glowed against their dark skin. Seeing us, cornered, they looked frantically around for a route of escape.

Behind them the brushes thrashed to and fro and the yelling of a slave catcher reached our ears. "This way, boys! The dogs got their scent. We'll get them niggers and string them up."

My eyes darted from the slaves to Whitney and we shared an astounded look. My pulse pounded in my ears. I wanted to jump into action, but I sat frozen like the slaves in front of me. What could I do? I'd barely had the thought before it was too late.

The dogs burst through the bush onto the narrow buggy trail, the men behind them grinning viciously at their triumph. They circled the slaves, chests thrust forward in superiority.

The boy clung to the man, their nostrils flaring in wild terror. As the nightmare unfolded before us, I prayed for them to disappear, to no avail. A whip whistled through the crisp morning air, snapping across the backs of the slaves. The sound sent our horses surging forward in fear. The boy's body convulsed in pain and he lost control of his bladder, the urine darkening the front of his frayed and patched trousers.

"Whoa, boys," Thomas said quickly, trying to calm the horses and steady the carriage. We grasped the sides to keep from tumbling out.

"Well, looky there, Pete," one of the men sneered, wadding a piece of tobacco into his cheek and using his tongue to rotate it into position before spitting the extra saliva in his mouth onto the ground, "the little black demon done gone and pissed himself." They threw their heads back, roaring in malicious laughter.

"I say what's the harm in a little more?" The one called Pete stepped forward; adjusting his trousers, he relieved himself on the slaves. Turning his gaze on us, he jerked his head and the other men advanced toward the carriage.

Thomas reacted instantly with a high-pitched "giddyup!" The horses reacted instantly to the reins lashing their backs by sprinting forward, sending Whitney and me tumbling back into our seats and leaving the men coughing in the dust stirred up by the carriage wheels.

Daring a peek over my shoulder, I breathed a sigh of relief as the distance grew between us and the evil intentions of those men. I tried to hold down the bile burning my throat. I closed my eyes tight, overwhelmed by my inability to help those slaves. They would meet a horrible fate today, I was sure. Their lives would be no more, and we, their only hope, had ridden off to avoid whatever those men intended toward two lone young women.

We grabbed our flapping bonnets to keep them from flying off as the carriage bounced down the rutted road. When we were sure the men weren't following, Whitney instructed Thomas to slow the pace. The horses sensed his hands relaxing on the reins, and at his soothing command, they slowed to a canter.

"Thank you, Thomas, for your swiftness," Whitney said.

"Yes, thank you," I whispered weakly.

"Willow, are you well?" Whitney nudged me gently.

"I guess." My mind was still on the slaves we'd left behind.

"We are fine. That's the main thing," Whitney said with a shrug, as if what we had witnessed was something you'd see any day.

"Those slaves!" I cried, aggravated by her attitude.

"I suppose they will go back to whomever they belong to," she said, leaning back and resting her eyes, letting her eyelids sink closed.

"Whitney!" I snapped, disappointed by her lack of compassion. "I thought with you being raised in the North, where human beings aren't property, your view would be different." Had I been wrong about her? "I thought we would have this in common."

Whitney sat forward. "Willow, don't sit there judging me. I don't want to see anyone hurt any more than you do. But common sense tells me we can do nothing when we are outnumbered. And we surely aren't strong enough to take on those men. Would you expect me to risk Thomas's life? The ways of the South are cruel. This I see clearly. Trust me, I do. But what can we do as women when we are the weaker sex?"

"We shout our demands until they are heard. Yes, we are obviously weaker than men. But try putting yourself in the shoes of a slave. Their voices are never heard. And more than that, they aren't seen as anything more than property, to be beaten, raped, urinated on, and treated lower than the lowest animals on this Earth. Tell me why this is all right!" I shouted. Hot teardrops squeezed from my eyes.

Thomas straightened on the carriage seat and turned to glance at me, and I met his gaze, saw his fascination in my passionate sense of right and wrong.

"I understand, Willow, honestly I do. And you are right," Whitney admitted, hanging her head in shame. "I suppose I've numbed myself to the horrors I see on Father's plantation. After the last few months of seeing it day in and day out, I guess I've found it useless to fight with Rufus about what I have seen him wreak upon the slaves. I have gone to Father many times, begging him to hire a different overseer. I have tried my best to help the slaves, only to find my efforts were in vain. I guess I became complacent because I felt hopeless."

"We can't become complacent, Whitney," I said in a calmer

tone. "If we want things to be different, we need to try to change the things within our power."

She looked away and thought for a moment. Then, as if struck by an epiphany, she said, "Help light the fire in the direction of change?" Her eyes lit up; a new fire had ignited within her.

Driven by our ambitions to make a small difference in this constrained world we lived in, we put our heads together in deep conversation for the remainder of the ride to town.

# CHAPTER Twenty-Four

AS WE APPROACHED THE EDGE OF TOWN WE CAME UPON A GROUP of slaves, shackled at the neck, wrists, and ankles with iron cuffs and chained together with a single long chain. The human train was most likely going to be held in a prison in town until they could be sold at auction or taken to the docks to be shipped out to other states. Charleston Harbor was the biggest port in the South for shipping goods, and it was popular with slave traders.

The slave catchers continuously prodded the slaves forward, degrading them with their words. An older woman in the middle of the line lost her footing and stumbled.

"Stop, Thomas!" I shouted. Not waiting long enough for the carriage to stop, I jumped down and hurried to the woman's aid.

Bending, I took her by the arm. "Let me help you, Mama," I said, gazing into her weary face. Her eyes lacked pigment; they were clouded over with white shadows. She was blind! The skin on the edges of her eyes held angry scars. Someone had burnt her eyes out!

The woman reached up and ran her agile fingers over my eyes, nose, and the contours of my face. She started to stroke the curls escaping my bonnet before she gasped and drew back in fear and confusion. "I'm real sorry, Miss. I figures you for a nig-ra." Her voice was jittery.

"I'm a friend, Mama. I see you're tired, but you have to get up." I struggled to help her stand and was relieved when the adolescent boy beside her offered his assistance. Our eyes met before he lowered his toward the ground.

"Thank you, Missus," he said, steadying the woman.

"What's going on here?" a slave catcher barked.

Startled, I jumped. Releasing the woman and stepping back, I turned to return to the wagon. Seeing the slave catcher, I stopped in shock. The swollen alien of a man was black as night! He wore a patch over one eye, and an evil sneer curled his upper lip.

It did not keep me from saying what was on my mind. Adrenaline coursed through my veins as my lip pulled up in a snarl of its own. "How can you betray your own kind?"

He shrugged his massive shoulders, further concealing a thick short neck. "Better them than me!" he growled, then spat toward the slaves.

This man was fueled with so much hatred he even hated his own race! He was unaware that with his inability to harbor any emotions but hate, the world had rejected him. He had become even less than the slaves he condemned. He did not belong with the white race or the black race. In his desire to belong in the white world and be a traitor to his own kind, he now stood alone, a man without a race.

Seeing the pity in my eyes, he turned and aimed his bitterness at the helpless backs of the slaves. They wailed in pain as he struck them and bellowed for them to get moving.

We entered Charleston with the group of slaves not far behind us. Whitney and I did not speak; our hearts were heavy. Thomas stopped the carriage in front of the general store, where men sat on the front porch smoking cigars, people-watching, and discussing everyday life. He assisted us from the carriage and we made our way up the few worn stairs and entered the store.

The shopkeeper, a bespectacled woman with an unnaturally long nose, stood behind the cash register looking haughtily at us as we came in.

"Afternoon, Miss Smith," Whitney said loudly.

"Girls," she said in a deep, detached voice.

We browsed through the bolts of silk imported from Thailand. My family crest was stamped on the board the fabric was wrapped around. These materials were imported on my father's ships, along with a lot of other goods in the store. We moved on to outrageous hats that sat on faceless heads on display in the large front window. We couldn't resist trying them on. We giggled as we checked our appearance in the floor-length mirror. I turned my hat over in my hand to see the price tag and was happy to see our crest wasn't stamped on it.

The door chimed as new customers entered.

"Well, what are the chances of the two most beautiful women in Charleston being in the same place at the same time?"

Seeing the reflection of Knox in the mirror, we returned the hats to the display.

"Knox, you have to come up with better lines. That's exhaustingly lame," Whitney said, her face pinched in disapproval.

I eyed the ice queen and had an insight. Whitney's rudeness toward Knox was her strange way of keeping him at arm's length as he threatened to melt her heart.

Unaffected by her meanness, he grinned.

We turned our heads as the door chimed yet again and Knox's sidekick entered.

"Hey, pal," Knox said, "these fine ladies have stated their interest in me!"

Bowden casually strolled over. "Is that true? Ya'll have declared your undying love to this old dog?" He snickered.

Whitney blurted an exaggerated, "Oh, please!" Crossing her

arms, she looked away.

"How are things at Livingston?" Bowden asked me.

I felt an iciness of my own. "Fine, thank you." I nodded politely, forcing a tense smile. I had promised him I would put our past to rest, and this would be the beginning of my effort.

After a few moments of relatively pleasant conversation, we paid for the items we had come for, and the gentlemen walked us back to our carriage. Bowden offered a hand to help me into the carriage. I thanked him as I arranged myself on the seat. Whitney swiped Knox's hand away and climbed in beside me.

"This was nice, Willow," Bowden said, and touched my arm, sending tingles through my body.

"It's a start. But yes, it was," I replied. "We'd best get back if we want to be home before dark."

"Thomas, on to Livingston Plantation," Whitney ordered.

The gentlemen stepped back and waved as we departed.

"Well, I'd say you are viewing Bowden in a new light," Whitney said.

"What do you know of it?"

"Oh, I don't know the whole story, but I do know the last time we were all in each other's company you could cut the tension with a knife. Care to fill me in?"

"Well," I said, "it all began years ago, in school..."

# CHAPTER Twenty-Five

## Mammy's Story

Henrietta was born into slavery. Leaving people behind was nothing new to her. Her mother birthed five children, including her. They were split up and sold off. She realized at a young age that she would never have a life filled with anything but pain. Henrietta developed a tough skin, closing her emotions off to survive the life dealt to her.

At the tender age of twelve, she was sold to a plantation in Georgia, to a cruel masa. She learned to detach herself from the world; making no friends, she kept her head down and worked hard. She hoped to go unnoticed and worked herself to the point of exhaustion as a way to keep her mind numb and her heart shut off. She did not feel alone in the world, she simply existed because human nature forced her to. She worked as a field slave from morning to dusk without a complaint. She ate and slept and started the process over again in the morning. This was what she learned defined life.

Two years after she arrived at the plantation, the masa brought home a new group of slaves. By this time she had been pulled from the field and given a new position as a domestic slave. Her duties entailed laundry, helping in the kitchen, and serving the main table.

That day she was hanging the bedsheets on the clothesline

beside the big house when the dust-covered group of slaves arrived. Curiosity pulled her to the corner of the house, where she peeked around the corner so she wouldn't be spotted. And she laid eyes on Big John for the first time. He was the tallest slave she'd ever seen. He stood proudly, his spirit unbroken by years of slavery. No marks scarred his glistening chocolate skin.

Later she learned he was a prince from West Africa, almost straight off the boat. He had made the unspeakable journey across the Atlantic Ocean that Henrietta heard other slaves describe as the ships of horror. They spoke of how the slaves were led onto the ships and stowed below by the hundreds; the living conditions were restricting and it was hard to breathe. Sometimes they were left for days before coming on deck for fresh air. Slaves begged to be killed to leave this life of misery behind. Some refused to eat, but their mouths were pried open with vises and they were force-fed. She'd heard slaves had found ways to end their suffering aboard the ships.

Her masa paid a high price to own a slave of John's strength and skills. Henrietta's interest surged whenever she saw him. He would give her a grateful nod and then continue on to his work. He worked part-time in the fields and the rest of his time as the plantation's medicine man.

The masa's infant son became ill and Henrietta was sent to find Big John. She went to the small cabin the masa allowed him to have all to himself. No other slave had this privilege. Masa said it was so he could tend to his patients and make his medicines. When slaves testified to the miracles he performed on them, he made a name for himself among them. The slaves looked to Big John for healing all their ailments, as did the masa and his family.

Knocking on the cabin door, she waited.

Big John opened the door and towered above her.

"Masa wants you up at de big house. De li'l masa is awful

sick," she mumbled. This was the first time they'd shared words. Stepping back, she took in the man who stood before her.

He disappeared into the cabin and returned minutes later carrying a sack, which she assumed held his medicines and the supplies he needed to treat the little masa. No words were exchanged as they rushed to the big house to help the child and spare themselves the wrath of the masa. Big John took the stairs two at a time and she scurried behind him. The head house servant, Lily, showed him toward the child's room, and Henrietta stayed in the hall, awaiting commands from inside the room.

The masa exited his son's room and his eyes looked at her with lust. That night his look was accompanied with determination, and it set her heart racing as he walked by. Without warning he stopped and pulled her body to him and with one hand squeezed her backside. As he pulled back he took her face in his warm, clammy hand and whispered in her ear, "You are ripe for the picking and I shall enjoy that very much." When he released her, she stood trembling. She had caught the eye of the masa, and this wasn't good. Her eyes wide with fear, she looked to Lily, who gave her a knowing look full of pity.

Big John stayed with the little masa that night and the next day, until his fever broke. He told the masa and the mistress the boy would improve, now that the fever had broken.

As Big John was leaving the big house to go back to his cabin, Henrietta met him in the hallway. "Will de li'l masa be all right?"

"Yes, Miss Rita, he will be fine," he said as he cut past her and was gone.

Rita? She had never received a nickname in all her years. She liked the sound of it as it rolled off her tongue.

She found herself inventing reasons to seek him out. At first their conversations were short and to the point. Big John seemed not to care much for her, but as time went on Big John flashed a smile from time to time. These smiles would set off long-buried emotions in her. Her brain warned her of the danger of letting her heart feel things that could cause her great pain. She couldn't pinpoint the moment she let her guard down, but she guessed it was the first day he arrived at the plantation and she had sized him up from the safety of the corner of the big house.

They spent many evenings on the steps of his cabin, gazing at the stars and speaking of his homeland. He told her stories of his tribe and his family. He had a mother, a father, and a younger sister. When his village was raided by the slave traders, he had been in the jungle hunting. The smell of smoke had caught his attention and he ran frantically back to the village, only to find his home in ruins. The bodies of men, women, and children of his tribe lay butchered on the ground. He went from body to body in search of his family. When he came upon his father's lifeless body he turned him over to find multiple bullets lodged in him. Big John held him and let out a war cry that reverberated through the night.

A blow to the back of the head sent him into a sphere of blackness. When he came to, he was chained to other tribe members, and people from nearby villages. Desperately he searched their faces for his mother and sister and not seeing them, his heart sank, wondering if they had shared the same fate as his father.

The slave traders ordered them up and they were marched from what remained of his village. His eyes searched the trees. Off in the direction he'd gone to hunt, his keen eyes spotted his mother with her arm around his little sister, watching them be led away. His heart leaped with triumph that they were safe, and he quickly lowered his head so he wouldn't draw attention to them.

"Do you think dey are still in Africa?" Henrietta had asked, placing a comforting hand over his giant one.

Focusing on the hand lying gently on his, he covered it with his free one. "Dey may have been saved dat day. But de slave traders began to infest my homeland long 'fore dat day. I fear dey suffered de same fate as my father, or dey have taken de ships across the ocean. I wish for dem death, above coming to a life lak dis. I may be spared of the cruelty in dis place 'cause I serve a purpose for now, but I watch dese white masters and no one is safe. At leas' in death, dey are free to sit along with my father in royalty. In dese lands, I am but a servant to dese white masters."

"We have to survive, John. Et be de only thing dat makes sense. I've been dead inside for too long. Dere be no joy in dat. We must find somepin' worth livin' for. We must live. Dey can't take our memories. In our hopes and dreams, we find life," Henrietta said, bewildered at the words coming from her own lips. This man before her made her soul want to live again.

The moon shone down on them, enfolding them in its light. He leaned in and placed a tender kiss on her lips. They were forming a bond of trust and opening their hearts up to the love they both felt. The next months passed with many evenings spent like this, including talks of marriage.

She started to notice the masa's eyes following her more openly when she was in the big house, serving the table or simply doing her work. He sought her out in the corners of the house, sometimes pinning her to the wall so she couldn't escape, and laying sloppy kisses on her neck and down to the tops of her breasts, visible in the lower-cut servant's uniform all domestic slaves were required to wear when serving the house. She would wiggle away, or someone would enter and he would back off. She shared her concerns with John about the masa's increasingly bold advances. John, still not used to being a slave, paced his cabin in angry frustration at the masa's nerve, and his helplessness in defending her.

One night as they were taking a walk within the bounds of the slave quarters that shielded them with some privacy, she found the courage to make an awkward request. "John?" She stopped him.

"Yes, my love?"

"I'm riddled wid fear dat I may not be able to hold off de masa's advances much longer. He is obsessed wid me, and evvy-where I turn, he finds me."

Concerned filled his eyes.

She licked her lips nervously. "I do not wish for him to be my fust. I want to belong to you. He can never have my body ef it already belongs to you. No matter what he does to me."

"Oh, my Rita. I'm honored by your request, b-but we aren't husband and wife," he stammered.

"Do you love me?" she demanded, placing her hands on her hips.

"You know I do, Rita!" The whites of his eyes shone in the moonlight.

"Den dat is all dat matters. Masa will not allow us to marry, but et is before God dat we claim ourselves husband and wife. We do not need witnesses, as he is de only one dat counts."

A smile grew across his face. "Well den, wife, I say we make you my wife in all ways!" He swept her into his arms and carried her to the tall grass, where he gently laid her down.

That night they became husband and wife in all forms be-fore God. They spent hours clasped together as one under the stars.

Henrietta's intuition had been right, for within the week she was alone in the kitchen when the masa entered. Fear clawed at her, and she looked wildly around for an escape route. She edged toward the back door, but he pounced on her before she had barely taken two steps.

"Your weeks of toying with me will stop now, nigger!" he snarled.

"I'm not toying wid you, Masa. I only wish to be about my wuk and be left alone," she pleaded, trying to escape his grasp, but his fingers burrowed into her arm.

"Left alone? You are my property to use as I see fit." He cocked his head, his eyes raking over her body.

"Please let me go!" she cried, panic choking her voice. Curling her free hand into a fist, she hit him repeatedly, trying to fight him off. "Oh, fight, little one. I like that even more." He chuckled and wrestled her around until her back was against his chest.

With one swipe of his arm he cleared the table, then pinned her facedown on it with one arm. With the other he raised her skirt and with one sharp, painful thrust, he was inside of her. The next minutes seemed like hours. Finally he found his release and withdrew. With a hard slap to her backside, he stepped back.

She never moved. She heard him pull up his trousers and then shuffle around the room. "Until next time, little one," he whispered in a thick voice. Then he was gone.

She lay there in pain and horror at his violation of her body. Lily found her that way and scurried to find Big John. He burst through the kitchen house door with Lily right behind him. Henrietta fell into the safety of his arms and wept as he led her away.

The rapes happened frequently, breaking her spirit once again. She learned to not fight to reduce the pain and his aggressiveness, willing her mind and spirit to go to the place where she had sent it before John entered her life. Her will to live was gone. Big John tried to comfort her but his words fell on deaf ears.

Her already crumbling world crumbled a little more when

she found out she was with child. She knew it was the masa's; she hadn't been able to let Big John touch her in an intimate way since the rapes started. Bitter and angry, she refused to love a child born of her masa's seed. She went to the witch doctor, as the slave woman who practiced such things was called, to rid herself of the babe. The witch was busy with another slave girl, and told Henrietta to return in a few hours. She sat on the front porch of the witch's shack, waiting her turn.

How Big John happened to pass by she wasn't sure, but when he noticed her he paused, knowing the steps she sat on were those of the witch doctor's. Not wanting him to try to change her mind, she turned her back to him and told him to go away. He would have none of it, and sat in silence beside her. When the witch came out he glared at her and plucked Henrietta from the porch, snapping, "She ain't gitting rid of de baby." He marched her away. She dug her heels into the ground and struggled with every step they took.

When they were alone he loosened his grip. He took her into his loving embrace. Scared and feeling helpless, she had cried, whispering over and over, "What will I evvr do."

Big John said they would raise the child as if they had made it together. They prayed the child would be born of a darker complexion so the masa and missus wouldn't know he had fathered the child. They knew Henrietta could not handle any more heartbreak. If the masa found out, the child would be sold or drowned in the river to cover up his shame at having a child with a nigger.

When her child was born, John handed her the baby bundled in a clean white cloth. She looked at her daughter with her straight, full hair capping her head like a summer bonnet, her skin wrinkled and new. She gawked up at her mother with round, unfocused eyes. Placing a finger in the tiny grasp of her baby, Henrietta discovered a love like no other.

John made true his promise to father Mary Grace as his own. He cooed at her when he held her and kissed the top of her little head. Henrietta loved to sit and watch him with their daughter. But with each changing month, Mary Grace's skin grew paler, and the slaves' tongues started to wag. Talk of the white blood in her daughter reached the big house.

One day the missus sent Lily for her. Lily found her in the kitchen house and Henrietta knew something was wrong by the meek way Lily approached her.

"Henrietta?"

"Yes, Lily?"

Lily hung her head and said, "De missus wants to see you and de chile."

"Why, Lily? What she want wid my Mary Grace?" Henrietta fretted.

"I'm not sho', but you bes' hurry."

Henrietta went to find the elderly slave woman who tended Mary Grace each day while she performed her tasks. Gathering up her sleeping daughter, she snuggled her tight against her cheek, inhaling her sweet baby smell. Her legs felt like lead as she pushed herself toward the big house and up the front steps. Fear threatened to cut off her air as she made her way to the study in search of the missus. She found the missus alone, waiting for her.

When Henrietta entered, the missus rose and came around the desk to stand in front of her. She reached forward to inspect the now wiggling and wide-awake Mary Grace. Unable to deny the child was fathered by her husband, she stepped back. Rubbing her forehead with her index finger and thumb as if to rub away tension, she addressed Henrietta. "I can't control my husband. I do not agree with the ways of men and what they think they can do with the women slaves. It is not holy before

God, and I will not be shamed by his sins in my own household. I will not separate you from your child, but you can't stay here, as he will only find you and father more of your children. If your child had been born darker, it might have gone unnoticed. A gentleman will be here this afternoon and you will be going with him. I need you gone before my husband gets back tomorrow. I suggest you say your goodbyes. You're dismissed." She turned to gaze out the window.

Henrietta felt weak as she tottered out of the main house and down the front steps. How many times had she wished to be off this plantation and away from the masa? But to be separated from John—she couldn't bear it!

She hurried to John's cabin, hoping to find him there and not in the fields. Luck was on her side; she found him mixing potions, and he smiled with surprise when she entered. The smile faded when he read her face. "Rita, what is de matter?"

"We've bin sold, John. Mary Grace and I be leaving in a few hours on a ship headed to Charleston, de missus say."

"No..." he moaned.

"Et true, my love. I don't know how I gwine to go on widout you, John. I jus' can't bear de thoughts of losing someone I love again. I've bin strong for so many years until you came into my life. Den de masa, he broke me, and den dis here baby gal and your love healed me. Now I'm weak and breakable all over again." She wept with overwhelming grief.

His feelings of grief at once again losing his family took over, and her African prince fell to his knees and a cry of anguish split the air. The sound sent Mary Grace into screams of her own, and with this Henrietta and John both tried to comfort her.

That afternoon the man arrived, and it was the last time she saw Big John.

She was sent to Charleston, South Carolina, and stood at

auction waiting for her next master. She knew she and Mary Grace could be sold as a bundle or split, whatever the buyers wanted. Terror at the thought of losing Mary Grace made her hold her infant tighter. She looked out over the crowd, praying God would show her mercy this one time in her life. Her eyes settled on a tall, handsome blond man; beside him stood his exceedingly pregnant wife, lightly holding his arm. She was petite, with dark, wavy hair framing her face, her eyes green and enchanting. There was a kindness in those eyes that Henrietta held onto. The woman gave her a smile of compassion and tugged on her husband's arm. He lowered his ear to her and then looked at Henrietta. What happened next was a whirlwind, ending with auctioneer yelling, "Mother and child sold to this gentleman here and his wife!"

Thus began Mammy and Mary Grace's story at the Livingston Plantation.

# CHAPTER Twenty-Six

A WEEK HAD PASSED SINCE OUR TRIP TO TOWN. I DECIDED TO PAY Whitney a visit and asked Jimmy to ready a carriage. Mary Grace would accompany me to the Barry Plantation.

The groomsman and footmen stood ready to manage the carriage as Jimmy brought it around front, stopping at the carriage stone. "Gentlemen, we will not require your services today, as I would like James to drive us," I told them. They did not question my request and bowed in acceptance.

"But Miss Willow, your father for sho' frown on dat," Jimmy said.

"Well, Father is not here and I'm in charge." I smiled wickedly.

Mary Grace joined us with a cheerful, "I'm here, Miss Willow."

The open carriage ride along the ocean coast to the Barry Plantation was beautiful and serene. I inhaled deeply of the salty ocean air and settled in to enjoy the ride. Freedom from scornful eyes set Mary Grace and I to daydreaming aloud of what we wished life was like. From his perch on the rich brown-leather seat, Jimmy could hear our girlish chatter. Every once in a while he would chuckle softly and shake his head. We rode along without a care in the world, and it was like we had stepped into another time: a time when skin color didn't restrict Mary Grace and Jimmy from being my friends, in a world that looked on us as equals.

"James, what would you do with your life if things could be different?" Mary Grace asked.

"Well, gal, I would own a piece of land out in no man's land and maybe git a hog or two. I'd have a garden as far as you could see and maybe a dog for company."

"What about a wife?" I piped up.

"Nah, don't have much use for a wife," he snorted. "You womens are a lot of emotions and wuk." This sent Mary Grace and me into fits of giggles.

"What 'bout you, Mary Grace? What would you do?" Jimmy said.

"Gray and I would have our own little place with five children running around, causing us worry. I'd raise them to be strong-minded and teach them to read and write. Gray and I would grow old together, rocking on our front porch in our matching rockers," she said dreamily, staring out over the ocean.

Tears welled and I tried to nonchalantly brush them away before they spilled over, not wishing to spoil the moment. Their dreams stirred emotions I'd carried near and dear to my heart for the Negro race since I was old enough to understand the world viewed us as different.

How simple were the things they wanted, but how impossible to them it must seem. Things white folks took for granted, the Negroes only dreamed of. Their desires were not grand, just the simple human right to be free. Mary Grace and Jimmy held no malice for my kind; they only wanted to be left alone to live in peace with no masters.

# CHAPTER *Twenty-Seven*

THE BARRYS' MAIN HOUSE SAT UP ON A HILL OVERLOOKING THE plantation. The home had been remodeled in the new design, with three large, Greek-inspired columns supporting a portico at the front of the house. The white shutters were open, letting in the morning sun. The home effused pleasantness. So why couldn't I shake the turmoil plaguing me as the carriage rumbled up the drive toward it?

As we drew closer I noticed there were no sounds of laughter, no small children playing alongside their mamas as they worked. There was no murmured conversation from the slaves. The yard in front of the plantation didn't show any signs of life, which seemed odd for a working plantation. Chills ran through me and my scalp prickled. Mary Grace shivered beside me as if someone had walked over her grave. We looked at each other and I saw my anxiety mirrored in her eyes. Jimmy's eyes were sharp as he looked around the plantation, and I noticed his back stiffen. I fought down the desire to flee as Whitney stepped out on the veranda.

"Willow," she called out as she hurried down the steps to open the carriage door.

"I thought I'd take my cue from you and stop by for a visit." I smiled, uncertainty prodding at me as I glanced around.

"I'll take that Southern belle right out of you, Willow Hendricks."

"That's what I'm afraid of. Father will be fit to be tied if you rub off on me." I laughed, imagining his face.

"Well, we have one life to live. We may as well live it."

Whitney's home lacked the grandeur of Livingston. The foyer was cold and echoing. As Whitney led me along the corridor away from it, I stopped to study the large portraits hanging on the walls.

"Kind of creepy, if you ask me," Whitney said, stopping and turning to look with me. "All these dead people looking at you as you go about your day. The funny thing is, these people aren't even relatives." She snorted. "Father acquired these before we moved here."

Perplexed, I looked from her to the portraits. "Why would he hang them here?"

"To gain social status. He has gone as far as to make up a story about each person in the portraits. He expounds on the Barrys' great legacy to his guests. My father is all kinds of shady."

I shook my head in puzzlement. "That is one of the most bizarre things I've heard."

"Trust me, I agree. Enough about Father, as I'll never figure him out. What do you say I get us a glass of lemonade and we go for a walk by the creek? It's the only view worth seeing around here."

"Sure, that sounds lovely," I murmured, trying to sound cheerful because, frankly, I couldn't wait to get out of this house.

"I'll be right back." She disappeared down the hall.

The uncanny silence made the hairs stand up on my arms. Wrapping my arms around myself, I tried to rub away the chill. If the walls could talk, I believe they would whisper of the evil that happened in this place.

Glad to see Whitney return, I eagerly took the crystal tumbler she held out. We retrieved our parasols in the foyer and stepped outside.

Jimmy stood watering the horses and Mary Grace wasn't anywhere in sight. Maybe she had friends here that she'd wandered off to find. My nerves were once again on edge.

Rufus rounded the corner of the house from the field behind it and his eyes fell on Jimmy. He paid Whitney and I no mind as he drew up his horse and sneered at Jimmy, "Mule, take your thieving ass out back. No black pigs are allowed out front."

"Rufus!" Whitney warned. "Who do you think you are, speaking to my guest's driver in such a manner?"

"Only good nigger is one with his back down and ass up in the fields," he declared.

"You go back to the fields where you belong, and let me tend to matters here." She slapped his mare's rump, and the horse took off at a gallop, nearly toppling Rufus from the saddle.

"Jimmy, I would prefer you take the carriage around back while we are gone," I instructed, choking down the worry niggling at me. "And please keep your eyes open and find Mary Grace. Mammy would never forgive me if something happened to her."

"Yes, Miss Willie."

# CHAPTER Twenty-Eight

TO REACH THE CREEK WE PASSED THROUGH THE CENTER OF THE slave quarters. The living conditions were not fit for animals, let alone humans. There was a stench in the air of uncleanliness and human waste. I covered my nose with my handkerchief. The shacks for the slaves were exactly that: they were barely standing and in colder temperatures, I doubted they would protect the occupants from the elements. We walked by the whipping post, which stood in the center of the quarters. This post appeared to be put to frequent use, as it was stained with years of dried blood, and fresh blood from some recent punishment splattered the ground around it.

There was little movement in the quarters. An elderly slave walked by carrying a water pail balanced on his shoulder. Lack of nourishment had hollowed his face and left his body a walking corpse. But it was the sight of the side of his face that drew a moan from deep with me. Horrible cruelty had been inflicted upon him. The skin on his face pooled like a long-burnt candle. He walked by, his face dull and devoid of any emotion. A middle-aged man stood hunched over homemade crutches. His right foot had been cut off at the ankle, leaving an ugly nub. He'd probably tried to run. I'd heard of masters meting out this punishment on runaways. We passed slaves clothed in tatters that scarcely covered their bodies. The dead walked in the form of slaves on this plantation. I couldn't handle the sight of this place anymore. I hastened my steps to leave the quarters behind me.

I slowed when we reached the creek, turning to Whitney to demand in a shrill voice, "How can you live here and allow this to go on?"

"Willow! Stop right there. Hear me out before you cast blame on me," Whitney said, her voice rising defensively. "I do not believe even you understand how much slaves have endured. You've spent most of your life away at school. When you are home, you've been restricted to your plantation, which is a far cry better than most, and therefore you too are sheltered. If we are going to make a difference, we need to have all blinders off. I wanted you to see the actuality of how slaves not on your father's plantation, or who aren't owned by good masters, live. I moved here a mere three months ago. I begged my father to make the living conditions better. To show mercy like your father does. It's no use. My father is no better than Rufus.

"Do you know how it feels to stand by and see your own blood behave like a monster? The shame, the guilt, and the dread I feel every morning I wake up? I feel like I'm living in an inferno. Father punishes the slaves and forces the twins and me to watch. I can't protect them from it and when they cry and turn away he pulls back their heads and forces them to look. He says it will make them stronger." She paused, her expression disheartened. "I am not from here. I have not long been subjected to this and within weeks I tried to block out their faces. The helplessness was too much—until the day you made me view it in a different light." The unceasingly strong Whitney fought back tears, and agony twisted her lovely face as she looked at me.

Remorseful, I hugged her. "I'm sorry, Whitney. Forgive me for judging you. I know this isn't your doing."

She sniffled and pulled back. "I suppose in time I will learn to adjust to how things work in this part of the country," she said, drying her eyes.

We strolled along the creek; removing our shoes, we dipped our toes in the cool, refreshing water, trying to put the devastation of the slave quarters tucked behind the hill out of our minds. Wading knee deep out into the middle of the creek, we splashed each other, and the shock of the cool water took our breath away.

Our dresses and petticoats heavy with water, we staggered up the bank and plopped to the ground. No words passed between us. We sat lost in our own thoughts.

Movement beside a big boulder caught my eye. Squinting, I focused on the area but saw nothing. I scoured the bushes around the boulder—nothing. Then, as I started to turn away, I saw a dark face peek around the boulder before darting back behind it.

"Whitney," I whispered, keeping my lips still, "we are being watched. Come."

"What?" Whitney whispered back, rising with me.

Like sleuths set on solving a mystery, we crept toward the boulder. We rounded it to see two slaves, a woman and a child, crouching with their backs to us, peering around the boulder toward where we'd been sitting. Spooked by our sudden disappearance, the woman looked wildly around, searching for us.

We stepped into their view. They jumped like startled rabbits at the sight of us. The young woman pulled back, her arms going around the child—a boy of about seven years—as her eyes darted from side to side, looking for an escape route.

I raised a hand in reassurance. "We are friends."

"We mean no harm," Whitney said.

The woman pushed the boy behind her, shielding him from us. Her face was taut with fear and her gaze flitted about, never settling on us. Sensing the woman felt cornered, I slowly dropped to my knees; Whitney followed suit.

"You are runaways, aren't you?" Whitney edged forward.

The woman became even more skittish; seeing her start to panic, I smiled and said, "Please let us help you. We will hide you. You can't stay here. Right over the hill are men who would surely cause you harm." I motioned toward the Barry Plantation.

The young woman studied us, trying to determine if I spoke the truth. Then her body relaxed and her face softened slightly as she decided we were not a threat.

"I'm Willow," I said, "and this is my friend Whitney."

The woman's voice came out like a croak at first. Clearing her throat, she tried again. "I'm Georgia and dis is my brother Sam."

The boy came out from behind his sister. He was handsome, and dressed in finely tailored clothes, now dirty and torn. He had to be a domestic slave to a wealthy family to be wearing clothes of that quality.

"How long have you been running, Georgia?" I asked.

"We've bin running for five moons, Missus."

I could only imagine what struggles the two had faced. The low country was surrounded by swamps that went on for miles; they were filled with all kind of dangers. I'd heard of slaves taking to the swamps to shield themselves from the slave catchers. Life-or-death desperation gave them a will and strength most people didn't possess. Georgia was one of these brave souls.

"We need to hide you somewhere safe and out of sight." I turned to Whitney for her suggestion.

"They can't stay at our plantation—Rufus would sniff them out for sure."

I agreed with her; it was the last place we could hide them. "Maybe I should take them to my plantation, as Father is away for at least another week. Which would give us enough time to figure out what we can do."

"The question is, how are we going to sneak them past Rufus's hawk-like eyes?" Whitney frowned in thought before her eyes widened, and she grinned. "I know a place. There is an old well I stumbled upon a while back, not far from here. We can lower them into that and when it's dark, come back for them. I can't help you at night, as Rufus does his nightly rounds and he will be suspicious if he sees me slipping out in the dark. But we can find it from this creek in minutes."

"All right, it's not like we have much choice," I said. My insides were tied in knots—we had made this promise, and there was no turning back. I was not a risk-taker but I had just become ears-deep in danger.

"You all wait here. I'll go find some rope and food." Whitney pushed herself up and scurried off.

Nervous, I looked at my new responsibilities. Their faces held hope. How our roles had changed—their faces were now relaxed and mine was taut with worry. I heard my racing heart pounding inside my skull. I leaned back against the boulder and closed my eyes, trying to slow my heartbeat. A few minutes passed before I opened them.

Sam had seated himself a few feet away and was playing with a stick and some rocks. Georgia sat with her eyes riveted on me. When our eyes met, she looked away and shifted her position. She let out a quiet groan.

I noticed the blood on the back of her dress. "Georgia, are you hurt?"

She nodded as she raised her skirt high enough for me to see her leg. It was bandaged with cloth she'd ripped from her skirt, and blood seeped through the cloth. "Hound's teeth got de bes' of me." She grimaced, straightening the leg.

"We will get it attended to as soon as we are safe," I assured her. "What plantation are you from?"

"None 'round here, Miss. We hid in de back of a farmer's wagon for de bes' of a day of ets travels. We've bin walkin' ever since. Four days back we took to de swamps to shake off dem slave catchers after one of dem hounds got in snapping distance of me."

"I can't begin to imagine what you have been through, Georgia. Were your masters cruel?"

"Yes, Missus," she said, and softly told me what they had suffered. "When de masa start coming to our cabin I thought he's lukin' for me, but I saw his eyes lukin' to my brother. He be sick wid wicked thoughts. Since dat day, I made sure to allus keep Sam close to me. Then one day I be catching a slave wench's baby and when I got back, my brother's gone." She shook with emotion. "I hurried real fast to de big house. I do not care 'bout nobody but my li'l brother. I found him in de masa's study, dressed in dose clothes." She nodded toward the boy. "De masa, he was half dressed, with his trousers undone." She lifted the hem of her dress and buried her face in it.

I was sickened by the implications of what she had witnessed. I drew her into an embrace.

Sam, seeing his sister in distress, moved to her and rested his small hand on her shoulder. "What's wrong, Georgia? Why you be crying?" he asked innocently, then he narrowed his eyes at me, looking to place blame. "What did you say to her?"

"Nothing. Your sister is overjoyed that you are safe."

His eyes softened. "Et will be all right, Georgia. You tuk real good care of us. Missus says et'll be all right." He lifted his sister's face and gave her a toothy smile of encouragement.

She laughed at his award-winning smile. "Yes, li'l brother."

Whitney returned empty-handed and I prickled with unease. "You didn't get the supplies?"

"Oh, you have yet so much to learn about me, Willow dear,"

she drawled, turning and lifting the back of her skirt waist-high. There, hanging from her waistband, was a small satchel. Whitney pulled it free and dropped it on the ground in front of me.

I took a peek inside. "That's all well and good. They won't starve. But how do you suppose we are going to lower them into the well?" I asked sarcastically.

Whitney gave me a look of exasperation as she twirled around and hiked up the front of her skirt. Sure enough, there was a coil of rope hanging from the front of her petticoats. I had once again underestimated her. I smiled at her cleverness. What better way to get past Rufus and his goons unnoticed?

"I do believe I love how your mind works." I laughed with nervous happiness and Whitney quickly hushed me. "I know. Sorry." I lowered my voice and said, "Let's move. We've taken long enough."

As Whitney had promised, the well was only minutes from the creek. When we reached it, we peered down the dark hole. I was relieved to see it was bone dry.

Working together, we lowered Sam down first. When it was Georgia's turn, she stepped back, concern pulling at her face. "Come on, Georgia, we have to hurry," I insisted, scanning our surroundings. It had to be my imagination, but my skin crawled, as if someone watched us.

"I'm scared of heights, Missus," Georgia said, edging farther from the well.

Whitney glanced over her shoulder. "We don't have time for this, Georgia," she said, her tone sharp with impatience. "The longer you're in the open, the more we are at risk of being discovered. Now move along."

"Whitney." I narrowed my eyes at her, afraid her attitude would threaten the trust we had formed with Georgia. I rested my hands gently on Georgia's quivering shoulders, affirming our status as friends. "I know you are scared, Georgia, but you need to find the courage you used to help your brother escape. You can't give up yet."

She looked from Whitney to me, then nodded.

"Thank the good Lord," Whitney said with a sigh. Taking Georgia's nod as her cue, she moved forward, tied the rope around Georgia's waist, and we lowered her down, digging our heels into the ground as we struggled against her weight.

"When it's dark, I'll be back," I called down.

"Yessum," her voice echoed back.

# CHAPTER Twenty-Nine

BACK AT THE PLANTATION, WE HURRIED THROUGH THE SLAVE quarters and were almost back to the house when Mary Grace's cry reached us: "No, Masa, please don't."

Frantic at the panic that was evident in her voice, I ran as fast as my heavy, soaked skirt would allow.

I heard Jimmy's voice. "Masa, Miss Willow won't take much lakin' to you harming her nigra."

"This way," Whitney squeaked, pulling me toward a nearby woodshed.

"Shut the blazes up, nigger. Go away and mind your own business." I recognized Rufus's voice.

I heard the sound of the first punch as I rounded the corner of the shed, quickly followed by the second, which I saw Rufus deliver to the side of Jimmy's face. Yates and Dave held Jimmy's arms behind his back. Mary Grace was pinned by fear against the shed, her blouse torn and her breast exposed.

*I'll kill him!* I seethed. "Mary Grace, to the carriage," I demanded and when she hesitated, I yelled, "Now!" Mary Grace snapped out of her daze and bolted past us, holding her blouse closed.

"Release my slave this instant," I yelled at Rufus's cronies. "And if you have any wisdom in those knuckle-brain heads of yours, you will not say another word."

The men knew better than to harm us or they would answer

to Mr. Barry. They loosened their grip on Jimmy, who jerked his arms free and moved out of their reach.

Turning my anger on Rufus, I clenched my fist tight and with all my strength, I swung it square at the center of his nose. He squealed as his nose made a crunching sound and started squirting blood. "You broke my nose!"

For a second I was amazed at my own strength, until the pain throbbed through my hand. I suppressed the urge to groan and shake out the pain.

Whitney barged in to back me up. "Get yourselves back to the fields, you idiots." Her nostrils flared.

I examined Jimmy's face.

"I'm all right, Miss Willie."

"To the carriage. We leave for Livingston immediately."

"Yes, Miss Willie," he said, keeping an eye on the men, unsure if he should leave us unattended.

"It will be fine, Jimmy. They know better than to harm us. My father will have their hides if they are stupid enough to touch us."

With one last look at the men, Jimmy scampered away.

"A nigger lover, aren't ya, pretty one?" Rufus jeered, his voice muffled by the dirty handkerchief he held over his nose. "It all makes perfect sense now. Well, you'd better watch your back, Missy, because I will find you and there will be hell to pay. I promise you that." He glared balefully at me.

His threat was real and it quickened my heart. But I willed myself to remain steadfast; I couldn't let him see that his threat rattled me.

Whitney pushed herself between us, her height allowing her to tower over the smaller man. "Are you threatening a guest on my land?" She gave him a shove backward. "I will inform my father of this. And you know how Father's social status is everything to him. Let me assure you, you will suffer his temper, and we both know that isn't pleasant, now, is it?" She boldly moved forward. "I'm sure you are aware of how powerful a man Miss Hendricks's father is." She smirked, looking him up and down.

A nerve twitched in Rufus's face. It did not change the bold, unspoken warning in the last look he gave us before he wandered off. We had made a deadly enemy, and it terrified me.

# CHAPTER *Thirty*

As the Barry Plantation shrank with the growing distance, I collapsed against the carriage seat. Mary Grace let out a soft moan, and I slipped an arm around her. She rested her head against my shoulder. The carriage ride of earlier was but a memory, pushed aside by the stresses and worries of the day. No words passed between us on the solemn ride home.

Livingston seemed like a breath of fresh air as we pulled up. Mary Grace exited the carriage in search of Mammy. Pulling Jimmy aside, I examined his face. "Go to the ice house and find some ice to apply to your face."

"Thank you," he mumbled, but he didn't immediately leave. "I see somepin is on your mind."

*Old buzzard. Can't get anything by him.* I grinned. Speaking quietly, I set my plan in motion. "I need a covered wagon ready for tonight. Park it behind the old barn on the north side."

"Miss Willie, what you up to now?" Concern flooded his face.

"I can't tell you. Please make sure you have it ready at dark, and be discreet."

"Yessum," he said. Mumbling under his breath, he led the horses away.

I waited in my room until the house grew still before

slipping down the back stairs and out a side door into the night. I scanned the darkness to make sure it was clear before I beelined it for the north barn.

The wagon stood ready, as I'd requested. Jimmy appeared to be nowhere in sight, and I was relieved, as I'd half expected to have an argument on my hands when I arrived.

Under the cover of darkness, I drove the wagon over the back field until I got to the track that led to the main road. The narrow track was barely wide enough for the wagon to fit through, and I struggled to keep the tree branches from slapping me as the horses pushed through. The branches clawed and scraped at the wagon.

The pressure of anxiety and fear made me so tense my muscles ached, and I started to question my own sanity. I was a woman alone at night. There was no telling what I could come across on the roads. Could I even lift the runaways out of the well? Say we made it back to Livingston: how would I keep them hidden without anyone finding out? I couldn't risk Mary Grace, Jimmy, or Mammy finding out, for their own protection.

"Willow Hendricks, you have done lost your mind," I huffed.

I talked courage into myself as I bounced along on the hard wagon seat. My inexperience at driving a wagon caused me to grip the reins tight. My knuckles were white and my hands ached from the stress. The light from the lantern hanging on the front of the wagon seemed dim in the pitch-black night.

I almost missed the white cloth Whitney had tied at the entrance of the path leading to the well. She'd placed it low in the brush where no one would notice unless they were watching for it. I turned the wagon down the rocky path and thrashed side to side as the horses pushed forward.

The meadow came into sight and I drew the wagon to a halt at the end of the path, using the trees for cover. Climbing down,

I unhitched the lantern.

Scuffling came from inside the wagon.

I froze. My mouth went dry, and my heartbeat pounded in my ears.

"Miss Willie, et's me, Jimmy." The whisper came from behind the wagon, followed by a thump as his feet hit the ground.

I didn't know if I should cry or hug the fool! "Jimmy, you scared the dickens out of me. What are you doing here?"

"I needed to be sho' you weren't gitting yourself into trouble wid dose lofty ideas you allus gittin'." A grin crept across his face.

Relief washed over me at the sight of him. He was heavenly. I cried and laughed and crushed him into a massive hug. "It's not safe for me to be here, let alone you, a slave." I pulled back, frustrated that now I had endangered him.

"What you up to, Miss Willie?"

"I guess there is no keeping you safe now," I grumbled. "Come with me; I'll show you."

Leaving the lantern on the floor of the wagon under the seat, I grabbed the rope and we crossed the meadow toward the well. It was so dark we stumbled along, and I wished I had the lantern to guide the way, but I knew the risk was too great. My feet got tangled in the hem of my skirt and Jimmy grabbed my elbow to catch my fall.

At the well I called down, "Georgia, Sam, it's Willow."

A swishing sound echoed from below and then a reply came. "We here, Miss Willow."

I slumped against the stone wall of the well, relief overtaking me at the sound of her voice. I turned to Jimmy, who stood dumbfounded. I lifted a hand, requesting his silence. "Don't start, Jimmy. We had no choice; they needed our help. Now, let's tie a loop and lower it down to them. We need to get out of here fast, before Rufus and his men find us."

He nodded and stepped up to do my bidding. Georgia helped send Sam up and as we pulled her up, I was grateful for Jimmy's stubbornness. Whitney and I had underestimated the strength it would take to pull someone out of the well. It was hard enough to lower Georgia down, but to pull her up proved to be ten times harder.

When Georgia toppled onto the ground, Jimmy helped her up and without hesitation, he hustled them toward the wagon. Goosebumps peppered my body as I looked around and once again felt as if I were being watched. I shook my head. Such ghoulish thoughts would drive me mad. The sliver of moon provided little light, making it useless to scan the darkness, but my overactive mind made me sprint toward the wagon, spooked by an eerie feeling that I was being stalked.

We hid Georgia and her brother in the wagon under an oilcloth. "Jimmy, you go in the back too. I won't have you seen if we encounter someone on the ride back."

"No, Miss Willie. Et already luks amiss for you to be out for an evenin' ride, but a 'oman alone for sho' be a sign dat somepin' up."

"Ugh…you're right," I huffed, annoyed. With all my efforts to protect the ones I loved, I hadn't thought of this.

We clambered up onto the seat and turned the wagon in the open field. At the edge of the road, I told Jimmy to stop so I could retrieve the white cloth marking the trail. Then we continued on our way back to Livingston.

When Jimmy pulled the wagon up beside the barn, I jumped down with a hand from Jimmy. The plan was to move the runaways into the house without being detected while Jimmy got the wagon and horses tucked away.

Leading Georgia and Sam, I sneaked up the back staircase

like we were thieves in the night. I had warned Georgia and Sam to not say a word and tread lightly, as Mammy's and Mary Grace's sleeping quarters were down the hall and the slight creak of a floorboard could wake them. No one was the wiser as we crept up the stairs.

When I had securely closed the bedroom door behind us, I sagged against it, relieved to be in the safety of my room. We had made it—but what was I going to do now?

"Tonight, you will stay in my closet, out of sight. Tomorrow we will get you out. But right now, we need to attend to your leg, Georgia," I said, ushering her over to sit on the bed.

I reached under my mattress where I had hidden the bandages and ointment I'd secured earlier in the day. After I'd cleaned and bandaged the wound, we prepared to settle in for the night. Taking down some of the extra bedding Mammy stored in my closet, I helped Georgia make a comfortable pallet for her and Sam.

"I know you are probably hungry, but we can't risk going back to the kitchen and being found out. Will you be all right until morning?"

They nodded with silent gratitude. Both showed signs of fatigue. Wishing them a good night, I closed the door.

I prepared for bed swiftly. Climbing under the covers, I leaned over and blew out the lamp on the night table. I lay awake beneath my silken sheets. My head was spinning with dire possibilities as I analyzed how we were going to get them away without anyone finding them. Whitney would come by tomorrow, and we would solidify the plan we had contrived earlier. With that thought, I fell asleep.

# CHAPTER Thirty-One

Morning arrived all too soon and I was awakened by a knock at the door. I sat up in an immediate panic. "Oh, no!"

The door opened and in came Mammy. "Chile, et is 'most nine o'clock. What are you still doing lazing in dat dere bed?" She pulled the velvet drapes back and sunlight spilled in, blinding me with its brightness.

"Mammy!" I complained, covering my eyes.

"Well, you gotta git up and git on wid your day." She frowned at me.

It was unusual for me to be in bed past five o'clock. I was thankful that I was able to quickly form an excuse. "We had a hard day yesterday, Mammy. Didn't Mary Grace tell you?"

"You mean 'bout dat Barry overseer trying to hurt my Mary Grace and beatin' on poor ol' Jimmy? Dat man be a low-life good for nothin'. De devil is in his eyes, I tell ya," she said, fluffing a pillow, sending its tassels swinging fiercely before she placed it back on the ivory chaise lounge in the corner.

"It was overwhelming, Mammy. And I was so scared for them. Do you mind bringing me a tray in my room? I think I'll have breakfast in bed today." I felt a tinge of guilt as Mammy eyed me with genuine concern.

"I'll be right back, chile. You jus' lay your head back and rest." She leaned down, tucking the blankets in around me as she had done every night when I was a child.

Mammy left to prepare my breakfast.

I thought back to the time before my twelfth birthday. It had been a nightly routine for Mammy to come and wish me good night; she would sit on the edge of my bed and pull my covers up under my chin before tucking them snug around me. After a brief chat, she would blow out the light.

I recalled saying to her one evening, "Mammy, I'm a grown woman now, and I don't need you to be swaddling me in like a baby."

Mammy had smiled a sad smile before replying, "All right, Li'l Miss, as you say."

I noted her sadness and jumped up and hugged her tightly. "But I will always love you, Mammy, like you were my own real mama." I declared my love with the pureness of a child.

Mammy kissed my forehead and said, "You real sweet, angel gal." She blew out the lantern and ever since that night, Mammy never came again to tuck me in.

The door opened and Mammy entered carrying a silver tray. A single yellow rose lay beside the dishes. Breakfast was a feast for a queen, with two hard-boiled eggs, a slab of ham, a bowl of fresh-cut fruit, and two slices of thick toast served with jam and honey, along with a glass of orange juice and a cup of coffee. Mammy always tried to spoil me with food; it was her way of showing love. She set the tray down on the nightstand.

"Thanks, Mammy, this looks amazing." She smiled and patted my shoulder affectionately before shuffling out of the room and closing the door behind her.

As her footsteps faded off, I threw the covers back and scrambled to the closet. Georgia and Sam sat huddled together, their faces anguished.

"It's safe. Come out." I beckoned, then guided them to the

bed. "Sit." I handed them the tray.

"What 'bout you?" Sam asked around a mouthful of toast.

"You eat. I will eat something later. But make sure you leave a little, so Mammy doesn't suspect I have grown a second stomach." I winked at him, giving his wooly hair a tousle.

The two devoured the food in no time. Behind the privacy screen, with Georgia's help, I dressed for the day. After a quick use of the chamber pot, Georgia and Sam returned to the closet. The sun shone through its small window, providing light in the claustrophobic space. Seated at my vanity, I braided my hair and tied a red ribbon on the end of the braid before heading downstairs.

The house was alive with activity. House slaves scrubbed the floors and I was mindful not to step in the areas they had recently cleaned. I found Mammy and Mary Grace dusting in the library.

Mary Grace looked up as I entered. "Morning, Miss Willow." Then her brows drew into a frown at my appearance.

"What?" I smoothed my hair.

"Your hair, it's farm-girl plain," Mary Grace said boldly.

"Mary Grace!" I laughed at her playful insult.

"Mama said you wanted to relax for a spell or I would have come and fixed it properly."

"Well, it's done, and it will do fine for today." I chuckled at her sass.

"Hello?" I heard Whitney's voice before she ducked her head into the room. She held my parasol in one hand and a parcel in the other. "Thaddeus told me I could find you in here. He was going to show me in, but I insisted I'd show myself. I hope you don't mind."

"Whitney, what a surprise," I said with a smile.

"You left your parasol yesterday. I thought I would stop by and personally deliver it."

"Thank you, but you didn't have to."

"Well, honestly, the other reason I came is I'm going into town today to pick up that new dress I told you about. The one I ordered from Paris. Would you like to join me?"

"Do you ever sit still, Whitney?" I teased.

"When I'm dead I will sit still. Until then…" She grinned.

"That settles it, then. We are off on another adventure." I left the library with Whitney on my heels. In the hallway, she quickly beckoned for me to follow her upstairs.

In my room, Whitney tore open the parcel she had brought, revealing clothing for Georgia and Sam.

"Clever girl," I said.

"Well, ya know!" she bragged, striking an exaggerated pose.

"Stop!" I giggled, giving her a playful shove.

Opening the closet door, I handed my hidden guests the clothing. When they were dressed, they emerged from the closet, and I filled them in on the plan.

"We will take you down the back stairs and through the sitting room, as the French doors open onto the back field. It's our best chance of getting you out of the house without being seen. Once you get to the trees there is a trail you can follow, and it will take you out to the main road, where we will be waiting to pick you up. Understood?"

"Yessum," Georgia replied, tightening her arm around her brother.

Whitney and I watched from the sitting room as Georgia and Sam ran toward the trees. I stood willing them to reach the tree line, and exhaled as they disappeared between the trunks.

Whitney quietly cheered. Then, grasping my hand, she said, "Let's get on with it."

# CHAPTER Thirty-Two

WHITNEY DROVE THE WAGON THROUGH THE GATES AND along the road toward the two humans lying in hiding, hoping for a chance at freedom. Minutes down the road we came to the path I knew all too well from the many years I'd used it to escape Father's disapproving eye.

"It's clear," I called out as the wagon halted.

Two eager faces appeared. Georgia and Sam emerged and dashed to the back of the wagon, keen to get out of sight. Then Whitney urged the horses into a trot.

Reaching town, we headed to the dock in search of Knox. Whitney and I had decided it was worth the risk. I knew Knox to be a man of integrity. A little piece of me was also counting on his growing affection for Whitney. We would use whatever measures necessary to secure his help. Since Knox worked on the ships in the harbor, it made our chances of getting our cargo out on a ship to New York or Boston high. We were taking a leap of faith on Knox, but had no other options or ideas.

Whitney trotted off to find Knox, leaving me with the wagon. Hours seemed to pass as I waited. I became antsy as the time ticked by. *What is taking so long? We are sitting ducks here*. I grew increasingly fidgety. Then I saw her, and Knox came trailing behind.

"Your father's ship, the *Olivia II*, leaves in a few hours, headed for New York," she whispered. "Knox agreed to help us get them safely aboard."

"Father's ship! Are you crazy?"

"Shh!" Whitney warned, glancing around.

I felt sick. What were they thinking? Father would kill me if he found out. Literally! They had signed my death warrant.

I looked to Knox as he approached. Sweat beaded his forehead. "How are we getting them on the ship?" I asked, fearing I was about to hyperventilate.

"Leave it to me. I'll handle it. Pull your wagon around to the warehouse at the far end of the dock and I'll meet you there." He turned and headed back the way he'd come.

We complied, then waited and waited for Knox to come back. Had we been wrong to trust him? I glanced at Whitney. She was biting her lower lip and trying not to pace—she'd take one or two deliberate steps, then stop, arms stiff at her sides, shoulders hunched, and visibly force herself to relax. I worried that the longer we sat in the open, the more attention we would draw. From my seat on the wagon bench, I looked around. *Knox, where are you?*

Minutes later, I caught sight of him strolling toward us with a burlap sack slung over his shoulder. I blew out a breath. The barrel-chested brute of a man was the best thing I'd ever seen.

"Knox, what took you so long?" Whitney growled, coiled like a tiger ready to pounce on its prey.

"Land sakes, girl. You can't send them without any food."

"Oh." Whitney lowered her eyes.

Knox added an, "Oh," and looked at us, offended. "You two thought I snitched on you, didn't you?"

"You were taking so long we got concerned. It's not like we dropped this into your lap after giving you time to digest it all," I retorted.

He brushed it off. "We need to hurry." He opened the locked

door to the warehouse with a key. I wondered about his access to the key, but we had no time for the little details. My agitation was growing by the minute, and we needed to get out of sight.

"Come on, it's safe." Whitney slapped the side of the wagon.

I didn't know if it was my nerves or my mind playing tricks yet again, but the hair rose on the back of my neck along with the ghostly feeling of eyes on me. I cast a quick glance around before urging the slaves to move. "Hurry, inside now." I grabbed a dawdling Sam and lifted him from the wagon.

The building looked to have been vacant for years. It was gray with a heavy layer of dust and cobwebs. Several large crates were stacked off to the side. Knox nodded toward them. "We'll use one of those crates to get them aboard the ship." He then addressed Georgia. "Once you know the ship has left the dock and you are a few hours into your journey, there are tools in this sack to pry the crate open. There is enough food for a week in here too, if you portion it right. After that, you are on your own."

"Bless you all!" Georgia cried, tears welling in eyes that gleamed with hope as she wrapped an arm around her brother.

I smiled at her, then rested my gaze on Sam. Stepping forward, I cupped his chin in my hand and looked into his innocent eyes. "Go find your freedom, young Sam. Make a difference in this world." With the tip of my index finger, I lightly tapped the end of his nose.

"I will, Miss Willow." His smile reached his eyes.

"All right, you girls need to move that wagon out of here. A friend who works alongside me will be here any minute to help load the crate onto the ship."

"He won't think it's strange that you have a crate going out of this vacant warehouse?" Whitney asked.

"No, too many years of taking opium has made him simple in the head, but he is strong as an ox. Now, move that wagon out of here." He wiped his hands on his pants.

We got the wagon away from the dock and hidden from any curious eyes. Then we went to the dock cafe and found a seat by a window where we had a clear view of the *Olivia II*. We had no appetite, but ordered anyway. We needed to blend in. Whitney tried to make light conversation, and I did my best to follow. But my stomach was knotted with worry. We picked at our food as we waited.

Lunch turned into tea and dessert as we endured the next two hours. Whitney's feet were mindlessly tapping a staccato rhythm on the floor beneath our table. The noise was drawing attention. I reached under the table and placed my hand on her knee to quiet her restless legs.

I spotted Knox first. He was stopped at the bottom of the ship's gangplank. The ship guard must be questioning him. The guard walked around the crate Knox and his friend carried on their shoulders, inspecting it. My churning stomach threatened to spill my lunch, and I covered my mouth to suppress it.

The ship guard stepped aside and allowed Knox and his helper to pass. Whitney and I shared a look of relief. I slumped back in my seat, staring into space. They had made it that far, but they still weren't out of danger yet.

Another hour ticked by before the ship left the dock. When the ship was but a speck in the ocean, we paid the bill and left.

Knox appeared out of nowhere wearing a look of triumph. "Well, Whitney, now I expect you to hold up your end of the bargain." He grinned deviously.

"Yes," she said, her face turning rosy. She promptly climbed onto the wagon.

I glanced from Knox to Whitney in puzzlement.

"Let's go, Willow," she said in a tight voice that discouraged any discussion on the topic.

Knox offered me a hand up and with a wave, we were off.

"Do you mind telling me what your end of the bargain is?"

Whitney's hands clenched the reins and she looked at me with narrowed eyes. "I agreed to allow him to pay me a few visits."

"A few?" I said, arching a brow.

Exasperated, she replied, "I agreed to one at first. Then he tried to bargain with me to start a courtship. After we dickered back and forth, it was settled at a few visits."

I laughed. *Why, Knox Tucker, you sly old fox.* He was brilliant and I loved it.

Whitney glared at me and jabbed my ribs with her fingers, sending me into further fits of laughter.

CHAPTER

**Bowden**

He knew something was gravely wrong the day he came home from school to find his grandpa sitting with his face buried in his hands. He moved slowly toward him.

"Grandpa, is everything all right?"

His grandfather looked up at him, his eyes burdened with an unfathomable grief. He pulled a patterned handkerchief from his pocket and blew his nose loudly. "Sit down. I need to tell you something."

Bowden sat down and waited for his grandpa to speak. The silence was palpable, the ticking of the grandfather clock in the corner unnaturally loud.

Clearing his throat, his grandpa spoke. "There is no easy way to say this, Bowden—" His voice broke. Bowden recalled the way his grandpa's hands shook uncontrollably as he said, "There has been a terrible accident, son. Father and Mother have left us and made the journey on to heaven."

He sat unmoving, focusing on his grandpa's face as it floated farther and farther away. He heard the muffled sound of his grandfather's voice but couldn't decipher the words coming out. Stone, his three-year-old brother, and Bowden had been left in their grandpa's care while their parents were away. Guilt-ridden, now he thought back to the morning his parents had left. In the wee hours of the morn, his mother had come to his room. Annoyed at being awakened, he'd grumbled as the light of the lantern shone in his eyes.

"What?" he whined.

"We are leaving, love. I wanted to kiss you goodbye and tell you I love you."

"I love you too," he mumbled between yawns.

"I want you to stay out of trouble and help Grandpa with Stone."

"I know, Mother," he said, wishing for the light to go away so he could return to his slumber.

His father darkened the doorway. "Bowden, mind your manners," his father said sternly. He'd been a laid-back kind of father, but stepped in to back up his wife in her discipline of them.

"Yes, Father," he said with a hint of sarcasm.

His parents hugged and kissed him goodbye. Bowden had been too selfish to care and hadn't let them know how much he loved them. As they left his room his mother turned one last time and smiled, her eyes shining with love and admiration. "I'm proud of the young man you are becoming, Bowden. I'll miss you."

"I know." He threw his pillow over his eyes to ward off the light. Why was she always such a sentimental woman, with her "I love you" every day and her over-the-top number of hugs? She didn't need to restate it every day. He wanted her to get out of his room and let him sleep.

Stone had not truly understood that they were gone. He asked for their mother and father from time to time. Then the images of them faded from his small mind. Bowden swore to live every day to the fullest, and love Stone as they would have. He realized the importance of what his mom had done. She told her boys every day how much she cared. The words of his mother had healed his heart of the unbearable guilt and shame he carried for his behavior the last time he saw them alive.

After his parents' death, his grandpa sold the family's properties in Texas and moved them to Charleston. He purchased a plantation that needed a lot of fixing up and owned fewer than twenty slaves. His grandpa had been a very smart businessman and turned the run-down plantation into a thriving business. He always said, "Profit is key. You treat the slaves right, and they will return it tenfold. You mistreat them, you may as well burn your money." Bowden took his advice to heart.

Bowden wanted to be a doctor and his grandpa sent him off to the University of Pennsylvania to study. He received his degree as a medical doctor and had plans to travel back to Charleston to spend the summer with his grandfather and Stone when word came that his grandfather had pneumonia.

Bowden returned in time to see his grandfather before he passed, but now Stone and Bowden were again left without a guardian. He gave up his dreams of being a doctor to take on the responsibilities of running the plantation. He had shadowed his grandfather as he'd run the plantation over the years and understood the basics of running one. Soon he found that he had inherited the instincts that had made his grandfather a savvy businessman.

The Armstrong Plantation thrived under his dedication and became a little town of its own. He believed in giving the slaves a reason to walk with purpose. On his plantation, the slaves with families had their own cabins. Slaves were allowed to have gardens to supply extra food for their families. Some slaves had a few hogs and chickens. Marriage between slaves was openly permitted. He strictly forbade his overseers to abuse the slaves. He struggled to find employees who were willing to abide by his guidelines. He began to lean more on Gray. Gray was a man of quality and wisdom, driven by a desire to learn.

---

Today Bowden waited by the dock for Knox. Knox was always slow as cold molasses. He did things at his own pace, forcing the world to wait for him. Finally he spotted Knox sauntering along without a care in the world. From his seat on his horse, Bowden watched him. This monstrosity of a man with hands the size of bear paws was as harmless as a newborn calf. He was soft-spoken, and there was a goodness about him that drew you in.

When Knox couldn't be found at the ship docks he was often at the Armstrong Plantation. Knox lived simply in a humble apartment over the general store. Bowden had offered him land to build a house, but Knox refused. He walked through life without responsibilities and found contentment in his work at the docks. Bowden couldn't relate to this side of his friend. Financially securing a future for his brother, himself, and hopefully one day a wife had become Bowden's own purpose in life.

"Afternoon, Bowden," Knox said when he got closer.

"Hello, Knox. It's about time you rolled out of bed."

Knox scoffed at the gibe.

Bowden dismounted, smiling fondly at him. "What have you been up to, old friend?"

"Well, there is something I've been meaning to share with you." Knox's expression grew serious.

His seriousness put Bowden on alert. When Knox wasn't teasing and carrying on, it meant something major had happened, or was about to.

"All right," Bowden said, not sure if he wanted to hear what Knox said next.

Knox motioned him to follow him to an area off the busy street. There, Knox glanced around before focusing on Bowden. "Willow and Whitney were in town a few days back. They came to me with a sticky situation."

"What sticky situation?"

"You know Willow; she's had a mind of her own all our lives. Well, Whitney and Willow came upon some runaways out at the Barry Plantation. The master of the slaves was trying to do ungodly things to the young boy, and the sister ran with him. The girls hid them until they could help them get away."

"They did what?" Bowden blurted loudly before he caught himself, and in a hushed tone asked, "Where are the slaves now?"

"We put them on a ship headed to New York."

Bowden removed his hat and ran a hand through his hair. He kicked at the dirt with his brand-new cognac-colored boot. He cursed under his breath and paced a few circles before coming back to stand in front of Knox. "Do you realize the danger they put you all in?"

"What was I supposed to do? They came to me already neck-deep in trouble," Knox shot back.

Bowden knew Knox was helpless against the spitfire Willow and probably half scared of the outspoken Miss Barry. *Helpless bastard.*

"Bowden, relax, it's done. Ain't no use you getting all worked up over it now," Knox said, putting a hand on his shoulder.

Bowden gave him a sour look and exhaled, twisting his neck side to side, trying to relieve the tension tightening it. "Knox, you could have been in a pile of trouble if you got caught. I hope this isn't going to become a habit of Willow's and Whitney's. Because next time it may not go so smoothly."

"Those two are quite the team." Knox chuckled in admiration. "One is as fiery as the next. But Whitney—" He whistled and let out a whoop. "It would take some kind of man to tame that one."

"Well, if I didn't know better, I'd say you have taken a mighty liking to Miss Barry."

The tops of Knox's ears reddened and he shrugged. "I find her interesting; no man would ever be bored with a woman like her. Besides, she does all the talking. I'd never have to worry about odd silences anymore."

"That is true. Maybe you will call on her one day?"

Knox released a booming laugh. "You have underestimated me, my friend," he said.

"Have I?" Bowden lifted an eyebrow.

"Well, you don't think I helped them out of the kindness of my heart, do you?"

"Yes, of course I do." He was all too aware of Knox's soft side.

Knox widened his stance as if to accentuate his manliness and said, ever the jokester, "She couldn't resist me so I told her I would allow her to court me."

Bowden threw back his head and roared. "I bet you did, Knox. I bet you did."

Knox grinned.

"Get your horse and I'll meet you on the road home," Bowden said.

Usually Knox's lightheartedness set the mood for the day, but Bowden's thoughts dwelt on what Knox had told him as he mounted his black stallion and made his way through town.

# CHAPTER Thirty-Four

I RODE LIKE THE WIND. THE ADRENALINE PUMPED THROUGH MY BODY as my horse galloped across the valleys and hills of the countryside. There were no boundaries to confine us. My hair hung loose under my hat. I held tight to my horse's mane, riding bareback in a pair of Father's trousers. I laughed to myself as I envisioned the veins popping on his forehead if he could see me now.

I slowed my mare to a trot. "That's a girl," I said, stroking her neck.

Weeks had passed since Georgia and Sam left on the *Olivia II*. In a newspaper I found on Father's desk dated a few days after their escape, I read a reward notice submitted by their master. I grew more determined with each passing day to help my fellow humans. I had found my calling in life, and I would do whatever it took to answer it. I would not sit idle and do nothing.

Jimmy never spoke a word to me about what I had done. I wanted to shield him from discovery of his involvement, so I left things between us unsaid.

I hadn't seen Knox since we said our goodbyes on the dock. He'd helped us once, but it didn't mean we could count on him in the future. My growing concern was that Knox would inform Bowden of our deeds. Bowden's and my friendship was on delicate ground, and trust had yet to be established. The fewer people who knew our secret, the better.

The sound of someone approaching on horseback snapped me out of my thoughts. I shielded my eyes from the sun so I could see who was riding toward me.

Speak of the devil. Bowden!

He reined in his stallion and flashed me a friendly smile. "Good afternoon, Willow."

"Hello, Bowden." I returned his smile.

"Out for a ride?" He peered at my riding attire.

"Yes, there is nothing like a morning ride." I knew I was a sight to be seen in the too-big trousers. Women wearing men's apparel was frowned upon. But it wasn't my first time, and it surely wouldn't be my last. The trousers allowed me to ride more freely.

"How is your brother, Stone? He must be getting big now."

"Stone started his tutoring abroad this year. He is thirteen now and I want him to have all the opportunities possible. He is a good boy with a tender heart. I don't know if the South is right for him." Bowden's voice held sincere concern for his brother.

Bowden had grown into a respectable businessman, and he was a good and decent human. He wasn't overly handsome, but more a man of average looks. No longer was he a young, mischievous boy, but a man who took my breath away.

How had I allowed this to happen? The walls I built up to protect myself were crumbling. For too long I'd carried anger because a young Bowden Armstrong had broken my heart along with my pride with his childhood prank. I'd always known this, but had never wanted to admit it to myself.

As I looked at him now, I tried to still the butterflies in my stomach. His hand rested lightly on his thigh, and his other held the slack reins. My heart was telling me to stay, but my head urged me to run. I quieted the voice in my head warning me to flee.

"Some days, I wonder if the South is for me," I said solemnly.

"So I hear."

My heart stopped. *He knows!*

"Knox?"

He nodded. "Knox told me of the cargo you sent out on one of the ships bound for New York."

"I see," I said grimly, my eyes searching his face. He sat composed and unreadable. "Well, I'm going to go so far as to say you never reported us?"

He stared directly into my eyes and I held his gaze, unmoving. "Willow, I…I am not against what you did. I know those slaves' story. I guessed your views long ago. My concern is that you will get caught. I don't want any harm coming to you." He looked away, but not before I saw the worry on his face.

"I appreciate your concern, Bowden." I meant that.

"I want you to know you have a friend in me, Willow," he confided, moving his horse close enough to take my hand.

I commanded my body to stay perfectly still, but feelings of vulnerability made me retreat to my place of comfort. "I am grateful for your friendship, truly I am." I gave him a small smile, gently retrieving my hand.

"That gives my heart great happiness." Reining his horse around toward his plantation, he looked at me one more time and said, "I like us like this, Willow."

"Me too." My smile widened as I realized how much easier we were together.

"Why don't you and Whitney join Knox and me this week? We could tour the countryside and maybe take a ride by the ocean."

"That would be nice. I'll discuss it with Whitney."

"Very well; until then." He tipped his hat.

I nudged my horse toward home.

# CHAPTER Thirty-Five

Bowden and Knox rode into Livingston around midmorning.

"Morning, ladies," Knox called, waving his hat in the air. He was obviously in high spirits.

I waved back from our seat on the porch swing. Whitney just watched them, her expression reserved.

Bowden's face was hidden in the shadows of his tan-colored hat. His wavy locks shone briefly in the sunlight as he tipped his hat. "Ladies."

The men slipped from their saddles and we went to meet them.

Jimmy rounded the side of the house with our horses in tow. He handed me the reins. His intelligent hazel eyes caught and held mine. I knew what he was thinking. I gave his hand a secret squeeze. Jimmy was too wise and caught on to my inner thoughts. He told me once, "Dat boy done gone and bruised your pride, gal, dat is all. You let your guard down and you'll find he's a good man. He's not jus' any white man. I see how he luks at you all dese years. Dat boy's got et bad." I paid him no mind and had even gone as far as thinking he might have touched the bottle that day.

Lately, I had begun to think maybe Jimmy was right. Bowden might be different from the rest of the males I'd met. I respected no man in this world, Jimmy being the exception. Trust didn't come easy for me. Could I allow my heart to trust this man who stirred feelings in me?

I glanced across the top of my saddle and saw Bowden's keen eyes witnessing the exchange between Jimmy and me. Ignoring him, I adjusted my stirrups. As I prepared to mount, Bowden stepped up, offering me a hand. When I took it, its warmth sent a frisson of pleasure through me.

We spent the next hour riding the countryside until the ocean came into view. We tied our horses to nearby trees and gazed out at the blue water stretching for as far as the eye could see. I moved away from the men, and Whitney followed. I sat down and untied my shoes, then removed them and my stockings. Proper or not proper, I was going to enjoy this day. Time spent in this relaxing environment was too short, in my opinion.

Whitney stood above me, contemplating my actions. I looked up at her. "Well, I'm not coming to the ocean without dipping my toes. Whitney, you of all people are worried about what people will think? Besides, there is no one around for miles."

No more pondering needed. Whitney plopped down beside me and started removing her footwear. "Your father would have you locked away for this, Willow," she commented mildly.

"I want to be free, Whitney. What harm is there in showing our toes?" I tucked my stockings into my footwear.

"There isn't, but if prying eyes were around, this would stir up some gossip. You know how people are. And you are the one of the two of us that has a chance at something good in life."

"Since when do you care about idle gossip, Whitney Barry?"

"I don't." She smiled.

"Well, today I don't either."

We laughed and, throwing propriety aside, walked over to join the men.

Together we strolled the shoreline. Conversation flowed

effortlessly amongst us. Whitney and Knox soon fell behind, leaving Bowden and me walking together. We walked without talking. I loved how the soft, sugary grains of sand squeezed between my toes. The ocean was the most peaceful place on earth. The silence between us seemed natural in a place so serene.

Bowden spoke first. "The relationship between you and your slave, Jimmy—how does your father see it?"

I stopped and turned toward him as I tried to determine his intent. Seeing no ill will in his open expression, I walked on, taking another few moments before I replied. "Jimmy is more than a slave to me. I neither care about his bloodline nor his race. He is the one man in my life I trust. He has shown me constant love and support."

"Willow, words like those could be the end of you."

"You are right, Bowden. For Jimmy's sake, I must keep my feelings under wraps."

"What of your sake?"

"I am working on reining in my openness. I am aware I need to avoid drawing attention to my views."

"Your fondness for this slave is dangerous in the presence of the wrong people."

"I'm beginning to understand that." Even amongst friends, I needed to be more careful, because who knew who was watching? I had so much to learn.

"You're not a careless woman. But remember, everyone isn't always as they appear."

"You make a valid point, and I shall heed it."

I found myself enjoying Bowden's company, the more time I spent with him. It was as if he had read my thoughts when he said, "This is refreshing." Stopping, he placed his hands on my shoulders and turned me to him. He gazed long into my eyes. "I'll spend a lifetime making it up to you, Willow." His fingers on my shoulders rubbed back and forth.

This closeness felt so good and so right. No warning came to my head as I considered this man before me. My heart cried, *Yes, spend a lifetime making it up to me. I wouldn't mind that at all.* I unchained the feelings I had carried for him since childhood. Bowden didn't seem to be such a threat anymore. Was this the start of something more?

All too soon, he released my shoulders. Strangely saddened, I stepped back to put a comfortable distance between us, and we resumed our stroll.

Now I wanted to understand more about Bowden Armstrong. "Do you think you will ever leave Charleston?"

"I used to think of it, but then my grandfather died, and the plantation and Stone became my responsibility. Why do you want to leave?"

"Let's sit for a while," I said.

He obliged, stretching his legs out and leaning back on the palms of his hands. I sat down beside him and drew my knees up, wrapping my arms around them. I rested my chin on top. "Sometimes, I feel like this way of life is swallowing me up. And the relationship between Father and I has always been strained. I'm scared to be in the same room with him." I sighed. "I want to run as far away as possible from Livingston. But other times, I truly love my home. I believe I'm meant to be here. Maybe my calling in life is to be a voice for the slaves." I cast a glance at him.

His jaw was clenched. He never turned to look at me but said, "You need to tread lightly, Willow." He picked up a handful of sand and let it run through his fingers.

"We have discussed this already, Bowden," I said, irritated.

He shifted to face me. Reaching out, he pulled one arm from my knees and took my hand in his. My heart skipped a few beats as I looked at him. In a gentle voice, he said, "Because you matter to me, Willow. You always have."

I couldn't breathe; I started to panic inside. I was vulnerable to this man again and it terrified me. "Bowden…I…" I gulped.

Whitney and Knox's timing was impeccable. I pulled my hand back as they approached and rose, grateful that the awkward moment had been broken. I did not dare look at Bowden; I knew my reaction wasn't what he wanted, and I was too much of a coward to look him in the eyes.

Whitney picked up on the tension and cheerfully said, "I'm starving."

"Well, I say let's eat." Knox smiled fondly at Whitney.

Suddenly famished, I eagerly agreed.

We returned to the horses. Knox retrieved the picnic lunch they had prepared. Whitney and I spread out the blanket tied to the back of Bowden's horse. Bowden unpacked the cheese, fresh bread, dried meat, and fruit they had brought, along with a bottle of wine and glasses. As we ate, the awkwardness I'd created faded away and we became four friends engaging in free-flowing conversation about our lives. It was the beginning of an unbreakable friendship.

On the ride home I sorted out the afternoon in my mind. For the first time in life, I belonged. In those three, I'd found loyal and trustworthy comrades.

# CHAPTER Thirty-Six

CHRISTMAS WAS AROUND THE CORNER, AND THE PLANTATION hummed with anticipation. The Christmas season was my favorite time of the year. At Livingston, we hosted the most extravagant banquet in the county. People came from near and far to attend. I spent months planning for the banquet and put my heart and soul into every detail. Father allowed me free rein with the planning and gave me an unlimited budget. It was important to me to make Christmas memorable for every guest who visited.

The slaves and I decorated the mansion in holly and greenery, from the pillars marching along the front of the house to the spiral staircase, and the fireplace mantel in every room.

Our slaves' faces shone with a joy and excitement matching my own. They'd replaced their usual songs with Christmas carols, and I heard them throughout the plantation. My spirit soared. Each year at Christmas, Father made sure all the slaves received two sets of new clothes along with two pairs of new shoes. I ensured each slave received a special, more frivolous gift, be it new hair ties or perfume for the women, pipes, tobacco, and cigars for the men, and toys for the children. Everyone received some molasses candy wrapped with their gifts. I found personal delight in making the rounds to hand out the gifts. Giving is the greatest pleasure in life and the glee on their faces was beyond rewarding. Mammy, Mary Grace, and I would tear up the kitchen making Christmas treats and traditional dishes. These are my fondest memories.

This crisp morning before Christmas Eve, the three of us were baking in the kitchen house. I was up to my wrists in flour and daydreaming of spending these moments with my own mother. I considered how my life would have been with her in it—having her to go to about things that troubled my heart; sharing with her how my heart ached over Father's rejection of me; seeking her advice on my growing feelings for Bowden—

"Penny for your thoughts." Mary Grace tossed a sprinkling of sugar at me from the mixture in her bowl.

The sweet dust brushed the side of my face and I smiled at her. "I was thinking how grateful I am for you and Mammy. And I was thinking about my own mother and what it would be like if she were here."

"She'd be mighty proud of you, chile." Mammy beamed at me.

"Do you think?" I asked in a voice tinged with longing, searching her eyes.

The kitchen went quiet, as if a thick blanket had settled over us.

"Angel gal, your mama be jus' lak you."

"How, Mammy? How are we alike?" I begged, desperate for more information on the woman who was but a phantom to me. Never had I so much as seen a portrait of her—not even her handwriting. Was it Father's intention to erase her existence from the earth?

"She is in your smile. Dose dark green eyes and dat silky dark mane of yours is de image of your mama. Like luking in a mirror."

"Oh, Mammy!" This knowledge thrilled me. "What else, Mammy?"

But Mammy stiffened and ran a hand across the back of her neck. "Dat be all, chile," she said, becoming tight-lipped.

Confused, I wanted to besiege her with questions, but I knew Mammy, and the firm set of her jaw meant I would get no further. I glanced at Mary Grace, who shrugged and smiled as if to say, "I'm sorry." I glared at Mammy's back as she turned away. I was done living in the dark about my mother. I was determined to get answers, in whatever way it took to get them.

# CHAPTER
# Thirty-Seven

THE SWEET, WONDROUS SOUND OF A HARP DRIFTED UP TO MY room. I could hear the merry voices of my guests filtering up from below. Mary Grace was applying the finishing touches to my hair. She'd swept it up on top of my head and a mass of loose ringlets dangled down the back of my neck. I'd selected a stunning gold silk gown that accented my olive complexion. The off-the-shoulder gown exposed my shoulders, and the neck scooped low in a heart-shaped design. Mary Grace clasped a diamond necklace around my neck and its large emerald pendant nestled just above my breasts. I stood and regarded myself in the mirror and smiled, pleased with my appearance. Tonight I felt beautiful. Mary Grace held out the elbow-length gloves and I slipped them on and turned toward the door.

Thaddeus appeared in the doorway. "Miss Willow, your guests are arriving, and your father requests your presence."

"Please let him know I'll be right down."

"Yes, Miss." He bowed and left.

I took one last look in the mirror and smiled at the woman staring back at me, then swept out of my room.

I descended to the landing overlooking the grand main floor and paused to observe the guests. Mary Grace stopped a few feet behind me. She, along with all the female servants serving tonight, was dressed in a royal blue gown trimmed in silver—garments fit for any Southern belle. The male servants wore sophisticated black tailcoats and pants.

My ears picked up Whitney's voice, carrying throughout the room. I caught sight of her, cocktail in hand, conversing with a circle of guests including Bowden, Knox, Josephine, and Lucille. Bowden glanced up and caught my eye as I descended the stairs. His eyes lit up and his approving gaze followed my descent. I blushed beneath his intense stare. Knox and Whitney, seeing they had lost Bowden, turned to see what had stolen his attention.

I stopped to greet a few guests who stepped up to kiss my cheek and wish me a merry Christmas. Whitney boldly cut through the crowd to get to me, and pulled me to their merry little group.

"Willow, you are stunning, as usual," Knox said with a half-bow.

"Thank you, Knox. You look dashing yourself." His red cravat stood out nicely against his black tailcoat.

"I rolled out of bed looking like this," he said, posturing. His audience gave him his expected chuckle. He wasn't a refined gentleman and he had no mind to be.

"The plantation is so beautiful, Willow; it must have taken you weeks to do this," Whitney marveled, surveying the main floor.

"Thank you, Whitney. It does take a lot of time and energy, but I strive to give our guests an evening of splendor."

"Well, with the money you have, I would expect you can afford it," Lucille said, jealousy marring her forced jocularity.

"My daddy says Livingston is like its own empire, and you could marry and be set for life," Josephine added without malice.

I was uncomfortable with the attention and insulted by their impertinent focus on our finances. My eyes narrowed as a rebuke formed on my tongue.

Bowden stepped in, putting a halt to the conversation with, "Are you meaning to insult your hostess, ladies?"

"No, we are stating what we have heard," Lucille replied, placing a hand on her chest as if she were the one being offended.

Grateful for Bowden interceding, I forced a brilliant smile, playing the gracious hostess. "It's Christmas. Let's all enjoy the evening," I said before removing myself from the group. In no way was I going to let those two meddlesome girls ruin the evening I had worked so hard to perfect.

As the beautiful Mary Grace swept past with a tray of champagne, I reached for one. After a long sip, I blew out a deep breath and left the negative energy from the last five minutes of conversation behind me.

# CHAPTER Thirty-Eight

My eyes swept over the crowd until they met Kipling Reed's. He gave me a gracious, deep bow from across the room. Smiling warmly, I wove through the guests toward him.

"Kipling!" I said, holding my arms wide in unfettered happiness.

"Willow, always the belle of the ball," he said, leaning in to kiss my right cheek, then the other.

"I'm so delighted you could come."

"My sister and her husband recently moved here and they invited me to visit for the holidays, so it works out perfectly." He smiled cordially.

I was surprised at how swiftly we'd become close friends. We'd exchanged letters weekly from the time Father tried to marry me off to him. He'd become dear to my heart, and he understood me in a way most people did not.

"Let's get some fresh air. What do you say?" he proposed, offering his arm, which I readily grasped.

Kipling ushered me out the side doors into a patio garden that was a magical fairytale land of wintergreen and holly illuminated by the glow of numerous small lanterns.

"You outdid yourself, Willow," Kipling said, admiring the greenery and lanterns I'd meticulously hung from the beams sheltering the garden.

I was overjoyed at his appreciation. "You are too kind," I gushed, as heat invaded my cheeks. I veered from his compliment. "How long are you in town?"

He grinned, recognizing what I'd done, but obliged me with an answer. "I head home in a few days."

"That disheartens me. This means we'd better make this time count."

"As if that matters to you, Willow Hendricks. You pinned me as a friend only from the moment I met you," he teased.

I laughed and shrugged. "But we are better off friends, don't you agree?"

He nodded, his wavering agreement making me wonder if he wished for more. I knew I would never view him in that light, and needed to be honest to avoid giving him a false impression. "Have you made up your mind yet on making the move to New York?"

He laughed, again aware of my steering the conversation. "Yes. I don't share the views of my fellow politicians. With the help of my father, I purchased a printing shop in New York. I figure I can use the newspaper business as a stage to make progress in the world. The plan is to put the politics aside, maybe for future use." His eyes were aglow with the excitement of his next venture.

"Progress? What kind of progress are you hoping to achieve?" Intrigued, I turned to him.

He stopped and regarded me intently. "I'm a good old Southern boy, Willow, but my heart isn't in the South or the way things are done here." He tilted his head, searching my face for a reaction.

I frowned, perplexed. Was he saying what I thought he was saying? Did we share the same beliefs? "I'm not quite sure I understand what you are implying, Kip."

He lowered his voice before he blurted out, "I'm an abolitionist."

What? No! Never would I have guessed. He'd never revealed these views before. I'd been oblivious. Unlike my amateur attempts, he'd moved forward, applying his wisdom and insight to effect change skillfully and quietly. *I should take a lesson or two from him.*

My voice cracked as I said, "I don't know what to say. You have taken me by surprise, Kip. I would never have known. I mean, after all this time. In the letters back and forth, you never said anything."

His face became reserved. "Well, one can never be too safe. Besides, I wanted to explain to you in person. So, has your opinion of me changed?" His brow knitted in concern.

I laughed wildly. He grimaced, taking my laughter as rebuke. "Quite the contrary!" I said quickly. "Let me assure you, dear Kip, in this our hearts align."

Now it was his turn to gape in puzzlement.

"What I am saying is, we share the same perspective on those matters."

Relief softened in his face.

We spent a few more moments in hushed whispers, until guests began streaming into the garden. "I had better play hostess and make my rounds." I gave him a wistful smile.

He took my hand and bowed to place a gentle kiss on my fingers. "Thanks for the lovely walk, my lady," he said in a carrying voice.

I noticed guests watching us and doing some whispering of their own, most likely wondering if we were courting. "Kipling, you have people staring."

"Mission accomplished," he said with a mischievous chuckle.

"Quick on your toes. I like it," I whispered through my teeth, then giggled like a silly schoolgirl. "I bid you good evening, Mr. Reed."

Turning slightly to put his back to the other guests, he shot me a private wink. Shaking my head, I grinned and reentered the mansion to go in search of the ever-dazzling Whitney.

My heart soared. I'd found an ally in Kip. He had connections and had agreed to be our eyes and ears.

When I found Whitney at the refreshments table, she bombarded me with questions. "Who was that?" she asked, looking in the direction of Kipling, who stood talking with Father and a few of Father's business associates.

"That's Kipling, the man Father intended me to marry. The one I told you about."

"Oh, yes." Her eyes gleamed with impishness. "Are you sure you aren't interested in him? He seems like quite the charmer, and you two seem to get on so well."

"No, I assure you we are only friends."

"Well, Bowden seemed to be stirred up as he watched the two of you interact as if you were long-lost lovers."

"Whitney!" I warned softly. "Stop."

"I'm simply saying from the moment you left us, his eyes followed you around the room. Then his face grew serious when you greeted Kipling. When you left for the garden with young Kipling, Bowden excused himself and went out the front door."

"Well, Bowden and I have only in recent months developed a friendship," I retorted, but my heart picked up its pace, and tingles coursed through my body.

Ever strong-willed, Whitney pressed on. "I believe Bowden has been trying all these years to make right his past wrongs because he is in love with you."

I squirmed with unease.

"I tried to question Knox on this, but he wouldn't say a word," she continued, throwing her hand up in frustration.

"Whitney, you need to keep your nose out of it," I said through gritted teeth. "The last thing I need is more tension. We can finally, after all these years, stand in the same room with each other, and I intend to keep it this way."

"Willow, I didn't mean to make you mad. Honestly, I didn't. Please accept my apology." Remorse darkened her pretty face, and she grasped my hands.

I scowled at her before my face split with a wide grin. "I know you have my best interests at heart," I said, and she beamed at my understanding. "But no more meddling. Agreed?"

"Agreed." She lifted her chin, exposing her lovely long neck.

"By the way, you pull off that gown swimmingly," I said, stepping back to admire her.

Whitney brushed off the compliment, embarrassment flushing her cheeks, but then she performed an awe-inspiring swirl of her classic black silk gown. The skirt of her gown was designed with layers of thin pleats; the bodice was modest, cut just below her collarbone. She had wisely chosen long, red silk gloves to give her a pop of color. She always had exquisite taste in fashion. Then it dawned on me that Whitney had coordinated her and Knox's evening attire.

"Why, Whitney, I do believe you and Knox planned your outfits for my party," I teased.

"What if we did?" She popped a dessert square into her mouth and wrinkled her nose at me.

"So, you two are courting. This proves it." I savored reversing her earlier intrusiveness as she blushed.

"You could say we are officially courting. But I will hear no talk of marriage. So don't even go there," she replied sternly.

Try as she might to deny it, courting led to marriage. But she could tell herself whatever she wanted to. "How exciting," I said.

"If you say so." She gave my arm a tug and wandered off to speak to someone who'd caught her eye.

I regarded her as she walked away, and a smile pulled at my mouth. This was Whitney's way of shutting down an uncomfortable topic.

# CHAPTER Thirty-Nine

THE COLD AIR MADE MY BREATH FORM FLUTTERING WHITE clouds as I walked into the splendid moonlit night in pursuit of Bowden. I pulled my fur wrap tighter around myself as the phantom fingers of ice stroked my shivering body. Laughter and music trickled out from the mansion behind me, giving the night a magical air.

I saw his shadow stretching from him in the moonlight. I admired his brawny silhouette from afar as he leaned against an oak tree, one leg casually bent, his foot resting on the trunk behind him. His gaze was turned from me, inspecting the dark horizon.

Cautiously, I approached him, my steps light and soundless on the half-frozen ground. "Bowden," I called softly.

He looked my way, his eyes consuming me. The usual twinkle in his eyes was absent, and that prompted a dull ache in my chest. "Evening, Willow."

"Whitney said I could find you out here." I paused and searched his face.

"I needed some air."

"Bowden, I need answers."

"Answers to what?"

"What are your intentions?" I boldly met his gaze.

"Intentions?" He appeared to be genuinely confused.

*I swear, men are simple-minded when it comes to the ways of women*, I thought. I blew out a breath. "How do you feel about me?" I asked, folding my arms across my chest.

"Why, Miss Willow, are you challenging me?" His eyes danced.

My eyes trailed over his clean-shaven face to the curve of his mouth. "Let's cut the small talk, Bowden," I demanded impatiently.

"I love you, Willow. I've loved you since we were children." He sighed as if wearied by carrying an invisible weight.

My heart surged. He loved me. But how—? We had been enemies for so long. My mind struggled to grasp the thought. My heart confronted me: *But, Willow, haven't you carried the same feelings?* "I don't know what to say…" I stammered, a lump forming in my throat.

"You need not say anything. I see how you care for the young man inside." I heard his jealousy.

Whitney's words rang true. Bowden misunderstood my relationship with Kip.

"You misunderstand, Bowden. Kipling is the son of a friend of my father's. We were to be married—" Anger flashed in his eyes. "Wait!" I held up a hand for him to hear me out. "Our fathers thought it was a wise arrangement and when I refused, Kipling took the matter to his father and the idea was scrapped. Though I turned down the proposal, we settled on friendship and we have become great friends. Kip knows I view him as only that, and he respects my decision."

Bowden looked sheepishly down at me before lowering his head. "Well, I guess I made a complete fool of myself, didn't I? I'm sorry."

I softened and reaching out, I took one of his hands in mine. "I won't hold it against you too harshly." I flashed him a flirtatious smile.

His eyes rested on mine. I saw his yearning. "Willow…I wish

to be more than friends." His voice was thick with emotion. He lifted his free hand and traced the curve of my jaw with a finger that came to rest on my lips.

My heart hammered in my ears, and my body yearned for his embrace. I closed the distance between us and he lowered his lips to mine for my first kiss. Fire surged through my body and I felt limp in his arms. His lips gently captured mine. I clung to him, feeling the muscles and warmth that lay beneath his clothing. It felt right, but yet wrong at the same time. Things would never be the same between us. In this moment of passion, we had yet again changed the dynamics of our relationship.

I was the first to find the willpower to pull away from the kiss. I rested my head on his shoulder, listening to the drumming of his heart. I hoped I knew what I was doing. Could I trust a man with my heart? Trust didn't come easily to me, and it would take a leap of faith to follow my deepening feelings for Bowden.

I moved away from the warmth of his chest; with a wavering smile, I put distance between us. "We can see where this goes," I said.

"We can take it one day at a time, Willow," he agreed, acknowledging my wariness.

"Thank you, Bowden. Trust is hard for me, especially when it comes to a man."

"I understand and I'll tread carefully and respectfully. I will win your trust, my fair lady." He grinned. "Besides, you have a reputation for running."

I smiled. "I need to go back inside; Father will be looking for me. After all, this is my party," I said with a laugh. "Do you care to join me?"

He smiled affectionately at me. "I'd be delighted to have you on my arm, and to rub it in young Mr. Reed's face."

"Bowden!"

"One more thing before we go, Willow."

"What's that?"

He reached into the breast pocket of his coat and removed a beautifully wrapped gift. "Merry Christmas."

"For me?"

"No, I'm taunting you with it," he said sarcastically as he handed me the gift.

I glared at him but then eagerly took the present. I ripped it open and discovered inside a pair of leather riding gloves with the initials *WH* etched into the leather. My eyes grew wide in appreciation. "Oh, Bowden, I adore them. Thank you. But I didn't get you anything."

"No need for that. You have a lifetime to spoil me if this all goes well." He pointed back and forth between himself and me.

I laughed. "Fair enough." Placing my hand in the curve of the elbow he offered, I walked with him back to the festivities.

# CHAPTER *Forty*

THE RIDER APPROACHED LIVINGSTON AT BREAKNECK SPEED. Whitney and I had been visiting by the pond, feeding the swans when we saw him. Curious over his urgency, we headed for the house.

He had already slid from his horse and was speaking to Thaddeus when we arrived. "I'll see him now!" the bearded, copper-haired man demanded.

"Very well, sir, I will tell him you're here. If you will please wait here."

"I will not," the man snapped. His complexion reddened and his eyes flashed with impatience. He brushed Thaddeus aside.

"Excuse me," I said loudly as I reached the front steps. The man appeared not to hear me. "Excuse me!" I repeated, louder.

He swiveled. Recognition filled his face and he politely bowed. "The lovely Miss Hendricks."

"Have we met?" I evaluated the man before me. His face was familiar, but I couldn't place it. I believed him to be maybe of Irish descent. He was obviously greatly irritated over something, judging by his ill manners with Thaddeus.

"Gillies. Captain Gillies, Miss." He managed a pained smile.

Oh, yes. Now I knew how I knew him. "Thaddeus, please inform Father of our guest."

"Yes, Miss." Thaddeus hurried off to inform Father as Mammy arrived on the veranda, awaiting instructions from me.

"Mammy, please bring refreshments for the captain and Father."

"Yessum," Mammy said and waddled back inside.

"Can you state your business with my father, Captain? Father didn't say we were expecting company," I added, aware I was bordering on rudeness.

Father appeared, preventing any reply. The captain, upon seeing him, bristled like a porcupine. Father looked surprised by the captain's arrival. He attempted to conceal his shock and disapproval at the captain's unplanned visit by running a hand through his hair, though he pressed his lips together in a tight line. "Mammy, please bring those refreshments to the study, where the captain and I will deal with whatever required him to show up on my property without a proper invitation." He glared a rebuke at the captain.

Father turned his attention to Whitney and me. "Now, I expect you young ladies to make yourselves scarce and go about your day. Understood?"

"Yes, of course, Father." Like a dutiful daughter, I curtsied and Whitney and I made our escape.

Our retreat stopped at the corner of the house. I looked at Whitney. "What do you suppose that is all about?"

"I don't know. But your father seems none too happy about the captain being here."

"Hmm…well, I say we find out." I grabbed her hand and pulled her to the back of the house. Whitney was a willing participant.

We slipped in through the warming kitchen and crept down the back passage to Father's study. The massive mahogany door was closed. We placed our ears to the door to listen. The thickness of the door made conversation inside difficult to hear.

"What are you doing here? I told you to never show up

here." Father sounded anxious.

"The contact was murdered—gunned down in a back alley," the captain replied.

"So what happened to the shipment?" Father's voice shifted toward panic.

"The human cargo was delivered as expected. I wanted you to know our connection is void."

Mammy's hefty footsteps startled us, and we scurried into the sitting room to avoid getting caught eavesdropping.

I couldn't stop myself from pacing as an eerie suspicion chilled my blood. What was my father up to? "Shipment" and "live cargo"? "What do you make of that conversation?" I asked a wide-eyed Whitney.

"Your guess is as good as mine. But it sounds like your father is smuggling slaves for trade. I can't be positive because we could only pick up parts of the conversation."

My shoulders, already feeling leaden, slumped in defeat. Her assessment matched my fears. I stared at Whitney; her horrified expression matched what I imagined mine looked like. A cold resentment seeped into my chest. Were our sins as slave owners not bad enough? How could he do this?

# CHAPTER Forty-One

WINTER CAME AND WENT. SPRING WAS BOUNTIFUL AND THE plantation was filled anew with a net of greenery. The apple and cherry trees were masses of blossoms. The honeysuckle and camellias were in full bloom and their heady fragrances filled the air. The daffodils leaned back, their yellow bonnets gleaming like a morning sunrise. The lambs bleated after their mothers. A newborn foal struggled to stand on its wobbly legs; its mother stood tall and proud, letting out a long nicker. In the neighboring corral, twin calves suckled on their mother while she ate the fresh blanket of green grass.

Today was my nineteenth birthday. After a long winter, I decided to use my birthday as an excuse to throw a party with a few friends. Kip was in town and promised to attend. Mammy, as usual, insisted on making me a special birthday dinner, and I had requested shrimp and grits.

I was determined to let nothing sour my day. I strolled out of the main house and made my way to the kitchen house, knowing I'd find Mammy there.

The delectable tang of lemon filled the room and tickled my nostrils as I swept through the narrow doorway. Mammy was baking a square, four-tier lemon cake. Two layers sat on a cake platter, layered with white fluffy frosting. "It smells heavenly, Mammy," I exclaimed, inhaling deeply, soaking in the scent.

"I hope so, Miss Willow—et is for a special birthday gal."

Her smile was broad and gleeful.

I leaned over and kissed her round cheek before dipping my finger into the dish of frosting and sticking it in my mouth. It was smooth and buttery, with a hint of vanilla; the shredded coconut she'd added made it simply divine. The ends of the cake that Mammy had removed lay on the cutting board. Lifting a piece, I slathered it with the coconut frosting. My eyes closed involuntarily and a soft moan of pure enjoyment escaped my crumb-covered lips as I bit into it. "Oh Mammy, this is beyond the best thing I've ever eaten," I said after I'd swallowed the first mouthful.

Mammy grinned proudly. "Aw, shucks, Miss Willow, you do have a way of making your ol' Mammy blush like a newlywed bride."

"I'm only stating the truth, Mammy." I smiled warmly. "Any chance you know where the lovely Mary Grace is at this moment?"

"Dat girl allus off wastin' time. Her head is all swelled up wid dreamy ideas. Et ain't practical for a slave to be talkin' 'bout freedom. Dat dere Gray—good-lukin' boy, but he's done gone and filled dat purty head of me gal's wid dat nonsense," Mammy grumbled as she stoked the coals in the open fire.

I knew Mammy's worries for Mary Grace oftentimes consumed her. Mammy had grown complacent after all these years of being a slave. But I had to remind Mammy of her own words. "Mammy, a wise woman once told me that dreams are all we have in life. Mary Grace is a brilliant girl who should long for a future of freedom. Slaves should never settle for being property. You all deserve so much more. The chains forced around your neck are wrong, and this needs to be made right."

"Hush, chile," she warned, frowning.

"No, Mammy, you hush!" I retorted angrily.

Mammy's eyes grew round at my sass. I had both disturbed and bewildered her, I knew.

"As long as I breathe I will fight for the rights of the Negro race. You've loved me more than my own father. White, black, purple, yellow—who cares? We are all the same. We all walk upright, we breathe the same air, and we all have hearts that beat like the good Lord gave us. You are no different than us. No one, and I mean *no one* has the right to tell you what you can or cannot do. No one!" Frustration twisted my face. The delight shared between us but five minutes ago was lost.

"Shh, chile. Please, I beg of you. I don't want you to 'danger yourself for us. Your pappy for sho' hear you talkin' lak that, et be de end for you and your Mammy." Sorrow brought the lines out on her face.

"All right, Mammy." I lowered my voice. "I'm sorry for back-talking. I love you, and seeing that you have settled into and accepted this life fills me with such anguish."

"Et be my Mary Grace dat made me settle." Mammy's eyes flashed. "I know et ain't right, what de white mens do to us. I know fear has guided me most of my life. When dat gal was growin' inside of me I made her a promise to protect her. So far, I kept dat promise to my gal. When you hold a babe of your own you will understand dis."

I was silenced by her words, and there was no more to be said as she turned from me. I judged her harshly in my anger, but my convictions stood strong. I left the kitchen house without another word to the woman who had mothered me, loved me, and guided me without prejudice.

# CHAPTER Forty-Two

MY MIND WEIGHED DOWN WITH THE DISAGREEMENT MAMMY and I'd had, I meandered past the boundaries of Livingston. I had been upset at Mammy for losing the will to fight. For giving up. But was she not as helpless to the cause as I at first considered myself? The burden resting on my shoulders was crushing. My perception of these incalculable transgressions consumed me. But guilt now devoured my thoughts. No matter my feelings, Mammy didn't deserve my ill treatment, and I needed to make it right.

"Miss Willow," a female voice called out.

I jumped, startled, and turned. Mary Grace was jogging to catch up to me. Her flowered head rag was a rainbow of color in the bright sunlight. I held a hand over my eyes to shield them from the sun and waited, smiling in response to her infectious white smile.

"Mary Grace, what are you doing off the plantation?" I asked her as she arrived, breathless. "Mammy will be fit to be tied." I couldn't maintain my stern face; I was elated to have her company.

"I was chasing you. I was in the woods on the plantation gathering these." She opened her tucked-up apron; inside were various berries and wildflowers. "I saw you leave the grounds and have been calling out for you ever since."

"I never heard a thing. I've been all up in my head. Mammy

and I had some cross words, which I'm feeling right awful about." My voice quavered.

"Mama will be understanding. You can talk it out. After all, you be her 'angel gal,'" she mimicked, placing an arm around my shoulders in an attempt to comfort me.

I laughed at her teasing.

"I promise it will be fine." She gave me an extra squeeze.

I smiled at her, cheered by her optimism. "Thanks, Mary Grace. You always have a way of dragging me out of my own head. For this, I love you more than before."

She giggled and let her arm drop.

I peered around, realizing I didn't know where we were. I'd walked a great distance from home. "Mary Grace, I'm not sure where we are."

"You mean that?" She frowned. "When I followed you, I never considered getting back. I know the woods on the plantation like the back of my hand, but this is all new to me."

"I was wandering around so aimlessly, I never paid attention to where I was going." I'd never been good with directions. My anxiety rose. *Keep calm, Willow!* I drew a deep breath and took in my surroundings. If I panicked and we roamed around frantically, we would be lost for days, and I had no intention of letting that happen. I had ridden these hillsides and woods all my life, but the landscape looked a lot different from a saddle.

I led us back the way Mary Grace had come. As we walked, Mary Grace became skittish. At first I believed it was her unease at being off the plantation. This unknown territory, this adventure that didn't lie in the pages of a book, was proving to be too much for a sheltered slave girl.

I soon realized it wasn't just Mary Grace, as I got a case of the jitters too. I knew we were being watched. There was no doubt about it. Every fiber of my body shot warnings at me. I glanced around, trying to find the culprit or culprits whose prey we had become. "Something's wrong, Mary Grace, I can feel it," I said in a low, urgent voice. "We need to hurry." Mary Grace looked at me, her eyes wide with terror. I didn't wait; I grabbed her hand and dragged her along until she caught up and matched my stride.

I spotted them coming in from the left, the side Mary Grace was on. I opened my mouth to shout a warning but a whip cracked loud and encircled Mary Grace's waist, pinning her forearms. The tip of it struck along my neck. I screamed, dropping her hand, and instinctively raised it to cup my injured neck. Mary Grace let out a bloodcurdling cry of terror.

Two masked men approached and circled us. One held the whip that had captured Mary Grace, pinning her arms to her sides. The taller one roughly grabbed my arm, restraining me. I struggled to break free, but his grip tightened, his fingers digging into my flesh, securing my obedience.

Mary Grace began fighting like a frightened wolf trying to free itself from a hunter's snare. The shorter of the pair arrogantly sauntered up to her and pulled her head rag from her head. Her long hair bounced out and fell down her back.

"A pretty thing like you shouldn't be looking like no nigger slave. You should be stripped down to your lady bits and paraded around like the rare exotic beauty you are." A malicious laugh flowed from the mouth behind the mask.

Terror beyond anything I had ever experienced choked me. The short man turned to his burly, pigeon-toed accomplice and remarked, "Naked and a dog collar around her pretty little neck. What do ya say?"

The other laughed as the heinous idea appealed to him. The man who held Mary Grace captive took a fistful of her hair and jerked her head back.

"Stop! Release my nigger now." I choked off the panic rising in my tone. I glared with unrestrained malice at them.

The smaller man moved to stand inches from my face. His eyes were hooded by the mask, but a familiarity tickled at my memory. "I suggest you shut your big mouth, nigger lover. White or not, you will suffer the same fate as your nigger friend."

There was no way I could back down. My knees wobbled but I willed myself to call on an inner strength. I must try to save us from a dire fate. "I am Willow Hendricks, and I would suggest you, sir, release my slave, or my father will make you live to regret the day you were born."

The larger, pigeon-toed man chuckled, rolling his head to his partner. "She is feisty like her mama," he crowed. "Maybe she should suffer the same—"

"Silence!" the other man growled.

My mother? My brain seized on his words but I couldn't allow myself to delve into his meaning.

"I'm sorry…I didn't…" the larger man stammered to the other.

Seeing my opportunity, I swiftly reached up and pushed my thumbs into the holes in his mask, digging with all my strength into his eye sockets. His eyes squished and rolled under my thumbs as blood squirted out and ran down his mask in a crimson stream.

He screamed in pain and staggered backward. "My eyes!" he squealed, hopping around in a frenzy.

Catching the small man off guard as he stared at his mate, I sent a hard kick into his shin. He groaned and staggered away, loosening his grip on the whip.

I grabbed at Mary Grace, desperately trying to free her from the whip.

"No, Miss Willow, run!"

"I'm not leaving you!" I yelled, tears spilling down my cheeks.

The little man regained his balance and sent a punch to the side of my temple, knocking me off balance. The tall man moved into my line of sight and, fueled by my attack on him, he hauled back and sent a fist at my mouth. I choked off a scream as pain surged through my already pounding head. The blow split my lips and warm blood spilled over my teeth, filling my mouth with a metallic taste. I spit out a mouthful of blood.

"Miss Willow!" Mary Grace cried, struggling to get loose. Her captor yanked on the whip, sending her sprawling on the ground. She lay wrapped in the whip, her eyes wild with terror as the man turned to her. Her heels scrabbled at the ground as she tried to push herself away from him. Chuckling at her determination, he advanced, pulling on the whip to stop her from moving any farther. Kneeing and straddling her hips, he ripped open the front of her dress, exposing her breasts.

"No!" Mary Grace shook her head. "Please don't!"

"Don't you touch her! I'll kill you, you bastard!" I shrieked. I broke free from the man and ran to her, but my captor looped his thick arm around my neck from behind and squeezed. I couldn't breathe! I clawed at the arm like a woman possessed, but my vision blurred, and as he felt the fight leaving me he released my neck and shoved me to the ground. I struggled to sit up and clung to my throat with my hand, gasping for air.

"I'll teach you, you stuck-up, rich wench," he roared. Balling up his fist, he planted it between my eyes.

The impact rocked my head and slammed me flat on the ground. I lay there, crippled by pain. In seconds swelling set in around my eyes and he became but an obscure object in my narrowed vision. I tried to move to fight him off as he lifted my skirt.

"No, not her, only the slave," the other man bellowed.

Without the sense of sight my hearing sharpened, and I recognized the voice of Mary Grace's captor for the first time.

Rufus.

My world began to spin from the impact to my skull. The last sound I heard before I lost consciousness was the tearing of cloth and Mary Grace's scream.

# CHAPTER Forty-Three

THE PROFUSE LICKING DREW ME BACK TO THE WORLD OF THE living. I brushed a hand across my battered face to push away the furry head of the animal licking my wounds. The whine of a dog alerted me that Beau had come to search for us, but I sensed no human rescuers. I groaned as I became aware of the radiating pain hammering at my head. The groan grew sharper as fear clawed at me. I recalled what had happened before everything went dark. The men left me untouched. But—*Mary Grace!* I scrambled to sit up.

Fearing what I was about to find, I tried to open my eyes, but they were swollen to slits. Through my narrowed vision, I could see the sun was setting. "Mary Grace!" There was no reply. I started to gasp for breath and screamed her name before I started to hyperventilate. "Mary Grace!"

"Over here," came a weak reply.

Following the sound, I crawled to her. I peered at the outline of a figure curled in a fetal position. The figure rocked back and forth and as I drew near, I gasped. Mary Grace had been beaten almost beyond recognition. In her struggles, they'd fought to silence her. She clenched the front of her bodice together in an effort to hide her shame.

*No, please, no! Why?* I demanded of God the merciful protector. *Why do you allow the sins of mankind to be visited upon the helpless? Why!* I challenged angrily.

I reached out, gently touching my friend.

"Don't touch me!" She recoiled from my touch, instinctively protecting her body from further trauma.

"It's all right, Mary Grace. We will get help."

"How will it ever be all right again?" she asked bitterly.

"I'm so sorry, Mary Grace; I didn't mean it like that. I only mean we have to find help and make them pay for this."

"What does it matter, I'm a disposable slave," she said bitterly. "You were spared because you are white. Rape a nigger, no one cares. Rape a white woman and there would be a posse of white men out looking for the criminals. Tell me I'm not right, Miss Willow." She sat up, venting her resentment at me.

Tears spilled down my face. I fiercely tried to wipe them away, but they flowed like sheets of springtime rain. I knew she was right. We'd endured this exact reality. "I can't deny it, my friend. Please forgive me for this fact I cannot control," I pleaded feebly.

Mary Grace pushed herself up to sit with her knees drawn up, her arms hugging them tightly to her chest. Burying her face against her knees, she sobbed, the sounds gut-wrenching. Her body trembled.

I sat in uncertainty, not sure what I should do. My heart told me to comfort my friend, but she shunned my attempt. I sat for a few more moments, letting her be lost in her feelings.

"Mary Grace, we need to get out of these woods and find help," I said. "Beau has found us; he will know the way home."

Mary Grace controlled her sobs and she turned her face toward me. Both her eyes appeared sealed shut. "How are we to get out of here? I can't even see to walk." She sniffled.

"Let my eyes be your guide." My voice became a growl as my fear was replaced by venomous rage. "We will make them pay for what they have done."

"How do you suppose we do that? Who would care?" she snapped.

"I swear on everything that is holy and pure, I will get justice for you, Mary Grace," I said with a frantic determination.

Mary Grace shuffled to her feet. Through my swollen eyes, I noticed the broken arm that hung limp by her side.

My snarl of rage didn't sound human. *I will seek justice!* I swore silently.

"We need to go now," I said through clenched teeth.

Mary Grace nodded and allowed me to put my arm around her waist. She leaned on me for support and took the first step toward the plantation.

I called to Beau, "Come on, old boy, lead us back."

Beau eagerly led us in a direction I hoped was home.

# CHAPTER
# Forty-Four

WE HEARD THE POUNDING OF HORSES' HOOVES, AND I WAS certain help had come. Feeling Mary Grace tense beside me, I assured her, "I believe help is on the way, Mary Grace."

"Now I face my shame," she whispered, the words almost inaudible.

I swallowed hard.

As the three blurry riders pulled their horses to a stop in front of us, I was relieved to see the face of my father. I could recognize Jones from his posture in his saddle. How our overseer sat a horse had been ingrained in my memory from his years of service at Livingston. Bringing up the rear was a man unfamiliar to me. The stranger stayed back and his dark hat shadowed his face.

"Willow!" Father dismounted and rushed to me; genuine worry thickened his voice. "What happened?" He gently touched my face. His face was inches from mine, and I saw the deep lines worry had engraved on his forehead. He glanced from me to Mary Grace. "No!" Twisting away, he released me to pace back and forth. A whimper escaped the hulk of a man before it was replaced with determination much like my own.

Turning to Jones he ordered, "Jones, help Mary Grace to your horse."

"No!" I shrieked as Mary Grace retreated into the curve of my side. "Father, can I ride with her on your horse and you double up with Jones or with the other one?" I gestured to the stranger.

"As you say, Willow," Father replied. He looked to the other two men. "Let's take them home to Mammy. She will know what to do."

I breathed a sigh of relief when Father understood my meaning without me having to press the matter. I led Mary Grace to the horse, and Father helped her up before seating me behind her.

As the sun dropped below the horizon, we rode into Livingston. I saw Mammy pacing on the porch, anxiously waiting for the men's return. Jimmy sat on the steps with his head bowed, his hat twisted in his hands. Mammy cried out when she saw us. Jimmy caught Mammy's arm as she ran from the porch and they ran to meet us together.

We pulled our horses to a stop. Jimmy reached up to help Mary Grace down. Beside him, a weeping Mammy mumbled unfathomable words. As she beheld her daughter's face, a low moan escaped her.

Mary Grace collapsed into the security of her mother's embrace. "Oh, Mama..." She sobbed hysterically.

"We'll take care of dis, chile. Mammy promises." Arms tight around her daughter, Mammy peered over Mary Grace's shoulder at my father, her eyes pleading.

I looked from her to Father in time to see his nod of acceptance to Mammy.

Jimmy reached for me, but Father stepped in and tenderly placed my feet on the ground. He stood with his arm resting protectively around my shoulders. I don't know why I didn't cringe away, but maybe like Mary Grace, I sought the protection of a parent. The moment passed as Father snapped into action.

"Round up the other men. We hunt the men who did this."

He barked orders to Jones and the stranger who still hung back like he had something to hide. "Jimmy, take care of my daughter. Don't leave her side. Take a gun and I want you stationed outside of her door twenty-four hours—around the clock, understand?—until the men that did this are caught."

"Yes, Masa."

Depleted of all strength, I crumpled into the hollow of Jimmy's armpit. He pulled me close. A flood of emotions overtook me at the safety I found there. Father looked at us. He never said a word about Jimmy's arm encircling me.

He continued barking orders. "I want a man guarding every entrance to the house. Double the guard at the gate. No one comes in or out of this plantation without my knowledge," he said to the employed men as they gathered around, guns in one hand and their saddled horses' reins in the other.

Mammy's footsteps were heavy as she led Mary Grace inside.

Father came back to stand in front of me. He brushed my matted hair from my bruised, swollen face and cupped my face in his hands with a kindness alien to me. Those hands had inflicted so much pain on me. This close, I discerned Father fighting the conflict stirring in him. In his eyes was a strange tenderness, and in this gesture, I felt his love.

"Willow, you must tell me who did this to you."

I forced the words out. "There were two of them. They were masked, but before I blacked out I recognized the voice of Rufus, Barry's overseer."

He turned away and shouted instructions to his men. "Mount up. We will pay the Barry Plantation a visit." He swung up on his horse. "No man will touch my daughter or anyone on this plantation with such brutal force and get away with it. An attack on one of us is an attack on us all. Ride out!" He swept his arm forward, and the posse thundered off. The grainy cloud of powdered dust from their departure filled my mouth and nostrils.

Jimmy's voice broke through the noise of the horses as they rode down the lane and out the gates. "Come on, Miss Willie, we need to git you inside and cleant up."

# CHAPTER *Forty-Five*

I CLIMBED THE SEEMINGLY ENDLESS STAIRCASE, HEAVY OF HEART. Jimmy spoke no words. None needed to be said; his presence was enough. At my bedroom he opened the door and, grateful for the haven it offered, I entered.

Turning, I gazed at the man who'd been my comfort. He opened his arms wide and I stepped into their embrace. Snug in the cradle he formed around me, curtained from the world, I broke. I soaked his shirt with my tears. The horror of the last few hours washed over me.

"Mary Grace…" My wail was muffled in his chest.

How would things ever return to normal? What would Mary Grace's new normal be? She would never be the same. The unspeakable things that had been done to her…I feared what it would do to a tender spirit like Mary Grace.

I leaned back and studied Jimmy's eyes for answers. His face was anguished as he returned my gaze. "I will make this right, Jimmy. I warn you, I will not find peace until I do." The attack evoked an unnerving anger in me.

Nothing could escape the careful eye of Jimmy. Worry swept over his kind face. "Miss Willie, I don't lak de luk in your eyes."

I said no more. I thanked him for his assistance and closed the door behind me. His footsteps faded away down the stairs.

Seating myself at my vanity, I sucked in a breath at the woman staring back at me in the mirror. I did not recognize my own reflection. My long, silky locks were a chaos of mats, twigs, and grass. I grimaced as I ran my fingertips over my lips; darkened cuts marred my once perfect pout, which had doubled in size, the swelling reaching to my nostrils. My chin was crusted in dried blood that ran down my neck and stained the front of my white blouse. My eyes looked like I had been caught in a swarm of wasps, so swollen that my eyelids swallowed up my lashes and the inset of my eye sockets was no more. Red blotches rapidly darkening to bruises covered most of my face. I twisted my head to view my neck, and the strain on the angry gash made me wince. The mark from the whip stretched two to three inches along my neck and looped up behind my ear. In time the rest would heal, but the lash of the whip would remind me of this day forever. I swore to myself this mark would become a reminder of the part I needed to play in this song and dance we called life.

Jimmy returned and took up his position outside my room, and the butt of his gun hit the floor as he leaned against my door.

I went to the water basin and splashed water on my face. Using a clean cloth, I blotted at the open wounds. From the stand the basin sat on I retrieved some ointment and applied it to my wounds. I needed to find some ice to ease the swelling, but my thoughts clung to Mary Grace. My heart cried to run to her, but Mammy was the one she needed right now.

Exhausted, I crawled into my bed, reached for the afghan neatly folded across the bottom, and pulled it up, covering my head. *If only I could rewind the day,* I thought.

"Willow..." Whitney's voice broke through my blanket cocoon.

*Whitney? What is she—the party! Oh, no.* I scrambled out of the bed.

Father had left firm instructions that no one was to come

in or out. But I knew Whitney, and she wouldn't take no for an answer if she thought something was up.

I shuffled to the door and opened it a crack. Without looking up, she barged in, announcing, "They are turning people away at the gate…" Her last words trailed off as she whirled to face me. "Willow, for God's sake, what happened to you!" Her loud voice turned to a screech, her brows rising in concern.

"I'll explain it later. I hope the guards managed to keep the other guests at bay. Father strictly ordered no visitors."

"I was having none of that," she declared. "We met your father on the road and he blew right past us in a fury. We knew something was wrong. Then when we got to the gates, the guards said the party was canceled and wouldn't clarify why. After arguing for what felt like hours, I tried to bribe them, to no avail. So, we took that back trail we used to move Georgia and Sam out."

"We?" I asked, already dreading the answer.

"Bowden, Knox, and Kipling arrived at the gate around the same time. They were having none of it either. We were all concerned for you."

"No…" My shoulders slumped. "Something horrendous has happened. I can't have anyone here tonight. Please, Whitney, make them leave. I can't face them." Tears of frustration flooded my eyes.

"Willow, I don't think they will listen. We are your friends. I know you feel you don't need them, but you do. I know Bowden won't listen, even if I tried to get rid of them. He was tearing up the ground to get to the house. Bowden, the image of strength and manly muscle, was as weak as a newborn colt with worry over you. We ate his dust getting here. The guards at the door would have suffered blows if Mammy hadn't intervened."

My knees nearly buckled, and Whitney reached out to

steady me. I studied the woman before me. As blunt and overbearing as she was, she came with good intentions and she wasn't leaving without answers. "Rufus did this to us," I said bitterly.

"*Us?* Who else?"

I related with as much discretion as possible what had happened.

Whitney was speechless. Then she was spitting venom and declaring the price Rufus would pay for this.

Mammy's heavy footfalls sounded in the hall, moving our way. She tapped lightly on the door and there was a muffled exchange with Jimmy.

"Come in."

Mammy's face seemed to have aged ten years over the last hour—her worst fear had come true. In her arms she carried Mary Grace's soiled clothes.

"How is she?"

"My sweet gal may never be the same." Mammy looked away, the burden heavy on her shoulders.

"Mammy, I wish I could take it all away. She followed me. If I hadn't gotten cross and wandered off, this would never have happened." I lowered my eyes, focusing on a dust ball in the corner of the room.

"Chile, dis is not your fault. Dem Barry boys is de ones who hurt my gals." Mammy cast a chastising gaze toward Whitney and said, "What are you gwine to have your pappy do 'bout dis, Miss Whitney?"

Whitney quivered beside me. Mammy was in pain and torn with grief. She was lashing out. Whitney straightened and squared her shoulders, meeting Mammy's challenging gaze. "I promise you, Mammy, there will be a reckoning for the sins forced on Mary Grace."

I went to Mammy and took the clothes from her. "I will

attend to this. You go to Mary Grace. Do not worry about this house or anyone tonight, Mammy."

"You all right, chile?" She tipped her head and looked slightly up at me. "I'm sorry I didn't come to you, but Mary Grace say dey didn't touch you lak dat, and I jus' so torn—"

"No explanation needed, Mammy. I'm taking over your duties tonight." I wrapped my arms about her. I couldn't stay holed up in my room. I needed to keep busy or I'd go mad. "I love you, Mammy, and Mary Grace."

"We know it, chile." She patted my back and stepped back. "You do my gal a favor?"

"Yes, Mammy, anything—you name it."

"She is axing for Gray."

Alarmed at her request and my stupidity at not thinking of this beforehand, I gasped, "Oh my, of course! I never thought. I'll do it directly." Eager to be of assistance, I hastily left them to do Mammy's bidding.

# CHAPTER *Forty-Six*

"WILLOW!" THEIR HORRIFIED VOICES EXCLAIMED together.

In my haste to be useful, I forgot my friends waited for news. "I'm fine. Honestly, I am, and there are more important matters to attend to," I said. "Bowden, Mary Grace is asking for Gray. Can you fetch him?"

Bowden stood frozen in place, his face reflecting his dark and dangerous thoughts. His arms hung at his sides and his hands flexed open and closed.

Aware of the turmoil surging through Bowden, Kip said, "I'll go." He clapped Bowden's shoulder, giving it a firm, understanding squeeze. Before he took his leave, he came to me, grimacing as he saw my face up close. His jaw set. "Willow…we…I will be back." He exited through the double front door.

Whitney descended the stairs and stood by my side. From the corner of my eye I caught her gesture to Knox to follow her outside, leaving me alone with Bowden.

Silence filled the foyer. Unsure what to say, I moved to the parlor and sat on the red sofa there. I realized I still held Mary Grace's clothes clasped tightly in my hands. Setting them aside, I massaged my temples with my fingertips before raising my eyes to survey the room. Through the door to the left, in the dining room, I noticed the beautifully decorated table I had spent many hours fussing over for my birthday party. The small rosewood

Victorian center table held the gifts quickly discarded by my friends in their concern. My brain felt foggy and I longed to wake from this nightmare.

I sensed his presence when his shadow loomed over me. "Willow?" My name softly trailed from him.

"I'll be fine."

He sat beside me. Gently turning my face toward him, he investigated the damage. "Who?" he said through his teeth.

"Rufus and Yates. I would recognize Yates's pigeon-toed stance anywhere," I replied flatly. "They hurt Mary Grace in ways I can't speak of."

He understood. "Justice will be served, Willow," he said firmly.

I threw a sharp glance at him. "Justice for who, me? I was beaten—so what? What of Mary Grace? The law will do nothing about this matter. You and I both know that."

I hated this truth. I vowed I would never be defenseless again, and he was going to help me see to that. "Bowden, I would like you to teach me how to defend myself."

"What did you have in mind?"

Encouraged when he didn't shut me down, I went on. "I will not be vulnerable in a situation like that again. I want you to teach me to fight with my hands, and to shoot."

"Willow, I don't know…"

I glared at him in disbelief. "You have no idea what it feels like to be a woman," I retorted, angrily rising from the sofa. "As women, we aren't taught any skills to defend ourselves in any way. We are simply to be pretty accessories on a gentleman's arm. Never again will I sit back and do as I'm told. I will learn to defend myself, with or without your help. I will never be pinned to the ground and straddled like a mare. I escaped the horror of rape this time, but what about the next?" I was on the verge of hysteria. "Without the physical strength to protect my friend, I lay there while the girl I've loved like a sister screamed, helpless and utterly useless." I ended on a guilty sob.

He stood swiftly and his shoulders straightened. "I will teach you. Forgive me for the hesitation." He reached out and placed his hands on my shoulders. "Willow, I'm sorry if I gave you the impression I didn't care. I care more than I am capable of showing. I can't begin to understand what you and Mary Grace endured. I vow to you to teach you anything and everything you require."

I needed him. I knew it. My heart stirred as I gazed up at him. This man had declared his love for me, and more and more each day I was brought to believe his words were true. I had been unable to say the words back. In time, maybe? I cared for him like I'd never cared for anyone before. And gradually, he was gaining my trust and respect.

"Thank you."

He scooped me into his arms and nuzzled the curve of my neck, tenderly kissing the nasty welt from the whip all the way up to where it stopped behind my ear. His voice quivered with emotion as he whispered in my ear, "I don't know what I would do if I lost you."

The warmth of contentment filled my heart.

# CHAPTER Forty-Seven

Horses pounded up the lane as Father and his men returned. Alerted to their arrival, Whitney and I joined Bowden, Knox, and Kipling, who had eventually retired to the chairs on the veranda. The horsemen's silhouettes bounced up and down in the light of the moon, their bodies casting shadows like moving mountains across the open fields. They arrived in the center of the front yard, exhausted and tight-faced. Father dismounted promptly and dispatched his men around the plantation. "And be on high alert," he barked.

"What is it, Father?" His strained manner worried me.

"They weren't there. Barry said no one had seen them all night. They may have caught wind we were coming."

"They were masked, Father, and they didn't know I recognized them."

"Yes, I remember. This means they are still out there somewhere. We start our search again at first light. Not a stone remains unturned. If we can't round them up by tomorrow eve, then I will go to town and inform the sheriff of their wrongdoing. I will put out a reward for their capture." He licked his lips as he paced, his eyes fierce.

Who was this man? I'd never seen this side of Father before. Was it because Rufus dared to damage his property? Or did Father care that harm had come to me? Mary Grace was but a slave to Father; it couldn't be that.

Bowden approached Father. "Sir, we are at your service if you require our help here tonight."

"No, Bowden, we will manage for the night. But I will need your help in the morning. Get your rest tonight."

"Yes, sir. I'll leave Gray here to stay with Mary Grace," Bowden offered.

Father started to protest the black man sleeping in his house, but I silenced him with, "How dare you! Is her life not as important as mine because she is a slave?" I glared at him.

"No, Willow, I didn't mean…" Father rubbed a hand over his weary face. "Forgive me, daughter; I've been unable to think straight since we found you. I'm trying."

I capitulated at the look of hopelessness on his face. "Very well, Father. Gray will sleep in the house with his wife." I turned to my friends. "Thank you all for your love and support. Please make sure Whitney makes it home safely, will you, Knox?"

"Of course I will, Willow," a somber Knox replied.

We said our final goodbyes and when they'd vanished into the night, I excused myself and went inside.

Washed up and alone in my room, I realized I hadn't eaten since morning when my stomach started churning and I felt nauseous. I wrapped a dressing gown around myself and took the back stairs down to the warming kitchen in search of a light meal. The house was still and the lanterns were turned low.

A glass of milk in hand and a piece of my birthday cake in the other, I started for the stairs, but voices coming from Father's study drew my attention. The study door was closed, but there was no denying the heated voice of Father and that of another man. Placing my ear to the door, I listened in on the conversation.

"You had one job and it was to watch her, and you couldn't even do that." Father's angry voice said.

"Charles, I understand you're angry. Trust me! I'm upset

that she could've been harmed worse than she was. I've watched over her all these years and I failed her. If anything had happened to her…" I heard remorse in the man's voice.

"At least we share this in common. You need to leave. You've been exposed too long. My men and I will take care of the search tomorrow," Father said firmly.

"But I need to aid in the search, after what happened before, and now," the stranger replied.

"No!" Father snapped. "You made me a promise. I expect you to abide by your word. You should go back to the shadows where you belong."

There was shuffling, and the door handle moved. I ran into the darkness under the staircase, but peered out as the men exited the study. My heart jumped into my throat. The stranger from earlier? I tried to widen my eyes, wishing the swelling would ease so I could see more clearly.

No words passed between Father and the stranger as Father saw him to the door and closed the door behind him. He was too far away to see his expression, but his next words chilled me to the core.

"Oh, Olivia…why?" he wailed.

The voice of Father calling my mother's name drummed in my head like a gong as I lay in bed, staring at the ceiling. For years I'd speculated about my mother and longed to know more of her. Now—in one day—I had heard her mentioned more than ever before. I needed answers. Who was this woman who was being kept from me? The woman Father seemed to want to forget—but in a time of sorrow, called on? My mind was filled with questions, and I was determined to get answers.

# CHAPTER Forty-Eight

MORNING CAME, ANNOUNCED WITH STARTLING PUNCTUALITY by the rooster's crowing. Irritated at its effect on my pounding head, and the unpleasant recollections of the previous day that came rushing in, I groaned. No matter how fervently I wished for the memories to fade, the reality of it was undeniable. I sat up, catching my breath at a sharp surge of pain. I paused and looked around my room through the slits of my eyes. My vision seemed to be improving.

*Mary Grace!*

Kicking back the covers, I rose too quickly and had to sit back down as my head spun. When the room settled I tried again to rise, more slowly this time. I slipped into my dressing gown, tying the twisted silk rope around my waist as I went out into the hallway.

At the door to Mary Grace's room, my heartbeat quickened as I lifted my hand and knocked. Receiving no reply, I put my ear to the door. No sounds came from within. Slowly opening the door, I peeked inside the small, bare room to find the drapes on the only window still closed. On the chest between the two narrow beds sat a darkened lantern. Mammy's bed was neatly made; a lumpy form lay under the covers of the other. I slipped into the room and crept over to Mary Grace's bed. My friend lay with the covers pulled up to her neck, facing the wall. Standing beside her bed, I could see one side of her damaged face. I clamped a hand over my mouth, muffling my gasp as I stared down at her.

"Mary Grace, it's Willow." I knelt beside her bed. Not wanting to frighten her, I refrained from reaching out to wake her.

"Miss Willow..." she whispered in a sleep-heavy voice. "I'm sorry."

"Sorry for what? You're the last one who should be saying sorry."

"What I said to you—I was...I was angry because I was born a black woman and you a white. I took all my hate and pain out on the one white person who has shown me nothing but acceptance. I was wrong."

"Hush now," I said softly. "I understand, so let's not think of it again. I need you to know I am here and I love you. We will somehow get you past this, if that is even possible."

"One day at a time, Mama says." She rolled onto her back and moved the blankets back to free her good arm.

"I don't want to impose on you, and I feel helpless about what I can do to help."

"There is nothing you can do, Willow. I will need to work through this on my own. But knowing I have the love and support of Gray, Mama, and you will be the strength I will call on." Somehow tears managed to slip through Mary Grace's grossly swollen eyelids to slide down her cheeks. Inflammation had taken over her face, and the definition of where her cheekbones ended and the inset of her eyes began was nonexistent.

A shadow fell across the room and I glanced up to see Gray in the doorway with fresh cloths and a bowl containing ice from the spring house. Mammy was on his heels with a tray of food.

I rose and backed away. "I'll leave you to tend to her. I'll be back later to check on her." I placed a hand on Gray's arm as I passed.

"Thanks, Miss Willow, for being a friend to Mary Grace."

He bowed his head respectfully.

"Always." I smiled at the man who had stolen my friend's heart.

Mammy touched my face, concern in her eyes. "You all right, chile?"

"I will be, Mammy."

"All right, angel gal, I'll be down to git breakfast right away."

"No, Mammy, we will manage around here without you for a few days. I will take over and things will carry on as usual. Mary Grace needs to be your only concern."

"No, Miss Willow, dat's my job—"

"Mammy, let me do this. I need to keep busy right now." I reassured her with a small smile.

"Bless you, my gal, bless you." She bobbed a nod of gratitude.

Leaving Mary Grace to her loved ones, I went to prepare for the day.

# CHAPTER Forty-Nine

THE WARMTH OF THE SUN SALUTED ME AS I STEPPED OUT ONTO the back veranda, where the guards dutifully attended their post. It was unusually quiet this morning. The chatter and singing of the slaves were absent on this beautiful morning. The absence of Jones and his men from the plantation did not hinder its operation, as the slaves appeared to be effectively running the place themselves. Their dedication amazed and puzzled me.

A group of women with baskets on their hips passed me on their way to the river. A thin, pleasant-looking woman called out to me as she passed by, "Bless you and your household, Mistress." She curtsied.

"Morning, Sara." I returned a small smile and a wave. *Bless me?*

I sat on the swing on the veranda and contemplated the last few days. I longed to be a child, unaware of the realities of an adult's world. Becoming an adult brought with it an understanding of things I wished not to comprehend. Every day life seemed to become more of a mystery. I'd started to question everything. Father had been distant and hard on me since I'd reached the age where his word simply wasn't enough. Never one to follow another person's outlook on life, I began to search for my own answers. As I grew older his rules grew stricter and the isolation worsened. My questioning his love had been a constant, but yesterday when Rufus and his man had hurt me, I was convinced it was worry and love I saw in his eyes. Was the desire to be loved by my father the reason for that? Had I read more on his face than was truly there? It couldn't be out of compassion for a slave.

What about the conversation I listened in on over his selling of live cargo? Did he care simply because Mary Grace and I belonged to him? Then what of the stranger? Who was he? And why had Father hired him to watch over me? This meant I was not crazy—I *was* being watched. Then there was what Rufus's man had said about my mother. I reflected on his words: "Maybe she should suffer the same fate." What had he meant by this? Had they hurt my mother too?

I could never get any information from Father, Jones, or Mammy or any other slave on this plantation. I'd gone over the ledger of slaves purchased before my mother's death and questioned them all. I'd tried endlessly over the years, but their lips remained sealed. Had Father threatened them? As steadfast as I was in my need for answers, I couldn't help the gripping fear settling in me. Did I want to know? What if I didn't like what I uncovered?

I tossed my distraught thoughts aside as Jimmy climbed the steps. His old knees creaked as he sat down on the swing beside me. "How you doing, Miss Willie?"

"I'm managing, but I'm fighting an inner battle."

"What be de trouble?"

"You would be here for weeks if I told you all that is tormenting my soul," I said grimly.

"De slaves are calling you de 'angel up in de big house.'" He smiled proudly.

I frowned. "Why's that?"

"Dey knowed you tried to save dat slave gal from what happened. Dey say you never left her and 'cause of et you take dis here beatin'. Your name's falling from all deir mouths today." He gestured broadly, encompassing the plantation.

The slaves didn't see me as the failure I feared I was, and their understanding humbled me. I twisted my hands in my lap, fighting back the tears.

Jimmy patted my back. "Dere, dere, gal, et be all right."

"I'm going to hold onto that hope."

"I have a birthday present for you." He reached into his pants pocket and pulled out a slender piece of wood. A tiny hole at the top had been cut and a thin, worn red ribbon was threaded through, tied, and left long. "I know you lak to read, so I made you dis."

I received it in awe at the thoughtfulness and the beauty of the craftsmanship. It was a bookmark. He'd engraved wings on either side of the words:

*Fly, my little angel,*

*spread your wings and soar*

*Above the trees, may you find freedom,*

*A slave no more.*

I was dumbfounded. He could read and write! The words were misspelled, making it dearer to my heart. "I didn't know you could read and write." I looked at him, shocked at his willingness to share his secret.

He lifted one of his bent shoulders in a small shrug.

He trusted me! The realization filled me: Jimmy trusted me. My heart leaped with pleasure.

"It's beautiful, Jimmy, and the words are lovely." I ran my fingers tenderly over the wording, absorbing the meaning.

"I used to sing dat to my girl, Mag, from de day she was born." His shoulders slumped. "Some days I can't recall her face."

"I'm sorry, Jimmy, that life did this to you." Saddened by his sorrow, I wished I could ease the pain imprinted on his heart.

"Et is what et is."

"You chose to put her song on a gift for me."

"You're de only thing keepin' me gwine most days."

His honesty swelled my heart with unrestrained love. "You're as dear to me, Jimmy." I stroked his hand, resting on the swing between us, and today he never flinched from my touch.

"I don't know, Miss Willie. I've bin seeing dat dere Armstrong boy paying a lot of visits nowadays." He gave my hand a squeeze.

I laughed at his teasing. "Well, you two came storming in like the troops trying to take over the fort I built. My faulty walls have weakened, and I realized he isn't so bad."

"You can't fool ol' Jimmy. Dat young man's a li'l more all right den dat." He winked, then rose and sauntered away.

# CHAPTER

THE DAY SEEMED TO TICK BY LIKE THE HANDS ON THE grandfather clock sitting in the corner of the parlor. I had scoured the library for books on guns and defense techniques. The books I found, I tucked away in my room for reading when my vision fully returned. Now, in the parlor, cobwebs were forming inside my head; boredom and frustration built as I waited for news. The waiting had become unbearable.

It was late afternoon before the hunting party made it back. Gray and I met them outside when they rode up

"Well, did you find them?" I inquired of my father impatiently.

"No, Willow. I'm guessing those cowards hightailed it deep into the swamps. Those swamps are like a fortress. We went hours deep in them most of the day and found no trace of them. Bowden refused to give up. He and Knox are still out searching along with that Barry girl."

"Whitney?"

"Yes, the girl rode into Livingston at dawn, all saddled up, along with Bowden and Knox. She wouldn't listen to reason. But she did ride like a trooper and kept up as good as any man." He chuckled with amusement.

I would never understand this man. He appeared to be perfectly fine with Whitney following along on men's work. Unbelievable! I snuck a sidelong glance at him before speaking.

"I fear Rufus will be back to leave no witnesses."

"I too share your fears that he will find the opportunity to clean up unfinished business." His jaw locked firmly as he rolled it over in his mind. "He wouldn't risk coming here. First off, he would be outnumbered and Rufus tends to prey on the weak. We will remain on high alert until he is caught, and you need not leave the plantation without protection. Understood?"

"Yes."

"I will be going to town tomorrow to talk to the sheriff and I would like you to come with me. I'm afraid we may not get any justice, but it's worth a try."

I clenched my jaw. He was right and it heated my blood.

Later in the day, Whitney, Bowden, and Knox rode into Livingston. I raced partway down the lane to meet them as they rode in. "Any sign of them?"

The three shared a private glance.

"We will get him, Willow." Whitney forced a tired smile.

"The coward eventually has to come out of hiding," Bowden said.

And when he did, I would be ready. He could remain in hiding until my eyesight recovered, giving me time to learn self-defense techniques. Then I was going for him.

The little voice in my head mocked me. *You are but a woman; what can you do*? I hushed the voice. Stubbornness wasn't always a bad thing. I'd made up my mind, and no one was going to stand in my way. Justice would be served, even if it had to be by my own methods. I knew how this was going to play out. Mary Grace and I were women, and disposable. Her honor didn't hold much value. And I was not the one raped, so this would take precedence over the crimes committed on Mary Grace. Then there was the fact that we did not see Rufus's face, and they would take into consideration my state of mind at the time.

"Willow, are you all right?" Whitney's voice pulled me back from my thoughts.

"Yes. Thank you for all your help. We will take care of our situation from here. I bid you good night." I turned and made my way back to the house. Their questioning eyes burned into my back.

# CHAPTER Fifty-One

WE DOCKED OUR SCHOONER AT THE WHARF IN TOWN. Father escorted me directly to the sheriff's office. Opening the door, he ushered me into a room where the air was stale and smothering from the heat rolling in through the office's front windows. Seated behind a desk in the corner, the sheriff had his chair tipped back, his legs crossed at the ankles and propped up on his desk, his sleeping face covered by a weathered black hat. Loud snores escaped from beneath it, a series of grunted snorts and whistling exhalations as his chest rose and fell. The black boots he wore had seen many miles.

Hearing the door open and close he mumbled and sat up, dropping his feet to the floor. He pushed the hat up over his long, greasy gray hair, revealing the face of a man of around fifty years whose mouth seemed to be held in a permanent grimace. I'd never met the man before, but I judged from his appearance and mannerisms that he might not be effective in his job, due to his disregard for personal hygiene and self-respect.

*I guess we will soon find out.*

"Charles Hendricks, is it?" He scowled at Father, his eyes flicking between the two of us. He could not have missed my injured face, but his glance never rested on my face a minute longer than it did on my father's.

"Yes, I've come here about an attack on my daughter—" Father started, but the sheriff cut him off.

"You never took her in hand?"

His insinuation infuriated me. It took all of my willpower not to respond to his implication that Father should have "taken me in hand."

Father bristled. His nostrils flared and he glared at the sheriff with his eyes that were flinty and cold. "Of course not! I suggest you take a good look at my daughter's face before I excuse her, so we can have a man-to-man talk."

The sheriff wiggled uncomfortably under his deadly glare.

"Now that I have your attention," Father said, then turned to me. "Willow, will you please wait outside?"

I wanted to stay and listen in, but I knew better than to argue. I made my exit.

I found a bench on the boardwalk by the sheriff's office and seated myself. The streets were bustling with people. Patrons moved in and out of the general store and the bank on either side of the sheriff's office. Many eyeballed me as they passed by. I pulled my bonnet forward on my head, wishing to avoid their gawking, but the hat provided little coverage.

Two women walked toward me. One was bone thin; you could almost count her ribs through her corset and dress, and her face was masculine. The other had a pudgy face covered with pimples; her figure was rounded from too much groundnut cake and sweet tea. She stood shoulder height to her friend. Maybe it was the criticism written on their sour faces as they drifted toward me that caused my instant dislike of them, or maybe it was the words they said loudly enough that I'd hear them as they walked by.

"That's Charles and Olivia Hendricks's girl. I hear she ran off with another man when the girl was little. A scandal, for sure. The poor man never married again after the heartbreak. Such a waste, with a handsome man like him. Our loss, I guess."

Their spiteful chatter faded as they rounded the corner and disappeared.

I sat paralyzed as I absorbed their words. Anxiety filled me and I felt physically ill. Lost in a daze, I did not heed Father's call to me as he stormed out the sheriff's door until he repeated my name loudly.

"Willow, wake up. Let's get out of here, I said," he grumbled. "Willow, what's wrong with you? Looks like you saw a ghost."

"I—I need to get out of here," I managed to say, stumbling to my feet. I swayed as everything around me began to rotate.

"Willow?" Father caught me.

"Father, please, let's leave," I said into his shoulder, the words muffled.

He supported my weight as we walked toward the wharf. Minutes later, I regained my strength and pulled away from him.

"I'm good," I said blankly. Giving me my space, he withdrew.

On the schooner and heading out of town, away from prying eyes, I studied the face of my father. I didn't need to ask how things had gone with the sheriff. Father's glum demeanor said it all. It had turned out as expected. My will for justice pushed me forward with the plan I'd thoughtfully worked out over the last few days. The time had come to prepare and put my plan into motion.

# CHAPTER Fifty-Two

Over the next several weeks, my face repaired itself. No physical scars remained, but the slash along my neck remained an ugly red welt. Mary Grace's physical wounds healed, but her emotional ones were still close to the surface. She withdrew within herself and disconnected from the world. Bowden gave Gray a pass to come nightly to assist in lifting her spirits. She no longer wandered off to the forest. The spring in her step disappeared, and no dreamy light danced in her eyes. I tried to comfort her the best I knew how, but it seemed the only one capable of putting a smile on her face was Gray. I knew Mammy wanted to protect her, but Mary Grace needed to get out of that bed and live again or she would wither away. Mammy's wisdom in the matter seemed to be clouded with the overpowering desire to shield her.

Burdened and feeling despair, I sought out Mammy one evening. I found her in the kitchen house, cleaning up after supper. A slave from the quarters had replaced Mary Grace for the time being.

"Amelia, could you excuse us?" Mammy said to the girl when I flopped down at the table. She nodded and with a fumbled curtsy, she left.

"What's wid de long face, chile?" Mammy had stopped her washing of the table and now gave me her complete attention.

"I can't stand it, Mammy. I'm eaten up with guilt and anger

over what happened to Mary Grace. I witnessed it firsthand. I understand she is hurt in ways no one should ever experience. I'm aware even I can't begin to imagine her suffering. But she can't lie in bed forever. If she is to get better, she needs to be busy and fill her days or she will replay this nightmare over and over until she fades away. You know I'm right, Mammy."

She said nothing. Her face remained unchanged. But I saw her mind spinning over my words.

"Mary Grace is forever changed by this. Everything pure and beautiful about her, they took that day. But I love her too much to see them take her life too." I examined Mammy's face, seeking understanding.

She huffed and finally replied, "I know you're right, chile." She rested her meaty hands on the table and shook her head as if to clear it. "Time will be what et takes to fix my gal, and in time she will find her way back. But et won't happen in dat dere bed."

I blew out a breath of relief. "Yes, Mammy! Does this mean you will help me get her out of bed?"

"Yes, chile. You're a bright gal. You love my Mary Grace, dat for sho'." She grinned briefly before her face grew serious. "And chile, et ain't your fault, what dose bad men did. Don't be carrying dat guilt."

Tears spilled from my eyes at her words, and I feigned a tired smile. "I'm trying, Mammy."

"Dat my gal."

I left the kitchen house. The sun was setting and the sky became sheathed in vivid shades of pink and orange. I thought about the last weeks as I made my way to the house. Father had left on his ship the day after the trip to the sheriff's office and we'd never discussed the rumor the town ladies spilled. We did, however, speak about what took place in the sheriff's office after I left. The sheriff claimed his hands were tied and there was nothing that could be done, as I wasn't raped, and even if I had been, I didn't see our attackers' faces. Father said he wasn't finished with the matter, but he didn't want to stir up trouble while he was gone. The guards were to remain at their post until his return, but, overall, the plantation went back to normal.

Bowden honored his promise and taught me self-defense and how to handle a gun. Whitney refused to be left out. Knox and Bowden made a point to come by Livingston each day, and we spent hours over the weeks practicing. We led Bowden, Knox, and Jimmy to believe it offered us a sense of security, which it did, but it hadn't been our only motive. Thankfully, we were quick learners and my confidence soared with each passing day. I no longer considered myself powerless. Like Mary Grace, the attack had changed me. I was aware of the ugliness of mankind before Rufus and his man's attack, but now I regarded it free of the blinders of a young girl. Tonight I felt aged beyond my nineteen years as I carried myself up the steps and left the artistry of the night behind me.

# CHAPTER Fifty-Three

As expected, Rufus was overconfident and thought he'd gotten away with his crimes. He came out of hiding and returned to the Barry Plantation. Mr. Barry threatened that if he tried the stunt again, he would hang Rufus himself. With a reputation and status in society like Father's, Art Barry couldn't afford to make an enemy out of him. Whitney said her father also couldn't afford to lose Rufus because, due to the effectiveness of his cruel ways, he turned a handsome profit for Mr. Barry. So, he remained on the Barry Plantation.

This evening I reclined in the mahogany chair in Father's study. I traced my fingers along the supple tan leather and over the brass studwork. The lantern on the desk flickered low. I folded my hands under my chin as I reviewed my plan.

Whitney sat in the chair opposite, her gaze locked on me. "You ready for this?"

"We've waited long enough. Now he's let his guard down, there is no better time than the present," I said loudly, trying to bolster my spiking nerves.

She nodded.

"You are aware, once we go ahead with this, there is no turning back? If you follow me in this plan for justice, it will change who we are and who we will become."

"We do this for Mary Grace," Whitney said firmly. "What of Dave? He is no better than the other two."

"No; though he is no better than the others, he did not take part in this attack. Justice will be served only to the two involved. So, we stick to the original plan and no detouring from it," I cautioned her.

I reached down into the satchel I had prepared and stored under the desk. "I arranged for Jimmy, Jones, and Mammy to receive a little extra something in their evening drink." I smiled mischievously.

"How?" Whitney asked, her eyes wide.

"Mary Grace!" I called out.

Mary Grace entered the room dressed in dark trousers and an oversized coat. Her hair was secured beneath a hat that was pulled down low, half covering her ears.

Whitney gawked from Mary Grace to me, her bewilderment deepening. "Care to explain?"

I lifted a finger to Whitney to wait while I asked Mary Grace, "Did you turn down the lanterns throughout the rest of the house and deliver the drinks?"

"Yes, Miss Willow. Mama drank her tea and is passed out in her bed. I saw the confused look in her eyes before she dropped off and you know Mama—she is a stubborn mule—so I hope it's strong enough to keep her out for a few hours. I served a pitcher of moonshine to James and Jones. Last I seen of Jones, he was sawing logs on the porch of his cabin and Jimmy was staggering off to his shack. The guards received their own pitcher of my liquid sleeping potion." She cackled, her eyes alive with devilment.

"Perfect." I grinned. Our plan was coming together nicely.

"What of the stranger?" Whitney asked.

Oh yes, my bodyguard. I hadn't forgotten him. I'm sure he was acquainted with our efforts to learn defensive techniques and wondered what we were up to. I was alert and mindful in every step I took besides the training, as there was no chance of passing unnoticed by anyone in earshot of us. I had no idea when Father had hired the stranger, and time had not allowed me to get answers to the growing list of questions I had for Father. When he returned home I would confront him with the knowledge I had acquired. "Well, there is no telling where he's watching from, so we can't silence him. My hope is that he will see the lights have been turned down and will settle in for the night."

"And what of Mary Grace? How did she become part of this?" Whitney asked.

"She is a house slave, Whitney, and a sly one at that." I winked at Mary Grace, who smiled. "House slaves know more of what is going on in a house than their masters. They are taught to stand by silently and obediently, therefore witnessing everything unnoticed. They are a goldmine of information. This being said, their information has not worked in my favor thus far, as the answers I have sought for years remain a mystery." I huffed, then continued. "Thankfully it was Mary Grace who got wind of our plan and not Mammy. She refused to stay behind and I could not deny her her own justice."

Rising, I reiterated our plan as Whitney and I changed into the sets of father's clothing I had hidden in his desk drawer from Mammy. I'm sure God frowned on me for what I was about to do, but I couldn't think on that or I would turn back. I shook my head to dislodge the beseeching of my conscience, and we slipped out of the house.

Horses saddled, we walked them out the north field until we reached my escape trail. Mounted, we rode with haste to the Barry Plantation.

# CHAPTER Fifty-Four

RUFUS AND HIS MEN, TRUE TO THEIR NIGHTLY ROUTINE, HAD retired to play cards on the porch of his cabin. We could hear their drunken laughter from the low shrubs where we crouched, surveying our surroundings. We needed to catch them off guard to balance our strength against theirs. The heavily flowing alcohol would give us the advantage.

We moved into position, pulled the masks down to conceal our faces, and slipped into action. Whitney took the right corner of the cabin, and Mary Grace and I approached from the left. Crouching to move below porch level, we approached undetected.

The men were caught off guard; they froze as our guns pointed at their skulls and we cocked the hammers. "Not a word!" I growled in a deep voice. "Rise slowly with your hands in the air. One wrong move and your brains will paint the front of this here cabin."

The men fumbled to their feet, hands held high. Whitney and Mary Grace followed my lead and grabbed the back of their man's collar to guide him from the porch and out of sight.

The night graced us with a half moon and while the poor visibility gave us the cover we needed, we strained to see as we shoved the men toward our waiting horses.

We gagged the men and bound their hands together, tying the excess rope to our saddle horns. We quickly mounted and, with a click of our tongues, the horses broke into a trot. The men had to run to keep up with the pace of our mounts.

A quarter mile from the plantation, we reined to a stop and silently dismounted. I jerked the rope that bound Dave's hands. He stumbled and fell. I gave the rope a forceful yank to get him up, but he lay in a heap on the ground, peering up at me. Not wanting to give away our identity with our lack of strength, I pulled my pistol from the waistband of my trousers. I smoothly pulled back the hammer and aimed the gun at his face, gesturing for him to rise.

He frowned, misreading my silence as cockiness. He rose, his eyes never leaving my masked face. I gestured him toward a nearby tree with my gun, where I secured him with more rope. Tugging at my handiwork, I was satisfied he would be no threat.

Whitney and Mary Grace put Rufus and Yates on their knees. I retreated to my horse and removed the torch from a saddle bag, along with a small folded bundle. From my coat pocket, I took out matches and lit the torch. As light filled our immediate surroundings I saw the twigs and branches Whitney had skillfully built into a teepee-shaped pile earlier in the day. I set the torch to it, and soon brilliant orange and blue flames crackled to life. Sparks spit and shot up. We waited for the fire to heat up and then to die down enough to provide significant coals. I bent and unrolled the bundle I held. Lifting the large nail I would use as a makeshift branding tool, I laid it on the edge of the red-hot coals.

My heart pounded in my ears. *Are you seriously doing this?* My knees began to shake and a lightness filled my head. *No, be strong, Willow! You have to get it together.* Closing my eyes for a moment, I inhaled deeply. We needed to act promptly to minimize the time the men had to figure us out. If they saw a weakness, they would attempt to regain the advantage. I squared my shoulders and clenched my jaw.

I lifted a hand and signaled Whitney and Mary Grace to bring Yates and Rufus forward. They jerked the men up, encouraging cooperation by pressing the muzzles of their guns into the backs of their skulls.

Once they were kneeling in front of me, I looked into Yates's face—the face of the man who had laughed as he inflicted pain on Mary Grace and me. He stared back with unwavering drunken arrogance. I looked over his head to Whitney for the support I needed to go on. She nodded—she was with me. I cranked my neck from side to side and trudged forward to execute the plan.

I stared at Dave from behind my mask. He stared back, wide-eyed. I lifted two gloved fingers to my eyes, then pointed them toward Yates and Rufus, instructing him to watch.

I returned to the fire and my gaze hardened as I glared down at Rufus. He peered back through narrowed eyes. For a moment I considered how he'd chosen this path in life. What had happened in his life to make him this sadistic, ruthless man? No one was born evil. Somewhere along life's path, he'd developed into the poisonous man that knelt before me. The men made the choice to do what they did, as we made this choice now.

I nodded at Whitney. She grabbed a fistful of Rufus's unkempt hair and snapped his head back. I handed her the torch. From the breast pocket of my coat, I withdrew a blacksmith glove and replaced my left glove with it. Carefully I removed the brand from the coals. I glared down at the slithering snake in front of me.

My first stroke sizzled into his forehead and he sent up a muffled cry. The smell of burning flesh made my stomach recoil. Each quick stroke drew a fit of muffled screams. Rufus arched his back in agony.

The grueling task complete, I moved on to Yates, relentless in my justice.

Finished, I stepped back.

The girls nodded, prepared for what I did next. I stripped the men as naked as the day they were born, their trousers piled at their knees. Mary Grace untied the whip from her saddle.

Dave angrily bleated behind his gag. I twisted to him, widening my stance while tilting my head. Deliberately I put a hand to my jaw to imply he might be the next target. In the firelight I saw the new fear flickering in his deep-set eyes as he shrank back against the tree, his objection silenced.

Whitney cracked the whip and it lashed Rufus's bare back. He squealed like a pig. Whitney paused and he whimpered.

*Zap!* The whip cracked again.

I pushed down a groan as the whip tore at his skin. His punishment was a scratch compared to the pain he levied on the backs of the slaves of the Barry Plantation. This was for the crimes he and his men performed on them and for the violation of Mary Grace's innocence. I fantasized the castration of these men and shame gutted me at the sick desire for vengeance that had chewed at me for weeks. Was it not what they deserved?

These men might be capable of evils of that magnitude, but we were not. That was a sin we could not wash from our hands.

One final whistle of the whip slashed Rufus around his lower midsection as Whitney grew tired. It elicited a suppressed yet chilling scream. He grabbed at his privates and doubled over. Whitney stumbled back, looking at us.

My breath caught and I gulped for air. I felt like I was going to pass out.

Mary Grace, however, did not lose her composure. Never faltering in her was her burning desire for revenge. This night, that was unmistakable. It was evident in the force she applied to the first slash of the whip. She repeated it with almost the same intensity in the next twenty lashes she inflicted upon him until she withdrew, dropping the whip to her side. She turned without a word and mounted her horse.

I'd been determined that justice be served. We had achieved that. I hoped to shame the men in a way that would restrain them from future attacks, but I knew this was out of our control. After gathering any evidence that could lead them back to us, Whitney and I saddled up and rode out.

# CHAPTER Fifty-Five

No sleep came to Mary Grace or me that night. Morning drifted in and with it came the worries about yesterday. Had we made an effective impact without repercussions to us? Had the men realized we were women? If so, would this realization lead them back to us?

A single rider rode into Livingston around midmorning and I recognized Whitney's profile. As I walked to meet her, an anxious Mary Grace came out of the kitchen house. We shared a worried glance when we met at the near end of the lane and waited for Whitney's arrival.

A flushed-faced Whitney reached us. "Whoa…" she instructed her horse, then effortlessly slid to the ground. Her forehead was puckered and she turned from us, crossing her arms tightly over her chest.

I swallowed hard and looked from her to Mary Grace. Mary Grace's eyes were wide; her hand went to her waist as she started to pace.

*Oh God, it's over. We are finished.* I tasted blood and realized I had my lower lip clenched between my teeth.

"Whitney, out with it now. What's wrong?"

Whitney twisted to face us, her expression solemn.

My fears had come to pass. I pressed my hands to the sides of my face and joined Mary Grace in her pacing. Rufus and his men had won. We'd attempted to punish the men the law would allow to go unscathed, and we had got caught. Life was beyond unfair.

Whitney's laughter rang out, stopping me.

"Whitney, for heaven's sake, what are you laughing about?" I scowled as Whitney stood holding her stomach, giggles vibrating through her body. *She's touched in the head. Straight-out plumb crazy.* "Whitney, what happened?" I moved forward, took her by the arms, and gave her a shake.

She stopped laughing to speak. "As of now, we are in the clear."

"What? Then why were you—why the worried face when you rode in?" I coiled my fists in the folds of my dress, shooting her a deadly glare.

"I wanted to lighten the mood. You two resembled two taut-faced spinsters. Those miserable tight faces alone would sell us out."

"Easy enough for you to say! You learned what's happening firsthand while we sat here fretting, waiting for you to show up. Then you show up all smug, playing these sick games with us." I rocked onto my toes and glowered at her.

Her shoulders hunched and her next words were apologetic. "You're right. I'm sorry. Truly I am. Maybe I can make it up to you by giving you the news that Rufus and Yates will be fine. Rufus may not be a functioning man for a long while, or maybe never, by what the doctor says. The slip of the whip struck his manly parts and caused some damage—oops." She raised and dropped her shoulders while trying to suppress another giggle. A smile cracked across her face as she continued. "The story the men have fabricated is that half a dozen large masked men overtook them, and Rufus went so far as to say he believed they were slaves."

"Slaves?" Mary Grace folded her arms across her chest and

rubbed her upper arms anxiously.

This put a target on all the slaves from nearby plantations. This wasn't good. What didn't she get about this? "This is no laughing matter, Whitney! We can't have them spreading that lie, or all slaves will become a target. Then what we did was for nothing."

Her smile faded. "I honestly never thought of it like that."

"We need to stop this rumor right away, and I have an idea. Follow me." I hurried toward the house with them on my heels.

In Father's study, I outlined my idea. "I'm thinking we write a note, threatening we will be back to finish what we started if we catch the slightest hint that they're stirring up trouble. We can't let them sense the threat to the slaves drives our motives, as they've already labeled me a nigger lover. And chances are, it would point fingers back to us."

"Who are you supposing should write this letter?" Whitney asked as she plopped down on a chair in front of the desk.

"Mary Grace, of course." I grinned.

Their open-mouthed stares hastened my next words. "We must outsmart them. If they somehow involve the law in this matter, a note could lead back to us. Our penmanship on a threatening letter would seal our fate. But a slave who doesn't read or write would be the perfect cover-up. What do you say?"

Whitney considered for a long moment, then bobbed her head up and down. "I think you're onto something. Mary Grace can write the letter. I'll take it back with me and find the right time to place it in Rufus's cabin. As you said, we need to put out this fire before it catches and spreads out of control."

A short time later, Mary Grace and I stood on the front veranda, watching Whitney ride off. We were both lost in our own thoughts, and didn't notice Mammy until she was right beside us. We both jumped as she spoke.

"What's so heavy on your mind?" Her expression was grim and her eyes studied us with hawk-like intensity. Careful of the ears of the posted guards, she lowered her voice. "Et be a mystery to your ol' Mammy, how I got de bes' sleep I git in all my days last night. You wouldn't know anything 'bout dat, would yas?" She waggled a plump finger at Mary Grace and me.

"No, Mama. I brought you a cup of chamomile tea. Before I knew it you were fast asleep. I was guessing you were plumb wore out."

Mary Grace had always been a poor liar. I forced my eyes not to roll at her pathetic attempt to fool Mammy.

"Chile, I've had a lot of long, hard days and never went out cold lak dat before. You see, de funny thing is, I be talking to James dis mornin' too, and he must have had dat same good tea."

"What Mary Grace is trying to say is, we need you to hush this talk of blame, Mammy. There is nothing to worry about; everything is fine." I gave her a light smile.

Mammy held my gaze for a long moment before lowering her head. "You're right about one thing, angel gal. De less I know, de better." She turned from us, and in her hunched shoulders, I knew we had burdened her with worry. It saddened me, but it was for the greater good. Things had to change and in change, people would get hurt. It was inevitable.

# CHAPTER *Fifty-Six*

FATHER RETURNED A WEEK LATER AND WAS SOON NOTIFIED OF THE attack on the Barry men. I was present when he called Jones to his study to catch him up to speed on things around Livingston. I tried to hide my smirk at Father's reaction to the news: a loud chuckle and slapping his leg in delight.

"That is great news! I applaud the men who took care of those imbeciles." His green eyes glinted.

The attack changed things between Father and me for the better. That horrible day had opened his eyes, and he began to see things in a new light. He asked my opinion on things around the plantation. He called me into his study to chat, and though it was awkward for both of us at first, I recognized his attempt and suppressed the mixed emotions his efforts stirred in me. Learning to overcome my constant fear in his presence would take time.

Our letter achieved the desired effect, and the stories died down about the men in the masks. Things went back to normal on the plantation, and the guards were dismissed from their posts a few days after Father's return.

Today I planned to divulge to Father my growing knowledge about my mother. I hoped to get the answers I needed to the questions that still plagued my mind.

Now, seated on the window seat in my room, I lowered my book to my lap. Resting my forehead against the pane of glass, I inspected the activity below. I loved to read, but after days of being cooped up in this house, I was going stir-crazy.

*How much reading can one person do, anyhow?*

My eyes roved the whole of the backyard until they idled on Mary Grace pinning bedding on the clothesline. The unhappy expression on her beautiful face made my heart ache. While I watched, she raised a hand and briskly wiped at her eyes with the back of it. Was she crying?

I set my book aside and ran from my room. The vibrations as my feet pounded down the back stairs pummeled the walls of the narrow space. I swept out the back door and ran across the yard, ducking through the bed linens until I stopped beside my friend.

She paused as she was about to pin a sheet to the line. "Miss Willow? Did you need something?" She attempted to change her sad expression with a fake smile.

"Mary Grace, I saw you crying from my window. What's wrong?" I touched her arm as I searched her face.

Mary Grace's eyes darted over my face as she struggled with the desire to tell me versus staying silent.

"It's all right, Mary Grace. Whatever it is, you can tell me."

"I can't. I don't know what to think myself. I'm in a real mess now." She bent to gather another sheet from her basket of wet laundry.

I waited for her to continue.

Mary Grace straightened and glanced at me sideways as she positioned the linen on the line, her movements agitated. "I don't think I can handle much more of this."

I didn't grasp what she was getting at, but I stifled the impulse to push her to get to the point.

"I'm pregnant!" she blurted through gritted teeth.

I imagined grounding my heels in the soft earth beneath me to keep from staggering back at the sudden news.

"And I don't know if the baby is those monsters' or Gray's." She fired words from her mouth like a cannon on the battlefield.

"Did you tell Gray?"

"I can't bring myself to. What if he doesn't want to help me raise a baby that isn't his? How do I raise a baby when it could be a constant reminder of that day? My shame would forever confront me, every waking day."

"Gray loves you more than anything, Mary Grace. He will not turn you away." A wave of tenderness swept over me. I gently took her by the shoulders and turned her to face me. Her lovely face was twisted with the torture of what-ifs.

"I know he loves me. But it is a lot to ask of him or any man." Tears glistened in her eyes.

I peered deep into her troubled eyes. "Tell him, Mary Grace. You can cross the bridge of who the baby's father is when the baby comes. What about Mammy? Have you spoken to her?"

"No, you are the first. And honestly, I would've kept this to myself a while longer if you hadn't been spying on me." She tossed me a half-smile.

I sheepishly grinned. "I see everything, and don't you forget it. I've got eyes in the back of my head like Mammy."

The remark scored me a giggle from her, and her face brightened with a flicker of the old Mary Grace.

# CHAPTER *Fifty-Seven*

**Mary Grace**

WILLOW'S RETREATING BACK REKINDLED THE UTTER DESPAIR that had been afflicting her for days. Willow's heart was perpetually in the right place. She was attuned to the people around her; she radiated compassion and virtue. Of course Willow would see her crying and come to investigate. Mary Grace felt relief to have someone to talk with about the frightening life she now carried within her.

Later, when the linens were hung, she went in search of Mammy. Encouraged by Willow's supportive response to her news, she knew she needed to talk to Mammy and summoned up the courage to seek her out.

The first place she looked was the kitchen house, of course. It was the location for many heart-to-heart talks between Mammy, Willow, and herself. The aroma of baked peach pie filled the air as she entered the kitchen. But the usual delight Mammy's cooking conjured instead nauseated her. Slapping her hands over her mouth, Mary Grace ran out the side door and released the contents of her stomach, retching until she thought her stomach had turned itself inside out.

"For heaven's sake, chile. What is wrong wid you?" Mammy asked from behind her.

Lifting her apron, Mary Grace wiped her mouth. She sent

her mother a pleading look of despair.

Mammy's narrowed eyes grew big. "Sweet chile of mine—come inside and I'll fix you some ginger tea to sip on."

Flour from the pie crust Mammy had been rolling still covered the well-worn wooden table in the middle of the room. Mary Grace pulled out a chair and plopped down, her misery overwhelming her. Mammy fixed the tea and poured it into a dainty white china teacup accented with petite blue flowers. Placing it before her daughter, Mammy fixed one for herself and sat down, resting her fleshy hand over her daughter's.

"I'm with child."

"I guessed et be so." Mammy's eyes radiated heartache.

"What am I ever going to do, Mama?" She curled her arms on the table and buried her face in them. How could she do this? What would Gray say? How could she love this baby?

"I ain't gwine to lie to ya, chile; et's gwine to be hard. But you can do et. You are Mammy's chile. Your Mammy will be here. Don't fret dat purty head of yours."

"But Mama, how can I ever love this baby? If this child is one of those men's, I don't think I can bear to look at it every day without thinking of its pappy or of the innocence he took from me. Every time I look in its face, I'd see the monster and relive that night."

"Now, chile, I loved you."

"I know, Mama, and you never made me feel any less or that I was a burden, but I'm not like you. You're made of a different cloth. You're strong; nothing bothers you. You protected me from the world and I'm grateful. It's this pain I feel, this violation. I don't think it will ever go away. I don't know if I'll ever allow Gray to touch me again."

"Chile, life makes you strong. I didn't git strong on my own. Life did dis to me. I larned to shut off my feelin's to protect myself from de pain. I was dead inside. Mr. Adams may have raped me. I may have conceived you by him. But he wasn't your pappy. Big John, he is your pappy in evvy way dat mattered. He loved you 'cause you were part of me. If Gray is not de pappy, he loves you 'nuf to raise dat child in your belly together. Here on Livingston dat chile has a chance, jus' lak you did. You will love dat chile 'cause et is yours. You think of et as being all you, and if et be born a pure Negro baby, you rejoice in dat."

"Oh, Mama." Fresh tears spilled as she nodded in acceptance.

"Dat a gal." Mammy's calloused hand caressed her cheek.

Mary Grace covered it with her own and grasped at the love and support she'd received from the strong women in her life. "One day at a time, Mama, is all I can do." Mary Grace twirled the teacup in its saucer. The last of the hot liquid swirled in a circular pattern as she gazed hard into her tea.

"Dat's right, gal," Mammy soothed before rising to finish her work.

# CHAPTER *Fifty-Eight*

At supper that night, Father informed me we would be leaving at the end of the week for New York. News of a trip was music to my ears.

"Father, can I bring Whitney with me?"

"I think that would be a splendid idea. You could use the company, as I will be fairly tied up while we're there." He didn't divulge exactly what would be taking up his time, but I didn't waste any time trying to figure it out. My head was spinning with ideas for what Whitney and I could see and do in New York.

"I will speak to Mammy about bringing Mary Grace along to attend you, as well."

"I think we all would benefit from a change in scenery." I restrained my desire to run from the room and share the good news with Mary Grace.

Father grinned at my enthusiasm. "I like the dynamics between us, Willow. It's refreshing to have a mature, polite conversation."

He meant it as a compliment, but I bristled inside. That was all I'd ever wanted between us, but he was the one with the notions that had created years of unease and tension. Why had it taken a violent attack for him to finally treat me with kindness instead of as a bothersome hindrance? But I refused to mar the mood, and decided to wait to ask my unanswered questions. An adventure was calling to me, and I had no intention of messing that up.

"Yes, Father, this is the way I always envisioned our relationship to be. Hopefully things will continue this way." I smiled sincerely, raising my wine glass in salute. He followed suit and then we sipped the French burgundy wine.

The dinner started and ended on the same positive note.

Later I waited in my room for Mary Grace to arrive to prepare for bed. I was in my closet going through my dresses, trying to decide which ones I would take with me, when Mary Grace arrived.

"Miss Willow?"

"In here, Mary Grace."

She peeked inside.

"I have exciting news." I came out and clasped my hands on her shoulders.

"What is it?"

"Father is taking me to New York at the end of the week. He said I'm allowed to take Whitney—and you."

Mary Grace's face split in a wide smile, and a light long dimmed brightened in her eyes. "Truly, Miss Willow?"

"Yes." I beamed at her reaction.

"I've barely been off the plantation, let alone gone on a trip." Her excitement heightened.

"Things are different in New York than they are here. I think we would all benefit by getting away and forgetting things for the time being. So it's settled—we will go. Mammy will come to see our side with some convincing, I'm sure."

"You let me handle Mama." Mary Grace winked.

"I have no doubt you will." I chuckled at the determination on her face. "We are off on a grand adventure, my friend. This time we will step out of the book and experience it for real," I sang out as I whirled through my room in a waltz that ended when I dropped onto my bed.

Mary Grace giggled and came to sit on the bed beside me. "It will be different, and it will take my mind off my predicament." She looked down at her stomach.

I pulled her down beside me and wrapped my arm around her shoulder as we stared up at the ceiling. "Everything is going to be fine. You'll see."

"I hope so, Miss Willow."

It had to be. We would figure all of this out together.

# CHAPTER
# *Fifty-Nine*

WHITNEY REFUSED TO LEAVE THE TWINS BEHIND SO THEY, along with Mary Grace, accompanied us to New York. Surprisingly, despite her condition, Mary Grace fared well on our voyage. A boundless joy seemed to buoy her and I frequently heard her humming. Our plantation life seemed like another world entirely.

The noise of the city was vastly different from the rural peace and quiet we were accustomed to. Smoke from the factories created a haze that hung over the city. My eyes roved from the tall brownstone buildings that nestled along the streets to the streets themselves, packed with carriages and people.

Heavy traffic had carved deep ruts and churned the streets to mud. I lifted my dress as we crossed, but mud sloshed over my shoes and my feet quickly became wet. I groaned at the squishy feeling inside my shoes.

Whitney saw me curl my nose in disgust and chuckled. "Poor darling."

I stuck out my tongue at her. If not for her pretty face and her stylish clothes, I'd find her the annoying brother I never had. Beside me, Father winced at my unladylike gesture, but held his tongue.

We reached the boardwalk on the other side and walked toward the hotel, passing the peddlers who lined the boardwalk, hustling their goods to passersby. I did a double take when a shopkeeper who stood idly outside his shop openly invited a well-dressed colored man in to purchase his goods. The shopkeeper smiled at the colored man and even offered his hand in a firm handshake. The sign hanging on a wrought-iron arm above his store indicated the proprietor was a cigar maker.

Ahead of us, a horsecar loaded its passengers. As the last passenger stepped on, a black woman and her child rushed up to catch the car, filled with conspicuously white passengers. The conductor put out his hand to refuse her passage. I saw the woman dare to challenge him, standing her ground and demanding to be let aboard. I was too far away to hear the words they exchanged, though I could tell they'd become heated. Finally the conductor gave her shoulder a rough shove and the woman lost her balance and landed in a heap on the ground. The conductor simply turned and boarded the horsecar. Seconds later it was moving along the iron track. I looked back to the woman as she rose and grabbed her child's hand, then spun on her heels and stomped off.

We reached our hotel and checked in just in time to freshen up before meeting Kipling for supper. The twins were a library of stories from the journey and the sights they'd experienced along the way. Whitney's hands were full, trying to get them to settle long enough to put on their evening wear.

"I don't want to dress up." Jack defiantly folded his arms, glaring at his big sister.

"I don't care what you want, young man, put those clothes on and be done with it," Whitney said sternly, her expression no-nonsense. He pressed his lips together and started getting ready.

Father was in the lobby waiting for us when we came down. "You look lovely, my dear." He kissed my cheek.

Although his compliments remained foreign to me, it

warmed me to hear them. "Thank you, Father."

"How do I look, Mr. Hendricks?" little Kimie asked, twirling around while holding out the skirt of her yellow dress for Father's inspection.

"Yes, Kimie, you are the prettiest of all." Placing his black silk top hat on his head, he offered her his hand, which she proudly took and skipped out the main door with him.

# CHAPTER *Sixty*

THE CARRIAGE FINALLY RUMBLED TO A STOP IN FRONT OF A midsized building far from the main streets. In this neighborhood the streets were dark, without the gaslight lampposts that illuminated the main streets. The footman opened the door and gracefully bowed to us; offering a white-gloved hand, he assisted us out of the carriage. As I descended the carriage steps I glanced about, wondering why we were meeting Kip here.

"Father, I wonder why Kip would suggest we meet at a restaurant off the beaten path."

Ducking to exit the carriage without knocking off his hat, Father stopped on the lowermost step to make his own inspection of our surroundings. I saw my confusion mirrored in his eyes. Turning to me, he offered a wary smile. "I say we find out." He strode over to open the wooden door with a window in its upper half.

The restaurant was not like the brownstone buildings on the main streets, but simply constructed of lumber, with a few wide windows in its front wall. Through the windows I saw both Negro and white patrons at the white-draped tables. I sent an open-mouthed stare of shock at Whitney. She returned one of her own, then shrugged.

We followed Father into the establishment to be greeted warmly by a black man dressed in a crisp waiter's uniform.

"Good evening, ladies and gentlemen. A table for five?"

"Um..." Father's eyes darted around the room, scanning the diners who laughed and conversed over their meals. Skepticism had replaced his earlier jovial manner. Then his face relaxed as his eyes found Kipling, who was in deep conversation with a young black lady. "We are meeting Mr. Reed this evening," Father blandly informed the man.

"Ah, Mr. Reed; let me show you to his table. Please, follow me." The man guided us toward the table.

Kip glanced up as we approached and instantly stood to bow in a grand gesture accompanied by a boyish grin that put us at ease. "Well, hello, my Southern comrades. Welcome to New York. I hope you are ready for some fine hospitality."

"I missed you and your craziness, my friend." I offered a cheek as he leaned in to kiss it.

"I second that." He stepped back with a wide smile.

He kissed Whitney's cheek, then moved to shake Father's hand. "Mr. Hendricks, always a pleasure, sir."

"Likewise, Kipling." Father delivered a wavering smile.

Looking at the twins, Kipling frowned, resting his fingers on his chin in thought. "Now, who are these grown-ups?" They beamed up at him, and Jack stood up straight.

"Those rascals belong to me," Whitney said, and ushered the children to their seats.

"I would like you to meet Miss Ruby Stewart, my assistant and a godsend." Kipling placed a friendly hand on her back. She was tall for a woman, and dressed plainly, though tastefully. I guessed her to be in her mid-twenties. She regarded us with interest as she greeted us. Her eyes rested longer on me, and her brow furrowed. Then it passed as I smiled openly at her.

I glanced at my father, hoping he would remember his manners, as it was not our custom to address blacks by anything but their first name. Father seemed rendered speechless, so I quickly stepped in. "On behalf of us all, we are pleased to meet you, Miss Ruby." I held out my hand and with a firm grip, she shook it.

"You as well, Miss Willow. I've heard so much about you."

"Well, I hope he hasn't been filling your head with nonsense." I feigned a glower at Kipling.

"On the contrary, I assure you," she replied politely, and offered me a seat by hers.

When the waiter came to our table, Father, who remained uneasy, managed to order a bottle of wine.

Kip addressed the waiter. "And could we get an order of those lovely sweet rolls you make here with the pecan butter, my good man."

"Of course, Mr. Reed."

"I was under the impression from your telegram that Mary Grace was accompanying you on this trip too. I thought she would be joining us tonight." Kipling aimed his question at me.

"I, um, I was unaware how things worked here—I mean, I didn't..." I stammered.

Father took over. "What my daughter is trying to say is, this is not the norm. We do not dine with the blacks. No offense, Miss...?" He looked at Ruby.

"Ruby, sir. Ruby Stewart." She exuded remarkable confidence as she answered Father.

"Yes, Miss Stewart."

I grimaced at Father's bluntness and begged Kip and Ruby with my eyes to forgive his frankness.

Kipling spoke for them. "That is understandable. Do not forget, I am from the South too. I assure you, it is no different here. The free blacks are banned from almost all establishments. That's why we met here tonight. I was eager for you to meet my assistant, and as I said, I thought Mary Grace would be joining us. The owner is a Dutch woman who is open to providing work for the blacks, regardless of threats and boycotting by the whites. She opens her doors to blacks or whites alike."

"But why would these other, seemingly higher-class, people dine here if it is frowned upon?" Whitney asked.

"Because these folks are allies of the free blacks, and all blacks, at that. Many are standing in the fight for change and for equality. The abolitionist movement is rising even more than it was twenty odd years ago. Their voices are a powerful accompaniment to those of the blacks, and we are seeing the effects of standing united. We need to end the racial segregation and discrimination. The friction between the North and South concerning slavery is growing rapidly and spreading far and wide with every passing day."

Kipling's matter-of-fact explanation rattled me briefly. I gulped a mouthful of my wine as I eyed Father over the rim of my glass. I resisted the urge to squirm in my chair.

Father leaned back and observed the ambitious young man sitting before him, his expression thoughtful. "I would be careful who you become friends with, young Kipling," he warned.

I seethed inside as I waited for Father to indulge in his opinions of how things should be run. After all, he was a Southern gentleman, and this was our way. To my surprise, he glanced at me and smiled softly before steering the conversation to agreeable pleasantries. Father remained a gentleman. The conversation remained light and sophisticated at this mixed-race table, making for a delightful evening.

# CHAPTER
# Sixty-One

THE FOLLOWING MORNING, FATHER DEPARTED EARLY TO MEET with business associates on the affairs that had brought him to New York. At the end of the previous evening, Whitney and I had made plans to meet with Ruby at a coffeehouse in the same neighborhood.

The coffeehouse was small but quaint, exuding a homey atmosphere. The aroma of fresh brewed coffee and sweet pastries made my mouth water. The five tables were covered in bright yellow tablecloths, with bright bouquets of wildflowers in glass vases in the center of each. Both white and black patrons sat in the varnished maple chairs, some with their heads close together, scanning paperwork spread on the table in front of them, others conversing. Patrons at one table discussed the abolitionist movement and politics. Ruby had secured a table at the back and sat reading a newspaper. That in itself made me do a double take before going to meet her.

"Ah, ladies," she said by way of greeting, her smile transforming her face from ordinary to pleasant as she set the newspaper aside.

"Good morning, Ruby," I said, then turned to indicate Mary Grace. "I'd like you to meet my friend Mary Grace."

"Mary Grace, it's a pleasure," Ruby said eagerly, and stuck out her hand.

Mary Grace wiped her palms in the folds of her dress before

timidly offering her hand in return. Her eyes scanned the coffee-house, looking for an overseer or someone to object to her presence. I entwined her other hand in mine and lightly squeezed it, then nudged her toward the chair facing the windows.

After we'd ordered pastries and coffee, I smiled earnestly at Ruby. "So, if you don't mind, I'm interested in hearing your story." I was curious about her life as a free black woman in the North.

"Well, I don't recall much about my life before I came to New York," she began. "I was born a slave, this I know. There are images—memories that fade in and out of my consciousness. I remember bits and pieces of my journey by ship to New York, but those memories have grown vague too.

"Once here, I lived on the streets, stealing what food I could get my hands on, until my adoptive father found me and brought me home. My adoptive parents gave me a new identity, including giving me their last name. I received a full education at an all-black school. They raised me as their own, with no concern about my ancestors.

"That's basically my life in a nutshell," she finished, turning her attention to her food.

I sensed Ruby wasn't used to talking about herself. Thinking about what she'd said, I took a slow bite of my warm, sugary pastry, and widened my eyes as the incredible taste wrapped my tongue. I let out a low moan of bliss. The others looked at me. Wiping the sugar from my lips, I felt my face heat. "Sorry; it's so good." They laughed. "It tastes like home," I added. "Mammy is the queen of the kitchen," I declared proudly.

"You speak of her with affection," Ruby noted, her voice revealing her astonishment.

"Willow has a bond with many of their slaves," Whitney explained. "An abnormal relationship in the South, as I'm sure you can understand."

Ruby regarded us both with an expression of wonder. "Yes, I can imagine it would be," she said after a moment. "What about you, Whitney? What is your take on life in the South?"

"My father is also a plantation owner. He is not made of the same fine cloth as Mr. Hendricks. His weave is flawed and spun demon-tight." Whitney lowered her eyes. "He finds much joy in torturing our slaves."

I looked at her in surprise. Fine cloth? Was Whitney's coffee laced with spirits? How had she forgotten the conversation we'd overheard between Captain Gillies and Father about the selling of cargo? I was annoyed that she cast him in a shining light when he was no different from the rest of the plantation owners who accepted and benefited from the practice of owning humans. He openly traded and sold slaves—I had witnessed it all my life. Even as we moved toward mending our relationship, I remained certain he was wrong in doing this.

"As a respectable woman of the South, what is your assessment of how your gentlemen handle things?" Ruby redirected her gaze to me.

"They are complete and total failures," I replied bluntly. "We may be women, but we won't be silenced by our men. As Southern women, we are taught to be passive and submissive to our fathers and husbands. We are considered too tender to deal with men's issues. We are the property of our fathers until we marry and then we become the property of our husbands." Realizing I was raising my voice, I took a moment to calm myself.

"True to his upbringing, my father tried to instill submissiveness in me, but I've always had a mind of my own. I rebelled against that—and much to his dismay, I inherited his stubbornness." I chuckled. "He sent me away to a fancy boarding school when he found he couldn't control me. He cringes when I speak, but like most parents, he wants me to have the proper manners and etiquette to be accepted in society.

"I've learned to curb my convictions and passions and to use wisdom when engaging in what I hold dear to my heart. I present a façade to the world that is different from what I am on the inside—I can be the proper, well-mannered lady that the world wants to see, but I must live my own truth."

Earnest now, I leaned forward, glancing at Whitney to include her in what I said. "Times are changing. We do what we can, educating ourselves about what is happening in the country. We need to progress in our production to the level of Great Britain and France—even the ways of the North are more advanced than ours." Whitney nodded. "I believe plantation owners have come to rely on cheap labor to make an extra dollar. We have to change that. Machinery is the way of the future.

"And all humans, white or colored, should have equal rights. They should be paid a fair wage for their work. They should be able to decide whom they wish to work for. They should be able to own homes of their own and marry whom they please. No parents should be separated from their children because a master says so. They are all entitled to have a proper education. Slavery is wrong on so many levels." Realizing my grip on my cup had tightened, I consciously peeled my fingers free.

Whitney gently touched my arm to calm me as other patrons turned their attention to us. Then she leaned forward to rest her hands on the table and, in uncharacteristic Whitney fashion, said in scarcely above a whisper, "I agree with Willow. Speaking of the North versus the South, we may be neighbors, but the North is more advanced in the ways of the world. We seem to lack the education afforded to those in the North. Do you know how many white folk back home can't even read? We depend so much on slaves that it hinders us in the long run. We declared our independence from Britain, but where do the slaves stand in this country's independence? These barbarians who run the country need to wake up and apply change." I admired Whitney's frank and even tone.

Ruby raised an eyebrow at her bluntness and then added an opinion of her own. "Oh, don't deceive yourself. The northern businesses rely heavily on the South's cotton and your slaves. They are no better. The manufactures and factories use your slaves too; they just don't physically own them. What drives men is money and power. We need to stand and fight for the rights of all God's creations. He made all men in his image, not only the white men," she said bluntly and without fear.

Mary Grace looked on in awe as we uncloaked our perspectives on slavery. We could become victims of our rulers, or we could rise above the dictatorship in this country. In the humble little coffeehouse in a black neighborhood, we were simply a group of women who became empowered and encouraged to persist in our efforts to apply change to the sick affliction that had overtaken our country.

# CHAPTER Sixty-Two

## Ruby's Story

A troubled Ruby, garbed in a white linen nightdress, stood on the balcony of the cobblestone home she shared with her aging parents. Her head tilted back, she gazed up at the infinite sky, glowing with stars, the moon hanging like a luminous globe in their midst. She reflected back over the span of her life, and her chest lifted and fell with an almost perfect contentment. Life had blessed her with a lifestyle frowned upon by society for a woman of her coloring.

She couldn't recall her life before she came to New York. Frayed and rippled images would trickle in and out of her mind. She was skeptical of their value to her. She considered the likelihood the stories weren't hers and simply part of her imagination. Over the years she'd helped hundreds of fugitives, and their stories became a constant in her head—their lives before their escape, and the consuming fear they shared of their grueling journeys to freedom. Her parents believed that, due to her age when she escaped slavery, she had suppressed her memories of the trauma she herself had experienced.

With her ultra-dark skin, she didn't think she'd been the baby of a master; she was likely of pure Negro descent. She could not remember anything about her biological parents. Frequently a man with a face that was but a blur would come to her in her dreams. His voice was persistent and soothing, his hands steadfast and gentle as he smoothed back her hair. Then he would laugh a boisterous laugh, a sound that made an unbridled happiness bubble up inside of her and out her own mouth as an identical laugh. When nightmares terrorized her, this ever-loyal man would ride in as a black knight. He'd dismount and kneel, and she would run to the asylum of his arms. He would hum a velvety tune that vibrated in the chest beneath hers as her tears melted into the crook of his neck. When the tremors of her sobs rocked her awake, she would find her pillow wet and her heart burdened with a yearning she couldn't place.

In her early years, she had a reoccurring nightmare, flashes of running in the dark with dogs snapping and barking at her heels, someone pulling her along, a paralyzing fear compelling her to seek a hiding place. It always ended the same. A white woman with bewitching green eyes would pull her to her chest and whisper comfort. She hadn't had the nightmare for years—until the other night, after Willow Hendricks, exuding refined dignity, gracefully sauntered into the restaurant. Ruby's subconscious awoke. The shroud she'd hid the hazy memories behind parted and they returned with a vengeance. Because of Willow's fierce green eyes, so like those of the woman in her dream.

The voyage to New York had left Ruby with a phobia of dark spaces. Her stomach seesawed with the memories of gnawing hunger, the struggle to stay hidden for days on end in the pitch-black of the hold in the cargo ship. When night fell and she heard no human voices, she would slip up to the deck to inhale the fresh air. Any movement would send her scurrying below decks.

The night she returned from the upper deck and saw the whites of another pair of eyes looking back at her, she almost choked on her own heart when it leapt into her throat. The stowaway had hidden with her in the cargo area, and as sneaky as she had been, she'd never caught wind of his existence.

Will was around twelve years old, with ginger-colored hair and a peppering of freckles. He was an Irish indentured servant. He'd served his four-year contract and when it was up, his owner abandoned him to the streets. He aimed to get to New York to search for his mother, who was there serving out the terms of her contract. Will said they'd lived on the streets in Ireland with no family to turn to, and hoping for a better life, his mother had signed contracts for herself and her son.

Things took a sideways turn when they were at sea. Their owner offered up his mother's seven-year contract in a drunken round of cards and lost. His mother, broken and defeated, became disconnected from her son for the remainder of the passage to the Americas. But as he exited the ship with his new master, she ran to him and clasped him in her embrace, then leaned back and held his face between her calloused hands. Gently but earnestly shaking him, she'd made him promise that, when his four years were up, he would find her in New York.

He'd stood on the dock, blinded by tears as she screamed to him, "New York, me boy!"

He boarded the same ship as Ruby and set sail to New York with the ambition of reuniting with his mother.

At night when the noise of the crew faded and the only sounds were the waves against the hull and the echoing clap of the massive sails, Will stole above to gather food. Like a sly fox he crept up, threading through the bunks of the slumbering crew, and scampered back below without stirring a hair on their heads or a whisker on their snoring faces. Ruby grinned in elation when he returned unscathed, time and time again. With the craftiness of her newly discovered friend, the hunger slashing at her empty belly lessened.

When the ship docked in New York and they stepped out into the golden, sharp sunlight, she lifted her nose to the heavens and inhaled a deep, lung-filling breath. Will grabbed her arm and zipped her away. Roaming the streets, she began to tremble, and a new foreboding ate at her.

What was she supposed to do now?

Then she felt Will's arm around her small shoulders.

She spent the next year of her life living in the slums of Five Points with Will, stealing food and sleeping wherever they could find shelter. The streets were rampant with crime and danger. Will continued to protect and care for her. He was street smart and he taught her how to survive on the streets. Eventually, Will found a job as an errand boy, which paid little, but it kept food in their bellies.

The night the men came, they'd settled down in the makeshift shelter they'd crafted with the scraps of sails, a few pieces of broken lumber, and fraying rope. They'd lain on the frozen ground within their shelter with their bellies half full, satisfied that they would survive yet another day.

Rough arms seized Will through the back of the shelter and she scrambled out the front. Two men held Will pinned to the ground, but he was having none of it. He fought like a wild animal.

The grizzled, bearded man growled at his accomplice to grab her while he knelt with his knee on Will's throat to hold him down. For a moment Will ceased fighting; flashing fear-filled eyes her way, he'd cried, "Run!"

She hesitated, but as the other man started toward her, she turned and ran. The wooden blocks that were supposed to be her legs felt leaden, but she never stopped; she wove around obstacles, trying to lose the man pursuing her as Will had taught her. When she was sure she'd lost the man, she dodged in behind some broken barrels and sobbed softly so no one would hear.

*Will...* Her mouth parted in a silent cry. She was utterly alone in the world. She'd lost her only friend.

She leaned back against the old crate behind her and shuddered with both cold and fear. Will would often spoon his body around hers for warmth. When the nightmares came, he'd rubbed her back and soothed her fears with cheerful words. She had grown reliant on the safety he provided.

What would happen to him? Would she ever see him again? He would get away! Will was smart and strong.

The next morning she returned to their shelter. It now lay in shambles, and there was no sign of Will. She searched the whole area, to no avail. She checked their usual meeting spots but he was not there. She described him to the peddlers and panhandlers and asked if they had seen him. Some shoved her away in annoyance and others heard her out before shaking their heads. For the next month she returned to the area of their shelter at night and observed it from concealment. Will never returned.

Then came the day fortune smiled down on her. A peddler with a cart of fresh bread for sale caught her eye. Slipping up to the cart, she snatched a loaf and spun to scamper away.

"Stop right there, you thieving nigger!" he yelled, chasing after her. The pounding of his feet grew closer and closer.

Her head snapped back as he grabbed a fistful of her collar. She heard the thin material tear as he lifted her and turned her to face him, but he shifted his grip to a new section before she could get away. Dangling in the air, she glared into his beady eyes. He returned her glare, his mouth twisted with disgust and hatred. She panicked and kicked him in the stomach with all her might, knocking the wind from him. He released her and doubled over in pain. She ran like she had never run before.

She looked over her shoulder and grinned. Will would be

proud at how strong and fast her legs were. And then she ran smack into a brick wall. She would have reeled backward if a hand hadn't grabbed her upper arm to steady her. The wall was a human. Instinctively, Ruby started to struggle and claw at her captor.

"Calm down, little tiger, I'm not going to harm you," the woman said, laughing.

That was the day she met Amy and Joshua Stewart. Amy had won her with kindness and the promise of a big meal. Ruby, with nothing to lose, followed her home. Amy Stewart bathed her and dressed her in a simple cotton dress. It was the nicest dress Ruby had ever had. After a full course meal, Amy offered her a bed for the night. Ruby stared up at her suspiciously but then accepted, as the thought of spending another night alone was almost unbearable.

The Stewarts' easy, genuine ways won her over as night after night passed, until they asked her to stay permanently.

Unable to have children of their own, they treated her as if she was born to them. They were aware she was a fugitive and kept her profile low so she didn't catch the eye of any slave catchers. They read the ads for runaways, searching for alerts for girls matching her description. Her master never came looking. The Stewarts told her one day after she had lived with them a little over a year that her master had probably thought she was dead, because how could a child so young and alone ever survive?

Ruby smiled smugly that day and said, "He must be a dumb masa 'cause I outsmarted him."

The Stewarts glanced at each other and chuckled before resting their fond gaze on her. Amy said, "Well, young lady, if you are to remain here as our daughter, we need to have you properly educated. What do you think of that?" Ruby had bounced with excitement at the chance to learn.

The Stewarts never faltered in their promise to care for her. They registered her at a local black school, changing her name to "Ruby Stewart." They never legally adopted her, but to her, they were her parents in every way that mattered.

As abolitionists, they surrounded themselves with friends who shared their beliefs, and Ruby remained unreported as the fugitive she was. Born a slave but raised a free woman, she sometimes wondered who was peering up at the same star-filled sky, wondering about her and whether she was well. The only key she held to her past and the one thing she remembered was the name *Mag*.

# CHAPTER Sixty-Three

IN THE WEEKS THAT FOLLOWED WE ENJOYED ALL THE FINEST THINGS New York had to offer, from the theater and upscale restaurants to the museums. We shopped until we had filled several extra trunks for our journey home. The twins had a complete new wardrobe. Kimie, with a fashion sense like her big sister, found great delight in her new clothes. Jack, being Jack (and a boy), grumbled at the endless wandering of stores. Whitney treated him to a new toy to occupy him, which also kept his complaints to a minimum.

Our last few days in New York, we visited with Whitney's Auntie Em, who showed immense enjoyment of our company. Father remained in the city, attending to his affairs. Our time with Aunt Em ended too soon for all of us. We headed back to the hotel to prepare for our trip home.

When we arrived at the hotel, the front desk clerk handed me a message. I unfolded the stationery and read the brief, neatly scripted note.

*Miss Willow,*

*I know you will be heading home soon and I'd like the honor of meeting with you one more time. If you could meet me at the same coffeehouse as before, I would like to ask you a few questions. I will be there at two o'clock.*

*Ruby Stewart*

"Who is it from?" Whitney asked.

"It's from Ruby. She would like to meet with me at the coffeehouse. She said she has some questions for me." I lifted a brow in curiosity at Ruby's last-minute request.

The ear-piercing squeal of the twins as they raced around the lobby demanded our immediate attention.

"Jack, Kimie—come here this instant!" Whitney demanded.

The twins came meekly to her side. Whitney's exhaustion was evident. I watched her as she spoke firmly to her brother and sister on the manners expected of them in a public place. I admired the maternal love she had for her siblings and how she had taken full responsibility for them when they had no one else. One word described my dear friend, and it was "selfless."

"Why don't you all stay here? Mary Grace could use the rest and these rascals can relax and play in their room," I tousled Jack's hair. He grinned up at me, thrilled at the idea of not having to follow us on another outing.

He turned to Whitney and bobbed his head up and down. "Please, Whitney. Like Willow said, we need to rest. You girls pretty much wore out my good shoes with all your shopping."

Whitney and I exchanged a glance. The corners of our mouths turned up.

"I insist, Whitney," I said. "You are wiped clean of energy, and it would do you all some good to rest a spell."

I saw the conflicting emotions zigzag across her face—relief, yet uncertainty.

"It will be fine." I smiled, lightly resting my hand on her arm.

"You're right. These twins will be the end of my youth." She laughed.

The doorman signaled a hansom cab and it rolled to a stop. The doorman helped me into the cab, and I was off.

The driver helped me out at the coffeehouse. I paused to smooth my cream-colored taffeta dress while I peered through the windows. I saw Ruby. She gazed out the window, but her eyes seemed to be focused far away.

Lifting the hem of my gown to avoid the grime on the cobblestones, I strolled to the door and stepped inside. I showed myself to Ruby's table.

"Good day, Miss Ruby," I said as I seated myself.

"Oh, Miss Willow." Her eyes focused on me and she grinned sheepishly. "Thank you for meeting me on such short notice."

"Not to worry," I said. "You said you had some questions for me?"

Ruby nodded and paused while composing what she wanted to say. But instead of speaking, she looked at me bleakly and her eyes sought mine.

"Ruby, ask me whatever you like. What is troubling you so?"

"It's your eyes. I'm wondering if I've seen them before, but when I was a little girl."

"My eyes?" I frowned, perplexed. "I don't understand what you mean."

"As I mentioned to you, I don't recall my past before I came to New York. My childhood came to me in dreams and visions I can't piece together. They plagued me for years before disappearing altogether. When you walked into the restaurant, I had an eerie feeling I had met you before. Your face looks so familiar, but it's your eyes that have haunted me since we met. You see, in my visions I see a woman with the same deep green eyes. All these years, I've thought that my subconscious was trying to tell me something, but I've forced the thoughts away because they were too confusing and frightening to deal with. After meeting you, my turmoil has returned."

Stunned, I swallowed hard, uncertain what to say. I could not give her the answers she sought. "What is this woman doing in your visions?" I asked, hoping to help her sort out her thoughts.

"It's dark...we are running in a thick wooded area...it's damp and cold. I hear the barking of dogs and men shouting. As the scenes play out, I'm filled with a fear so great I can't move. The woman and child are running frantically, trying to escape the men and their dogs. During these visions, I am looking through the eyes of the child. In the next vision the woman and the child are hiding in tall bushes or grass, and the child is sobbing. The woman pulls the child to her and tries to calm her. Besides a direct view of the woman's eyes, that is all I see of her.

"It's the same visions over and over. In other dreams a man appears to me—like the woman, always the same man. He pats my head affectionately and his infectious laughter makes me laugh. Then when my dreams turn to nightmares, he rides in like a black knight and hums a tune that soothes all my fears. When I wake I'm drenched in sweat and tears, feeling a longing so deep, I can't eat or sleep for days." Ruby stopped and regarded me with tortured eyes.

"Do you think your mind is putting bits and pieces of your escape together?"

"That is what keeps rolling around in my head. It makes sense that someone helped me escape. How could a child so young make it all the way to New York alone? But then again... maybe it's not my story at all. Maybe it's me longing to know where I came from, and I'm pushing myself to make these visions my own past. Maybe this vision had to do with you coming into my life, and our lives will become intertwined in helping the slaves to freedom."

I came to understand her confusion as she voiced her thoughts. "What of the black knight? What significance does he play in these dreams?"

"Maybe he is my father...or maybe he is my Prince Charming." She tried to laugh playfully, but it didn't ease the confusion on her face.

"I'm sorry, Ruby, that I can't be of more help."

Her eyes grew sad. "It's all right. How could I expect answers from you about a past that has nothing to do with you? It's almost a relief to reveal the craziness in my head aloud to someone." She smiled softly.

As we boarded the train to return to Livingston, my mind returned to the conversation I'd had with Ruby. I knew how daunting unanswered questions could be, and how they could nibble away at your mind. As the train pulled out of the station, I glanced out my window and sent voiceless well wishes to my newfound friend, and the hope that she would find the answers she sought.

# CHAPTER Sixty-Four

WE'D BEEN BACK AT LIVINGSTON FOR A MONTH WHEN THE opportunity to approach Father with my long-delayed questions finally presented itself. We were sitting in the library that evening, the fireplace crackling and popping, washing the room in a cozy, welcoming glow. A lover of chess, Father studied the board, his chin resting in his hand as he calculated his next move. I considered the man before me; he'd spent more time lately doing right by me than wrong. He had softened, and the change made me want to do my part to mend the years of hurt and dysfunction between us.

My eyes traveled over the creases forged around the corners of his mouth and eyes. He was creeping up on sixty years. Did he ever relax? I regarded his rigid posture. Until lately, I'd never seen him laugh or find any enjoyment in life. He consistently exuded authority and had been serious and guarded for as long as I could remember. He'd provided me with all the worldly possessions a girl could want, but he held his feelings and love at arm's length.

"Willow, it's your turn."

"Oh, sorry." I dropped my eyes to study the board.

"Care to share what has tied up your mind?"

I picked up my rook and moved it to take his open bishop. "It's nothing. I was thinking of life and how it is playing out."

"If you could change something in your life, what would you change?" He tentatively held my gaze.

I fought the urge to squirm. Here was my opening.

"I would want to know of my mother," I said, my voice strained. "Please, Father, give me this bit of peace," I implored him, my eyes fastened on his. I noticed the change in them at my request. I tensed in anticipation of another rejection.

Father leaned back, inhaling deeply, and his eyes met mine. He clasped his hands under his chin, resting his index fingers on his lips as if pondering what he would say. Anxiety built in the space between us and pounded in my ears.

"Your mother and I grew up together. She was an only child to John and Grace Shaw, your grandparents. Your grandparents had your mother later in life and they doted on her. She was educated and smart. John sent her to the best school. The one I decided to send you to."

My heart fluttered in surprise at his words. We had attended the same school. But why? Why would he keep her from me, only to allow me to have this connection with her?

Father smiled in admiration as he envisioned my mother. He began to reveal the knowledge I'd yearned for all my life. "She could hold her own, much like you. She had a mind of her own and never backed down from anyone. Though pampered and spoiled by your grandparents, your mother remained humble and kind. She touched the lives of so many. She was intoxicating in her charm and didn't have to demand the attention of a room. She had a rare beauty. Your mother was physically beautiful, but her true beauty radiated from the inside out." His gaze grew even more distant, lost in time, and a smile transformed his face.

He loved her. I was certain of it now. But why the secrets? Why had he banned all knowledge of her from my life?

He shifted in his seat. *Continue,* I demanded in my head, and he did.

"You are the replica of her." His eyes glinted with respect

for her as he rested his gaze on me. "You have her beauty, and in you lies her spirit. You are everything that was pure about her. You also have her stubbornness and her determination to set the world right." His voice broke and the heartache he'd kept caged for so long began to escape.

I wanted to go to him. I wanted to wrap my arms around him. To give and find comfort. To be united in our grief and longing for a woman we both loved. But the years between us held me back. Instead I asked, "Father, what happened to my mother?"

Shocked, he whipped his head up. "You were told what happened. Why would you ask?"

"Yes, you told me she died of yellow fever, but there have been rumors…"

A sharp knock distracted him from his response. We looked toward the doorway. Jones stood in the passage outside the room. There was no denying the sheer relief that swept over Father's face.

Angry at the disturbance, I glared at Jones. "What is it, Jones?"

"Evening, Miss Willow. Sir, I need to speak to you about a matter in the quarters." He wiped his forehead with his sleeve.

"Very well, Jones," Father replied, standing eagerly to make his departure. "Please excuse me, daughter." He walked briskly toward the doorway.

"But…Father," I cried after him as I saw my mother fade before my eyes. Father disappeared without a second thought for me. *No!* Hopelessness swept through me. The tightly woven secrets Father had wrapped my mother in were threatening my sanity.

# CHAPTER Sixty-Five

FATHER OFFERED NO MORE INFORMATION ABOUT MY MOTHER. THE next day, desperately needing to lift my spirits, I had a footman saddle my horse and bring it around front. Whitney and I had grown accustomed to showing up unannounced at each other's home, and today I was going to do just that.

I thundered across the countryside in hopes of reaching the Barry Plantation in record time and slowed my horse to a trot when I reached the lane leading up to the plantation. The ride had not helped. I'd settled into a depression. Tying my horse to the hitching rail, I peered around. No one came to greet me. That was strange! Where was everyone?

I went inside in search of a servant to inform them of my arrival. The house was deadly quiet. "Hello," I called out. My voice bounced back to me. I had the uncanny feeling the house was smirking at me as I raced from room to room in search of any form of life. "Whitney!" I yelled.

Nothing. *This doesn't feel right.*

Fear crept over me as I wandered the plantation grounds. It was as if the Barry Plantation had been wiped clear of human life.

Then I heard wailing from the direction of the river.

Terror chilled my blood. *The children! Whitney!* I lifted my skirt and sprinted toward the river, images of the horrors I would find running through my mind.

Through the trees, I saw the reeds along the river. And more.

My hand flew to my mouth, stifling a gasp of revulsion.

Before me was a sight that would remain in my memory forever. Never before had I witnessed such savagery.

Mr. Barry and Rufus stood in the middle of the shallow river, each with a hand resting leisurely on his waist. They were grinning at each other. The water splashed fiercely around them, churned up by the thrashing legs and arms of the drowning man pinned beneath their boots.

As I rushed forward, I saw the white head of a gaunt black man surface momentarily. He fought for air and desperately clawed at the men's boots. Lined up to share his fate were two other slaves, aging women who'd outlived their usefulness to Mr. Barry. One's arm had been severed sometime in the past. With her only arm, she struggled to support the feeble woman who leaned against her. The one-armed woman's courage held me spellbound. She stood erect, proud and strong, staring straight ahead over the river toward the horizon. There was stubbornness in the chin she held up.

I scanned the crowd of plantation slaves until I found Whitney. She stood on the bank, her eyes squeezed shut and tears streaming down her face. Turned with their faces buried into her skirts on either side were the twins. Whitney was shielding them from the horror their father was performing.

I pressed my way through the slaves to Whitney. "Whitney!" I choked out as I cast one last glance at the old man. His body had given up its fight to survive. The men lifted their boots; the current caught the body as it surfaced and floated away.

"Willow…" When I reached her, she wrapped her arms tightly around me, and the young arms of Jack and Kimie encircled my waist.

"All right, children, let's go—now." Clenching my teeth, I shoved the three of them toward the trees.

"But…Father?" Whitney's voice trembled.

"Whitney, please, I know you're in shock right now, but let's get them out of here. Your father is so drunk with sadistic lust he won't notice you have gone." I looked at the elation shining on his face and knew the man was crazy. He had no empathy for human life. How Whitney and the children had endured living with him this long was beyond my comprehension.

We hurried through the trees to the path leading back to the house.

Kimie reached out and clenched my fingers tightly, her frightened eyes pleading. "Auntie Willow, can't we live with you? Can't you take us far, far away from here? I like your father—he's nice."

Saddened by her words, I peered over her head at Whitney. She stared straight ahead, her expression bleak.

"Yeah, Whitney, what do you think? Can we go live with her?" Jack asked his older sister.

"I wish we could, buddy." She rested a protective hand on his dark curls. "But Father would never allow it. We need to stay strong…we have to." She seemed to be encouraging herself along with the twins. "Never forget the horrible wrongs you have seen on this plantation." She stopped and turned to lift his chin, so their eyes met. "Jack, promise me you will grow up to be a man of honor. Promise me you will treat all people with kindness and respect."

"I will, Whitney. I swear to you, I'll never be like him. Not ever!" he swore with determination.

My eyes burned with unshed tears as I observed the small family grasping at some sort of security in their decaying world.

"Be the difference in the world. Don't let anyone tell you life has to be this way. Live by your heart and it will always steer you right," Whitney said before bending and kissing the top of his head.

# CHAPTER Sixty-Six

THE SLAVES WALKED SLOWLY BACK TO THE PLANTATION FROM THE river, their movements lethargic, their heads bowed. The ordeal at the river had snuffed out any hope they had left. The blackening skies rumbled in accompaniment to the shuffling of their feet.

Bringing up the rear of the group of slaves were Mr. Barry, Rufus, and his men. Their laughter seemed to pummel the slaves deeper into despair and constricted my aching heart.

Whitney, the children, and I stood waiting on the veranda for Mr. Barry. The men paused and peered up at us.

"Well, Jack, I say soon you will know all the ins and outs of running this here plantation yourself." Mr. Barry's smile at his son was detached and cold.

Jack remained silent, but his body language projected a coldness of his own as he regarded his father. He squared his narrow shoulders and stared long and hard at the men before him. I followed his intense gaze. Rufus removed his hat and mopped his forehead. Beads of sweat trickled from beneath the black bandana tied around his head. Partially visible was the word I had branded into it: *rapist*. I twisted to look at Yates, who also wore a bandana, trying to hide the disgrace advertised on their foreheads for the world to see.

My mark had made an impact! If not, these men would not have tried to conceal it. In this petty thing, I found a kernel of contentment.

The heavens above us opened and released torrents of rain, as if God were unleashing his fury at the wrongs done this day. It beat violently on the roof of the veranda. The men ran to avoid the storm, Mr. Barry sprinting past us into the house.

We seated ourselves on the porch swing. Kimie wiggled onto Whitney's lap. Whitney's chin rested on the top of her head, her finger twirling one of Kimie's blond curls. Jack sat between us, solemn and obviously troubled, his small hands clasped tightly together in his lap. I gently placed my hand over his.

"We fight evil in our minds, Jack. If we control our own minds, no evil can come in," I said softly, seeing the conflict tormenting his soul.

Confused, he peered up at me. "What do you mean?"

"I mean when bad people, like your father, Rufus, and his men, do the things they do, it's because they chose to do it. You may be his son, but don't think it means you can't be better than him. Look at Whitney—she is his daughter, but she is nothing like him. You keep your mind strong and when the little voices in your head tell you it's hopeless and you may as well fall in line with the ways of the world around you…find your own strength. Stand up and say no. You are the gatekeeper to your mind and your soul belongs to God. Art Barry is a man who helped your mother make you, but he does not make you who you are. You do! Keep faith in the goodness of mankind, all right?"

He smiled and looked thoughtfully out over the storm-drenched plantation. He nodded in understanding. "I think I get it."

My eyes wandered to Whitney's. She whispered, "Thank you."

Giving her a wistful smile, I nodded.

# CHAPTER Sixty-Seven

## Whitney

THE NIGHT OF THE UPRISING, HER FATHER, RUFUS, AND HIS MEN leisurely sat drinking whiskey and smoking cigars in the study. Art Barry mingled with his working staff as if they were his friends. *Creatures of darkness find commonality,* Whitney thought as she listened to their intoxicated, vulgar conversation drifting from the library.

"Whit?" Knox's voice broke through her thoughts. "Are we going to play the game with the twins or not?"

"Yes." She looked from the plate of treats the kitchen cook had prepared for their game night to Kimie, who sat cross-legged on the floor playing with her dolls, waiting patiently.

Jack, who had been outside playing until the sun went down, stomped the mud from his boots on the veranda before stepping into the foyer. Whitney frowned as he paused and closed his eyes before taking a deep breath and entering the library. "Hello, y'all. Sorry to have kept you waiting," he said, sounding old beyond his years.

Whitney arched an eyebrow. "Jack, are you all right?"

"I'm fine. I think it is a perfect night for a carriage ride." His grin didn't reach his dark eyes.

"But Jack, we are going to play some games," Knox said.

"We will later, but a nice ride will help me relax my mind.

So I can win." He smirked with mischievousness at his sudden, brilliant idea to get his own way.

Whitney couldn't help but chuckle at her dirty-faced little brother. Jack was always missing in action. His love for nature often had him off on a new adventure. She knew in his mind the farther he could be from the plantation, the better, and she couldn't help but agree. *I wish I could take them and run from this horrible place,* she grumbled to herself.

"All right, Jack, you win. I will find Thomas and ask him to prepare the carriage."

He let out a whoop and ran toward Kimie while calling over his shoulder, "Thomas is already out front, waiting." He grabbed Kimie's arm, pulling her to her feet. "Come on, Kimie, let's go."

Whitney and Knox exchanged a puzzled look. Gathering up a blanket for the children, Whitney handed it to Knox, then placed her straw bonnet on her head and tied the blue silk ribbons under her chin.

"I don't feel like a carriage ride tonight, Jack." Kimie stomped her foot. "I want to play with my dolls for a bit longer."

Jack slightly bent down, as if his three extra inches of height were far greater, and stared into Kimie's tear-filled blue eyes. "Now, Kimie, this is something your brother wants to do, and you know how Whitney tells us we have to think of others, right?"

"Yes," she said grudgingly, and pouted.

"Well, what are you going to do about it?"

"I'm going to go on the carriage ride." Angry, she folded her arms across her chest.

Whitney put her hand over her mouth to muffle her giggles at Jack's manipulation of his sister. So wrong, but oh, so funny. Knox's eyes lit up with his own mirth.

Kimie snatched the shawl and bonnet Whitney offered

her. Securing her own bonnet, she gave Jack a glare and headed outside.

As Jack had stated, the open carriage stood waiting. Thomas tipped his hat. "Evenin'."

When all of his passengers were seated and settled, Thomas took his place in the driver's seat. He hesitated, glancing around the plantation before shouting an order to the horses, and they were off.

Jack slouched low in the carriage seat, his wary eyes unwaveringly fixed on the house. The light of the plantation faded behind them. The carriage lanterns swung back and forth with the swaying of the carriage as they rode along.

Growing concerned at Jack's suddenly sullen mood, Whitney asked, "Jack, are you all right?"

He leveled a solemn look at her but nodded.

"Are you sure?" She saw panic beginning to surface on his face. "What is it? Tell me."

He searched her face before saying, "I know something very bad that is going to happen, but it will save a lot of people."

At his words, Thomas slowed the horses to a stop, "I knowed et, Miss Whitney! Somepin' bin amiss in de quarters since de river. Lots of whisperin' dat I was left out of. I got a feelin' in my bones dat somepin' ain't right."

Whitney gave Jack a stern look. "Jackson Barry, if you know something is happening, you need to tell me now!" She grabbed his arm firmly.

"Ouch! All right." He squirmed under her gaze before fixing his eyes on her. "On my way to the house, when I passed the big barn, I heard voices coming from it and I stuck out my ear and I heard them say, tonight they were going to end Father and his men while they sat drinking up in the big house."

"What?" Whitney and Knox said in unison.

"They are burning it and running tonight." He leaned forward, head down; sobs shook his body. "That's why—why I made Thomas take us for a ride, so we weren't in the house when it happened. I couldn't tell anyone because Father would do horrible things to them if he found out." The guilt and helplessness overwhelmed him and his sobs became cries of anguish.

Thomas, without waiting for a command, turned the horses back toward the plantation. "Thomas, to the Armstrong Plantation," Knox ordered. "We will need Bowden's help," he said to Whitney.

Fear twisted her insides as the horses ran at breakneck speed toward the Armstrong Plantation. The short distance to Bowden's homestead seemed to take forever. When they arrived, Knox almost tore the front door off, trying to get in. Whitney and the twins stayed seated in the carriage.

And then Whitney smelled it. It was happening.

# CHAPTER Sixty-Eight

Retired to the parlor after a luscious dinner, Father, Bowden, and I were in mid-conversation when the front door burst open and Knox barged in.

"Bowden, where are you?" he bellowed. Knox's perpetually laid-back manner had vanished.

Bowden dashed from the parlor to find out what had spun him into such a frenzy. "Knox, what is it?"

"Bowden, you must come quick. The Barry Plantation—it's on fire. The slaves, they've rebelled."

"Whitney? The kids? Where are they?" I screeched. Anxiety threatened to choke the oxygen from me.

"They're with me," Knox said, hurrying out the door.

Bowden grabbed guns from the cabinet. Tossing one to Father, we flew out the door, shouting orders for horses to be brought around.

"Make it quick. Gray, you and you come with me." He pointed to his overseer and the overseer's brother.

"Bowden, wait!" I cried, grabbing at his arm. "You can't harm those people. If only you saw what they went through. It's—"

"Willow!" he said sharply, cutting me off. "Not now. I know I can't stop you from coming, so get in the carriage." He snagged the reins from the slave's hand.

Saddled up, the men rode out.

"Children, stay here. Clara, please tend to them," I instructed the pretty house slave who stood on the front veranda, waiting to assist. I hurried the children out of the carriage.

"Yes, Miss Willow. Come on, chillums, let's see what we can git yas in de kitchen." She led them away.

I scrambled into the carriage, and Whitney and I were off.

I could see the flames above the trees, and heard their merciless howl as we raced toward them. At the Barry Plantation we raised our handkerchiefs to cover our mouths and noses as the intense smoke muffled our breathing.

"Oh, Lord," Thomas said as we took in the fire engulfing the house.

The heat from the fire had broken out the windows and flames spilled from them like murderous spirits seeking a soul to invade. The fire in the quarters chewed right through the pitiful shacks like they were dry cornstalks. The slaves must have already fled.

Father and Bowden came around front lugging buckets of water as we pulled in. "There is no way in," Bowden shouted to Father as we exited the carriage.

I looked from them to the house as a screaming man emerged from the inferno.

"Father?" Whitney murmured.

Art Barry's agonizing screams as the flames devoured his body chilled me to my core. I could not move. Bowden raised his gun and sent a mercy shot into the man and he dropped to the ground. The master of the plantation became but a charcoal corpse.

As her father's body burned, Whitney stayed unmoving. I gazed upon this woman who'd dealt with more in her twenty years than most do in a lifetime. The crimson destruction surrounding us was reflected in her eyes. "I'm so sorry, Whitney."

Her face hardened as she said, "I'm not. He got what he deserves. He can burn in hell with his kind."

I cast no judgment. I knew she would never want to see any human meet their end like this, even the sadistic man fate had given her for a father.

"The only parent I loved lies in a grave." She turned and strode to the carriage. Grief plucked at me as I followed.

"I sorry, Miss Whitney, for all dat you've lost." Thomas bowed his head respectfully.

"Thank you," Whitney grimly replied.

"Thomas?"

"Yes, Miss Willow?"

"Why did you stay?"

"I didn't play no part in dis trouble." His forehead pleated with growing worry.

"No, I didn't think you did, but you must have known about the slaves' plan? Why didn't you help and run off with the others?"

"Only de good Lord has de right to take a life. The Lord had a plan and he is part of et." He gestured toward the smoldering body.

"Why don't you run now, while you can?" I asked.

"Miss, I have nowhere to go. I am an ol' man, never had a family. Wouldn't know how to survive on my own." He shrugged his thin shoulders.

The house was lost. The men joined us.

"I fear I may find we are penniless. Father was never any good with money. We all hated this plantation, but at least we had a home," Whitney said.

"You all have a home at Livingston. Isn't that so, Father?"

"That big empty mansion could use some children's laughter." He settled an arm around my shoulders and I welcomed it.

"And Thomas?" Whitney asked.

"You and the children are the rightful owners of what is left of your father's plantation, and that would mean Thomas goes with you. He was with you and is innocent of this mess," Father told her. "You girls need to be aware, this isn't going to go down easy. It will spread like pollen in the wind and people will be on the hunt for the runaways. Things like this make people go mad. I need you to keep to Livingston until this ordeal is dealt with. Understood?"

"Yes," we said.

"Good. We will stay here until this fire dies down. I'll meet you at home."

We clambered back into the carriage and rode down the lane and away from the horror that used to be Whitney's home. I glanced over my shoulder. The slaves had purged all remnants of human existence from the Barry Plantation. There would be no more gruesome brutality here. My thoughts turned to Father's haunting words: "Things like this make people go mad." Fear magnified inside of me as I imagined what the repercussions would be for the slaves, if caught. *Run*, my mind cried mutely into the night.

# CHAPTER
# Sixty-Nine

FATHER HAD BEEN RIGHT. AS THE NEWS OF THE UPRISING SPREAD to neighboring plantations, the people of Charleston County went mad. The festering seed of hatred, sown so deeply, sprouted. With a grim face, Father had said, "They will come."

The next day, neighbors poured through the gates into Livingston. Father was the one they turned to; it was evident he was respected by many. Father tried to calm the venom stirring their blood.

Around midmorning, Bowden and Knox rode in, followed by six other riders; behind them came carriages with their womenfolk. From our position on the veranda, Whitney and I watched the growing crowd.

Growing tired of Father's voice of reason, a belly-heavy man with small, wire-framed spectacles resting on the tip of his nose climbed up on the front of a wagon. "Listen up, good people of Charleston," his voice boomed. The restless crowd turned from Father to the new man. "Mr. Hendricks seems to be suffering a little black-lover fever." He sent a warning glare at my father.

I glanced at Father. He didn't respond. He remained placid and unmoving, his back straight, his shoulders drawn back, his eyes fastened on the man.

The man went on. "Them niggers will pay for what they did at the Barry Plantation. We will incinerate them like they did to poor Mr. Barry and his men. Let it be a warning to anyone who stands in our way: these niggers are as good as dead."

The crowd erupted in a cheer, their fists raised, pounding at the air; they were hungry for Negro blood.

"Now, time's a-wasting. The longer we delay, the farther those murderous bastards get. Let's go!" he shouted.

The crowd thundered its approval. As quickly as they arrived, they left. Bowden, Knox, and Father stood watching them disperse. Father turned to walk away.

"Father!" I yelled to him as I descended the steps.

He stopped and half-turned to me. "What is it, Willow?" His eyes flashed a warning that stirred a memory of one of his earlier warnings. I continued cautiously. "Aren't you going to do anything?"

"What do you propose I do?"

"I suppose I expect you to help save those slaves. I know you can't stop that blood-thirsty mob, but there must be something we can do. I've seen the condition of the Barry slaves. Some can't have gone far; some may have doubled back to the Barry Plantation already."

"Willow, you are to do nothing. Do you hear me? Nothing!" His voice deepened as he moved toward me. "I will lock you in your room if I must. But you are not to leave this plantation. Understood?" He gripped my shoulders and shook me.

I gulped at his show of anger. We were back at square one. All the mending we had done to our relationship had vanished. I shifted my burning eyes to the ground and forced a nod.

"Good. I have things to attend to at the warehouses in town." The muscles at the corner of his mouth twitched. He released me and stepped back. Turning, he strode toward the wharf, summoning Jones to follow.

Whitney and I ran to the corner of the house and peered

around it. Father boarded the schooner and Jones climbed in behind him.

We jumped and yelped when Bowden whispered between our hovering heads, "I hope you ladies aren't getting any ideas." He and Knox had crept up behind us.

"Bowden, didn't anyone teach you not to creep up on people?" I sent a fist at his chest.

Bowden smirked. "You are aware, aren't you, that you become more irresistible when you are angry, Willow Hendricks?"

"Oh, puke!" Whitney said with a huff, pushing her way through the men.

"We've had about all we can handle for the day. Being women and all, this day has been a bit much for us. So, we will bid you gentlemen good day," I said in a honeyed voice.

"Oh…?" Bowden examined my intent for a moment too long.

"Bowden, Whitney's been through enough and the twins need her. So I suggest you stop trying to figure out what I'm up to and do something productive. Why don't you and Knox put yourselves to good use and go out there and see if you can stop whatever that deranged mob intends for those slaves?" I said, my tone more acerbic.

Bowden's expression sharpened to anger at my disrespectful response. "Do not speak to me like I am a child," he said, hurt.

Instantly regretful, I replied, "Father's behavior has upset me. You don't deserve that. I'm truly sorry." My lip trembled as I gazed into his face.

Bowden softened. "I gladly accept your apology." He gently stroked my cheek with the back of his hand. I leaned into it; turning my mouth, I tenderly kissed his knuckles.

"All right, lovebirds, let's get on with it." Knox chuckled good-naturedly.

When the men were gone, Whitney turned to go inside.

"Where are you going?"

Puzzled, she drawled, "Umm, inside…aren't I?"

"No, of course not. We are going out there to help those fugitives."

"But you said to your Father and Bowden—"

"I know what I said. But sometimes you have to take matters into your own hands when it comes to men. I told them what they wanted to hear, so they would leave."

Whitney arched a brow, then her head bobbed up and down. "Sneaky little wench, aren't you?" She giggled.

Blatantly disobeying Father's orders, we had our horses saddled and headed first for the Barry Plantation.

# CHAPTER *Seventy*

ALL THAT REMAINED OF THE BARRY PLANTATION WAS smoldering ashes. Relieved to find no sign of the mob, Bowden, or Knox, we roamed the grounds and the boundaries of the plantation in search of any trace of the slaves.

Some horses stood drinking from a trough that still held water. A few more horses and some cattle grazed in the fields, and a mama goat wandered nearby, her kid frolicking beside her. Chickens clucked and fluttered their wings as we meandered through them. Beyond the animals, there was no movement, no sign of humans. A melancholy I could not shake settled within me.

"There is no one here. Let's ride out," Whitney said.

Mounting up, we left. Not sure of where we were going next, we wandered the trails; leery of being seen, we moved with caution. My melancholy was turning into mind-numbing hopelessness.

We rode past a fresh trail heading into the swamps. The trampled ground had to be from the horses of the mob. Stopping, I signaled Whitney to take a look. She rode up beside me. "Looks like the trackers entered here. The slaves know more about these swamps than most of us. Makes sense that they would use the swamps to assist in their escape. What do you want to do?"

"I don't think we have a choice. We have to go in. Those slaves are my responsibility. I owe them this much to atone for the crimes of my father." Whitney guided her mount into the underbrush and slipped from her horse.

"We keep our ears sharp. That mob is crazed with vengeance—we don't want to spook them and become their victims," I said as I jumped down from my horse. We pulled the animals into the brush, out of sight of the main path, and tied them to a tree. Then we tucked the sides of our skirts into our waistbands to give us greater mobility in navigating the woods.

"All right, let's go," she said.

We had not traveled far along the beaten trail before a shot rang out. Whitney and I grabbed at each other, instinctively dropping to our knees. The shot was followed by a frenzy of shrill screams, and angry voices reached our ears. They were too distant for us to understand the words. Before we could process that the slaves had been found, a volley of shots split the air, sounding as close as a stone's throw away. Choked with fear, we dropped to our bellies to avoid stray bullets.

I clenched my eyes closed, wishing to shut out the unfolding horror. As gruesome images of what was taking place whirled through my mind, my tears began to fall. Opening my eyes, I turned my cheek on the mossy earth and saw Whitney's trembling hands outstretched in front of her.

Pain suddenly radiated through my back as someone literally ran over me. The fleeing slaves were unknowingly stumbling over our bodies. Someone fell on top of us and I gawked at the slave woman who sprawled across us, trapping us beneath her. She stared back, her eyes large with fear.

"Mary?" Whitney whispered.

"Miss Whitney?" She struggled to rise, and I saw hope in her dark eyes.

"Mary, we have to get you out of sight." Whitney sprang into action. "Willow, we can't hide her out here. We need to take her back to Livingston."

"But we can't leave them out there. What if…" I struggled to articulate words in my brain.

"Willow, snap out of it," Whitney growled, driven with desperation.

"All right, you go. I'll stay. You get her home and come back."

"I'll hurry, but you must stay out of sight." Without waiting for a reply, Whitney and Mary started running back the way we had come.

Shuddering, I glanced around. An eerie silence had fallen over the swamp. The ear-piercing shots had ceased and not a voice or a cry reached my ears. I found my feet and pushed farther into the swamp, my heart in my throat. A play of destruction performed in my head as I pressed on.

Raucous laughter and then a cheer rose from the mob. I saw movement ahead and sought cover as I edged closer, careful not to be seen. With my eyes pinned on the mob ahead, I missed the obstruction in my path. Stumbling, I went down hard. The wind was knocked from me and I lay sprawled on the ground for a moment before looking to see what had caused my fall.

A slave's body, riddled with bullets. His lifeless eyes gazed at the sky.

*No, no, no…* I moaned.

Tears stung my eyes as I placed a hand over his eyes to close them. "May you finally find freedom," I whispered. Stumbling to my feet, I forced myself to go on, crouching low.

I heard the leader shout, "We are done here. Justice was served. I say we all deserve a drink. Everyone is welcome back at my plantation." A gleeful roar went up.

I darted for cover as the mob tramped toward me. Ducking behind a cypress tree, I crouched down, holding my breath. I could almost reach out and touch them as they passed by. *Please, don't see me.*

The last human figure was long gone before I released my hold on the tree. I wiped my sweaty palms on the bunched-up fabric of my skirt. Alone and fearful of what I would find, I persuaded my feet to go on.

# CHAPTER Seventy-One

My senses were overloaded, dulling my desire to investigate the inevitable conclusion for the slaves. I fought the desire to turn and run. Run from what lay beyond my view. Something pushed me on. I parted the tall grass and my feet edged forward.

My imagination couldn't prepare me for what I found. I staggered back, a scream catching in my throat as my eyes beheld the massacre of the Barry slaves. Men, women, and children—the mob had left no survivors. Blood flecked the green foliage and shallow puddles of stagnant water were crimson with their blood. A man lay with his hand intertwined with his woman's. A grandpa and grandma lay tucked in each other's embrace. Beneath a mother's corpse, a tiny pair of legs protruded.

My stomach rioted. Vomit burst from my lips. Tears burned my cheeks and my vision blurred. And—I saw him. My watcher.

He stood in plain sight, his face shadowed by the same lowered hat brim he'd worn the last time. I'd forgotten about him for a time. Why did he now step from the shadows Father had confined him to? The stranger appeared to be fighting an inner battle of some sort as he watched me. For some reason, I didn't mind his presence. With him there, I didn't feel so small and abandoned in this gloomy everglade. The limited companionship he offered gave me a sense of comfort. I brushed away my tears.

As I walked amongst the dead, I deceived myself with the

hope that I might find a survivor. I bent and checked for a pulse again and again. And with each one, my heart descended further into despair. I checked over my shoulder for the stranger, to find he had faded into the shadows he had emerged from.

I dropped to my knees beside the mother and child and pushed the dead weight of the mother aside. The child was a boy of maybe four years of age. His hair had been shorn scalp-short. His small fist was clenched tight even in death.

*Why, God? He was but a babe. His life had barely begun.* I reached for the boy's hand and lightly enfolded it in mine. I stroked his wee hand, my fingers tracing his knuckles. Placing his hand reverently in his mother's, I caressed his innocent face with the back of my hand.

He blinked. His eyes opened and I wrenched back in alarm.

"Mama?" he said quietly. Then he saw me and he began to scream, "Mama!" He rose to his knees and saw his mother lying dead beside him, and released a gut-twisting wail. "Mama…" He gently shook at her. Then, as fear gripped his heart, he shook her with frantic intensity.

I slowly moved toward him and reached for him. His cries stopped and his small body became rigid when I touched him, but his head turned to look at me. "No, no!" He pushed my hand away.

"I won't hurt you," I said in a soothing voice.

"I want my mama," he whimpered.

"I know you do." He fought me as I cradled him to my breast. "Mama has gone to heaven. Do you understand that?"

He shook his head.

"Your mama is free."

"But Mama promised she gwine take me wid her." He hiccupped.

"Your mama was going to, sweet boy, but those bad men

came," I whispered. My heart ached as the child grew silent.

Minutes passed before I spoke. "We must leave this place now." I waited for his acknowledgment, but he remained mute. I struggled to stand on my wobbly legs, and guided us out of the swamps.

# CHAPTER Seventy-Two

WHITNEY MET US HALFWAY. THE SIGHT OF HER WAS A relief. Numb, I'd been concentrating on getting away from the nightmare that lay behind me. Reading the shock etched on my face, Whitney looked straight ahead as we headed home.

We rode through the gates into Livingston's comforting embrace. Mary Grace reached for the child I lowered down into her waiting arms. He had been silent since leaving his mother's body.

Hours later, bathed and fed, the child was still silent. But even numbed by shock, I noticed how the child turned to Mary Grace for comfort. When I asked, she readily agreed to provide him with whatever comfort she could. I watched her walk away with the child straddling her expanding waist.

The setting sun cast long lavender shadows across the plantation. I leaned against the railing on the back veranda, gazing out over the Ashley River. Fiddle music reached my ears from a group of slaves hovering around a recently stoked fire. Jimmy stepped from the forge. Arching his back, he stretched out sore muscles. Done for the day, he whistled a familiar tune as he headed in toward his cabin. Mammy emerged from the kitchen house with a basin of dish water and cast it in an arc over the grass.

My attention swung back to the river and the wharf as Father's schooner came into view. Time seemed to drag while I waited for it to dock. Jones secured the rope to the wharf, spoke a few words to Father, and wandered off. Father ambled toward the house, his head down, absorbed in his thoughts. Glancing up, he noticed me for the first time.

"Willow." He stopped abruptly and clasped his hands behind his back, but not before I saw the red blemishing the cuffs of his once crisp linen shirt.

My jaw set tight as I looked down at him. "How were matters at the dock, Father?" I asked, my voice heavy with sarcasm.

"Fine," he said as he ascended the steps.

I moved to him, quivering with hostility. "Liar!" I jerked on his arms, and his hands swung forward and dangled at his sides.

"Willow? What are you talking about?" he asked, alarm in his eyes.

"The bloodbath that took place in those swamps!" I swung my hand out, pointing in the general direction of the swamp.

Father tensed and his face contorted. "You disobeyed me! I warned you to stay put. But no, you can't leave well enough alone. You cannot…save them, Willow," his gaze met mine.

The fight left me. Hope was lost to me. Sickened that I was the daughter of a man like him, I fixed a stony glare on him. "As you say, Father."

He flinched. His mouth opened to speak, then closed again. His complexion paled and his face was suddenly tired and empty.

I laughed a dry, disheartened laugh. Pivoting on the tips of my toes, I strode into the house.

# CHAPTER Seventy-Three

A WEEK LATER, MY LIFE SHATTERED LIKE SPLINTERING GLASS. I knew something was terribly wrong when Jimmy charged into the house shouting my name. Startled at the sudden interruption, I dropped the book I had been reading.

"Miss Willie, come quick!" He staggered into the sitting room. Bending at the knees, he gasped to catch his breath.

I hurried to him. "What's wrong, Jimmy?"

"Et's your father, Miss Willie. Dere was a horrible accident. His carriage—"

"What? Where?" My fear rose at the news.

"Jones brought him back. He's sent for de doc."

I caught a glimpse of Father's bloody body as Jones and a slave carried him to his room.

"Find Mammy. And cloths and hot water—prepare for the doctor when he gets here," I ordered over my shoulder as I hurried down the corridor to Father's room.

Father's voice was weak, a gurgling croak as he said, "Willow…find my daughter…"

"I'm here, Father." I knelt beside him.

His body had been crushed beneath the carriage. As I observed his condition, I feared internal bleeding. *The doc will never make it in time.* I couldn't lose him. He was all I had.

"Mammy!" I screamed. *Please, someone help me.* I looked at my father's mangled body. Despite our differences, he'd always been a pillar of strength. My eyes roved the room, desperately seeking someone to help me.

"I must tell you something…" He coughed, and blood spattered from his mouth. "You…you must know the truth." His eyes brimmed with pain…and longing.

"Try not to talk, Father," I said softly, trailing my fingers along his face.

"No, you must know. I have always loved you. All I've done is to…to protect you. I did what I thought was right." His body convulsed and a moment later, he settled. He gazed past me, focusing on something behind me. "Ben, you must tell her. We have wronged her by…keeping the truth from her." His hand weakly waved someone forward.

A shadow fell over me and I looked up to see him. The man in the shadows.

"Father, please try to rest." I knew rest was a lie; he was failing. Tears pricked my eyes as I lifted his hand and kissed it.

"I'm sorry…Willow." His body stiffened with a wave of pain. "I'm sorry I didn't share her with you. Like your mother, you are the best of them." His grip tightened around my hand and a moan escaped him. His eyes closed, then flew open at some memory.

"Ben." He once again summoned the man beside me with his hand. The man moved closer and bent to hear the words Father whispered. "Get them out. The warehouse…the ship leaves tomorrow."

His words confused me. Who? Get who out?

Father's body stiffened once more, then it relaxed as the life left his body.

"Father!" My scream filled the room. My heart pounded in my head, blocking out the sounds around me. "No, please no…" I buried my face in Father's bloodstained chest. "I'm sorry,

Father. I'm sorry for being a disappointment. I'm sorry I couldn't be what you wanted me to be. I love you…" Sobs carried me away.

"Dere, dere, Miss Willie." Jimmy placed an ever-constant hand on my back.

"What shall I ever do?" My words were muffled against Father's chest. "I can't do this alone."

"Miss Willie, you ain't alone," Jimmy said in a soothing voice.

I was inconsolable. I gave way to my grief. Jimmy led me from the room as the doctor arrived.

In the passageway, I paused when Mammy spoke. "I'm sorry, chile, for your loss. Masa, he was de bes' masa, and we 'member him so."

"Thank you, Mammy," I murmured.

# CHAPTER
# Seventy-Four

I scarcely recalled the day of Father's funeral. It was a grand event, attended by many who came to pay their respects. As Father's friends and colleagues offered their condolences, I sat behind my black veil with my hands folded in my lap, nodding respectfully, a stiff smile painted on my face. I was grateful for the privacy the veil provided. Whitney stood tentatively by my side.

Sam Bennick, my father's lawyer and a close friend, approached me. I'd met him on several occasions when he came by to pay my father a visit. "Sorry for your loss. Your father was very dear to me." His light blue eyes reflected genuine sorrow.

"Thank you."

"I want you to know you aren't alone, and my office is always open."

"I appreciate that, Sam." He bounced lightly on his toes as he removed his timepiece from his front pocket. Glancing at me, he said, "Next week, we should get together at my office to go over your Father's will."

"Yes, that is fine," I said, knowing even in my grief that life would go on.

With Father gone, my responsibilities were greater. The plantation was a huge responsibility on its own, without adding on Father's businesses. How I was going to manage, I wasn't sure. Running a plantation with labor provided by slaves—something

I didn't believe in—was a battle in itself. I loved Livingston and the slaves on it were like my family, but how could I in good conscience turn a profit on the backs of slaves?

"He left you this." Sam handed me a small box tied with twine.

"Umm…thank you," I said as I accepted the box he placed in my black-gloved hands.

"I bid you good day," he said. Tipping the brim of his top hat, he left.

Later that evening I sat in the garden, gazing down at the box that lay unopened on my lap. I ran my fingers over it, fearful of what mystery the box would reveal.

Mammy appeared carrying a tray with the tea I'd requested. She placed it on the garden table and glanced at me. Her face radiated love and concern for me.

"Thank you, Mammy."

"Yes, Missus."

I looked sharply at her, taken aback by the formal address. "Mammy, I may now be the mistress of Livingston and you can address me as missus in formal situations, but please don't leave me. Please, do not let that change us." I was suddenly afraid. "No matter what becomes of Livingston, you are still my Mammy and my friend."

Mammy smiled fondly. "Yes, chile," she said, and a smile pinched the corners of my mouth.

Alone in the garden again, I untied the box and withdrew a thin, leather-bound book along with an envelope labeled with *My Willow* in Father's handwriting.

Turning the envelope over, I broke the seal and gingerly removed the paper within. I closed my eyes, breathing deeply to calm the nerves that churned my stomach. Unfolding the paper, I read:

*My dearest Willow,*

*If you are reading this letter, then my time in this life is over. I wish I'd learned to show you my love sooner. I regret every day that I couldn't. My pride has ruled much of my life and yours, making my decisions and my behaviors in raising you my biggest mistakes.*

*I've left you your mother's journal. In it may you find some answers to the questions you seek. Questions I was too weak a man to give to you. After losing her, I lived with the fear of losing you and in that fear, I guarded my heart and pushed you away for what I now realize were many wasted years. Don't let my mistakes hold you back. Know that you were loved by me.*

*All my love,*

*Charles Hendricks*

Struggling with the many emotions my father's words conjured, I folded the letter, then pressed it to my lips and kissed it. I missed him. Why did it take his passing for me to see how much? We had been each other's stumbling block in the relationship we had formed. Father, with his stubbornness and fears. But was he that much different than me?

On his deathbed and in his letter, he declared his fears and love. Maybe I would eventually find the healing in these words. Why had he spent so many years keeping me at arm's length? Why had he set out such restrictions on our relationship and why had his expectations always seemed unattainable? Would I find the answers in the pages of my mother's journal? Time could wait no longer. I must have the answers I sought.

Opening to the first page, I read the words so elegantly written:

*My Precious Willow,*

It was written to me. My heart leaped in my chest. It was dated a year after I was born.

As I scanned the pages of my mother's journal, I developed a new understanding of my father. I understood why he had kept this book from me. My mother's secrets, my father's shame, filled the pages. I found no resolution in the words filling the pages of her journal. The information this book held changed my past and my future.

# CHAPTER Seventy-Five

I REMOVED THE VEIL AND PINS FROM MY HAIR, ALLOWING MY HAIR TO fall down my back. Running my trembling fingers over my aching scalp, I gently shook my mane. Seated behind the desk in my father's study, I waited in anticipation for the return of Jimmy. I'd sent him to find the man that lived in the shadows. The man Father called Ben. The man who'd been the love of my mother's life, and my protector. My father.

Through the window, I saw him walking toward the house. He was tall like Father, I realized. Minutes later he entered the study and removed his hat to reveal a full head of blond hair. Where my father's hair had been thinning, his remained intact. His eyes were dark and burned with a yearning too long restrained. But I also saw in him a humbleness, a tenderness, as he gazed at me.

"Hello, Willow," he said. Though his mannerisms were gentle and kind, his tone was steady and confident.

"Hello…Ben?"

"That's right."

"You will have to bear with me as I am…well, I'm…" I lowered my eyes and cleared my throat before lifting my gaze once more to him. "This is all new to me, as you are aware. I have come to see we were both slaves to the shadows." I motioned him toward a chair in front of me. He obliged.

"Please, I refuse to waste another day in the dark. I can't go on like this. Please, tell me: who am I?"

He let out a long sigh before he began to speak. "Charles and my parents were family friends of your mother, Olivia's, parents. As children, we played together. I loved her for as far back as I remember and it was only later that I found out how deeply Charles also loved her. But she loved me.

"Your grandmother passed away when your mother was in her teens, so when your grandfather's health began to decline, he thought the right thing to do was to arrange a marriage for Olivia. She was the apple of your grandfather's eye, one may say. But when seeking a husband for her, he didn't give in to 'her girly woes,' as he said. Charles and I were longtime family friends of his family and became the front-runners. Charles had become a fine businessman and I was a student still in med school. Your grandfather decided Charles was the better option to give your mother the quality of life she was used to, and he was smart enough business-wise to keep Livingston profitable.

"Olivia was furious at her lack of control in the matter. I remember the day like yesterday. As Charles and I sat on that very porch out there eagerly awaiting your grandfather's decision, Olivia flew out the front door in a temper at your grandfather for even suggesting an arranged marriage. Like the day Charles approached you with a similar proposition." His laugh was carefree and unstrained.

I leaned forward, resting my elbows on the desk. Reading my urgency, he continued. "That evening your grandfather suffered a heart attack. Your mother blamed herself for it. Not wanting to cause your grandfather undue stress, she agreed to marry Charles. A few weeks after the wedding your grandfather suffered another heart attack, and that one took his life."

"Trapping her in a loveless marriage to Father?" Understanding filled me with compassion for my parents.

"Charles treasured your mother, but soon after the wedding, we found out she was pregnant with you. Olivia refused to keep the fact that I was the father a secret. We told Charles together. He didn't take it too well, as you can imagine." Ben lowered his eyes. "He was outraged. Your mother and I had shamed him. But being a man of honor and because he truly loved Olivia, Charles decided to keep Olivia's shame a secret. The neighbors and townsfolk already frowned upon her for her outspoken views. It was agreed I would finish school in Virginia, and Charles and Olivia would raise you together without my involvement.

"Olivia's love, the love of a mother, outweighed the love she had for me, and she agreed to Charles's offer. In those years, I remained absent from your lives. Until I received Charles's letter." He stopped, his eyes haunted.

"Letter?"

"I received a letter demanding I come to Livingston immediately."

"Go on."

"Upon my return, I found your mother was not here. Charles showed me to this study, but not before I got a glimpse of you playing with Mary Grace, in the parlor. You looked up at me with those eyes; they were like a gateway to the past. You stared at me as if trying to figure out who I was. You smiled and waved before turning back to your toys, and Charles called me in here."

"What did he want?" I leaned forward. The answer to my mother's disappearance was within my grasp.

"He told me that…umm…he informed me of…" Even now, after all these years, Ben struggled to give me the answers Father had kept from me—to tell me the truth.

"Please, do not withhold the truth from me," I implored him.

He was silent for a moment before he went on. "Your mother was murdered. Charles found her hanging from an oak tree a few miles from here. Hung around her neck was a sign that said 'Nigger lover.' With her hung the slave she'd been helping escape."

Nothing I'd imagined about my mother's death or disappearance could have prepared me for this. "I-I thought—" The room began to spin, and I felt the blood drain from my face.

"Willow?" Ben's hands turned me. His face was a blur, floating farther away. "Rita!" he yelled in a panic.

"What is et, Masa Ben? Oh, lands sakes! I'll git some water for de chile." Mammy's footsteps thundered rapidly away.

"I'll be all right," I said, resting my face in my hands. Tears had become a second language to me lately and today was no different. I cried for the mother I'd lost and for the father I never knew.

Mammy returned. "Move on outta de way, Masa Ben. Mammy take care of her chile."

Her words touched my heart. *Mammy…oh, Mammy…always faithful and devoted.* I cried harder.

"Now, now, chile. Evvything gwine be all right. Mammy promises you dat." She pressed my head to her bosom and let me cry a spell before lifting the corner of her apron and drying my tears. "Drink up, chile." She put the glass of water to my trembling lips and I reached up and held it myself.

Draining the glass, I handed it back to her. "Thank you."

She turned to leave, but I stopped her. "Mammy, did you know my mother was murdered?"

She froze. She sent a nervous glance to Ben, who nodded. Turning to face me, she said, "Yes, Missus. I knowed 'bout et all. Your mama was our friend. Jus' lak you. She did what's right by my people. She was right fine to me and my Mary Grace, from de day she and your pappy…Gawd bless dat man." She whispered a brief prayer before she went on. "From de day she made Masa Hendricks buy us. Den on her death she freed us." With her final words she looked me square in the eye.

*She freed us.* What in the world was Mammy gabbing about now? "Mammy, what nonsense are you talking about?" I returned her stare.

"Your mama give me and Mary Grace our freedom papers. Masa Hendricks, he never knowed until he go to de fancy lawyer's place and finds out for himself. Your pappy honored your mama and signed de papers giving his approval."

"But all this time…all these years…you have been free?" I frowned in confusion.

"Yes, Missus."

"But you stayed. Why?"

"'Cause I can't leave my gal behind."

"But Mammy, she was free. You both were."

"I knowed dat, silly gal. But I can't leave my other gal behind. I owe your mama dat much, and by den you trusted me and loved me. I told you, I love you lak you be born of my own body." Her smile encased my heart with the love of a mother.

# CHAPTER Seventy-Six

Yesterday had nearly been more than I could handle, with Father's funeral and the revelations surrounding my parentage. Breakfast with Whitney and the twins proved to be a challenge, as I struggled to focus on anything other than the wealth of information I had received. Today would prove to be no different, I learned as I pushed back from the table.

Ben appeared in the doorway.

"Yes?" I said, though there was a fluttering in my breast at the sight of him. My uncle…yet my father. Now that was a story Lucille would run with. I laughed inwardly, but my mouth formed a taut line.

"I hoped we could talk about your father's business affairs." He offered a reserved smile.

"Yes, I suppose that is an urgent matter. Whitney, children, would you please excuse me?"

"Of course. I have an appointment with the twins' tutor this morning. I'll catch up with you later." Whitney rose and tried to shoo the children from the room.

"But I don't want to do my studies today," Jack said, scowling up at Whitney.

"Me either," Kimie said as Whitney led them away.

Alone, I looked at Ben. "Would you prefer the study?"

"For what I wish to discuss with you, I thought maybe we

could take a ride," he said, looking uncomfortable.

"Oh, for Pete's sake! What now?" I grumbled.

"Your horse is ready outside," he said.

I changed into my riding attire and met him outside. He lifted me into my saddle, mounted his horse, and we were off.

*What does he wish to talk about that requires we speak far from any listening ears?* I wondered as we rode in silence, his mount leading the way.

When Livingston was far behind us, he reined in his horse. "Do you care to walk for a spell?"

Like Father, he was attractive, but he was far removed from Father's uptight manner. Ben Hendricks was open and unguarded. Maybe a lifetime spent being my overseer—my protector—had produced the love that radiated from his face. It filled me with hope and the desire to learn more about him.

Reining my horse to a stop, I slid to the ground. I waited for him to speak.

"I will get right to the point. You remember the words your father said before he—right before he passed?"

"He said a few things, as I recall. To which are you referring?"

"The words he whispered to me."

"Umm…yes?" I remembered his words, but I had dismissed them as the confusion of a dying man.

"As you know, he asked me to go to his warehouse at the dock."

"Right."

"In the warehouse, I found slaves."

"Slaves?"

"Slaves from the Barry Plantation. I was busy trying to keep up with trailing you on the day of the massacre, so your shock is my shock."

"Why would he go to the trouble of carrying dead slaves to

a warehouse?" I asked, confused.

"They were alive, Willow. That's what I'm trying to tell you. When he left on the schooner that day he didn't go to town, he went in search of those slaves. He came across the dead slaves in those swamps, but he didn't give up hope—he searched farther in the swamps. In the warehouse were four runaways he found out there. It's what he was talking about. Getting them out on his ships.

"The secrets we thought surrounded this family go deeper than even I knew. We have barely scratched the surface. I spoke to Captain Gillies and it seems after the death of your mother, Charles's focus turned to protecting you with a feverish obsession. The love he had for Olivia and the loss of her tormented him. Visions of her murder haunted him. It pushed him to want to make a change to this oppressed world we live in.

"Charles picked up the torch your mother left behind and carried it all these years. His ships, the warehouses, his unexplained trips, all were part of his efforts to free hundreds of slaves." Pride swelled in his voice as he explained the deeds of my father. Tears threatened to escape the corners of his eyes. "He was a hero, Willow. My brother, your father…" He reached out and pulled me into his embrace.

Welcoming the comfort of his arms, I rested my cheek against his chest. The years of yearning to belong fell away. In his arms I had found…acceptance.

# CHAPTER Seventy-Seven

THE SKIES WERE HEAVY WITH THE PROMISE OF SHOWERS, BUT when the sun peeked from behind the clouds, I admired the beauty its light cast upon Livingston. I had always loved my home, but now that affection grew with the full understanding of what Livingston stood for. It was a haven of hope in the midst of a land overtaken with hatred. I was free from the secrets that had enslaved me.

I felt uplifted by my understanding of the steps that had guided my life. In the stories of my parents, I found purpose and the inspiration to go on. I had to protect their legacy, the legacy my mother died for. I had spent too many years in confusion, longing for something that wasn't meant to be mine. She would remain a ghost of the past. Father's death had left a man to take his place. Even from the grave he was protecting me…his love reigned supreme.

Now, as I sat on the porch swing overlooking the plantation, my thoughts turned to Whitney. She sat beside me, her shoulders stooped and burdened with worries. An extremely pregnant Mary Grace waddled onto the veranda with the child from the swamps in tow.

In the hopes of relieving Whitney of some of her uncertainties, I smiled warmly at Mary Grace. "Mary Grace, would you mind taking Jack and Kimie to the garden for some sweet tea and one or two of those delightful shortbread cookies

Mammy whipped up?"

"Of, course Missus," she said. "Come along, children." She ushered them away, but not before I saw the slight bounce of old in her step.

The bond that she had developed with the boy whose hand lay secure in hers as they walked away brought tears to my eyes. In his sadness, she had found an escape from her own. Together they healed one another.

"Let's take a quiet stroll before those clouds give way," I said to Whitney, grabbing her hand. She tried to resist, but I pulled her along.

I released her hand when we reached the walkway around the pond. "I wanted to speak with you about what your plan is now."

Whitney walked on, taking her time to reply. "I've been giving it a lot of consideration. So much has changed. The funds left in my father's estate won't last for long: I need to find work and a place for the twins and me to live permanently. Aunt Em invited us to come live with her. But we aren't her responsibility and I want to stand on my own two feet. I've depended on people long enough; I need to be in control of my own affairs. I hate to leave you when your own world has turned inside out, but I can't expect to live off your family any longer."

"Nonsense. I figured you would say something foolish like that, Whitney Barry. I can't possibly run this place without you. I will hire you. Not out of the goodness of my heart, but because I need you as much as you need me. Besides, until recently, that house has been a house full of empty rooms. Now it seems to have become a home to a family of women and children." I laughed fondly at the irony of it all.

My fear of the future and what it meant for us all occupied an ever-expanding space in my mind. How could I ever do it all—run Father's business, this plantation, and sort through the still-unraveling extent of Father's involvement in the smuggling of slaves? I would not see all my father's and mother's dedication to breaking the bonds of slavery die in vain. Who better to help me carry the torch of progress…than my partner in crime?

# Slave Dialogue

Whar = where
Helt = held
gawd = god
larn = learn
bin = been
fust = first
axed = asked
seed = seen
allus = always
folkses = folks
knowed = knew
'oman = woman
purty = pretty
mussy = mercy
'bout = about
De = the
jus'= just
dere = there
chillum = children
wukked = worked
wuk = work
wid = with
'cause = because
Dey = they
Lak =like
Et = it
dem or 'em = them
'fore = before
'members = remember
Yessum (polite greeting to a lady)

Deir = their
Dan = than
Git = get
Gitting = getting
Axin' = asking
Dat =that
Somepin' = something
Warn't = weren't
'lowed = allowed
Cleant = clean
Atter = after
Evvy = every
sho' = sure
hangin' = hanging
evvything = everything
forgit = forget
tole = told
et = ate
'most = almost
Den = then
tuk = took
luk = look
mis'= miss
li'l = little
'nuf = enough
Gwin = going
bes'= best

# AUTHOR NOTE

Laws often changed throughout the 1700s and 1800s. In America, each state had its own laws. All of this can sometimes add a gray area to research: what laws were actually in place in what year, and in which state did the laws apply? And when did the laws change?

In the colonial and antebellum eras, only single women and widows could own property and sign contracts. When a woman married, her husband took ownership of her property—*unless* her family set up a legal settlement before marriage.

When researching for *A Slave of the Shadows*, my sources led me to believe that a slave owner could, in *his or her* last will and testament, set slaves free for faithful service. During my many trips to Charleston, South Carolina for research, I found nothing to deny that this was, in fact, the case. So, following extensive research, when writing the ending of my story, I had Olivia give Mammy and Mary Grace their freedom in her will.

However, in my recent studies, I've discovered that women weren't allowed to have wills. Then I came across the article "Married Women's Property Law: 1800–1850," written in 1982 by Richard H. Chused of the New York Law School, and realized it may not be as cut and dried as I'd thought. (This article will be posted on my website)

In 1820 the emancipation of slaves became even more restricted, and slaves could only be freed through an act of the legislature. In 1841 (five to six years after my fictional character Olivia's death) "The Act to Prevent the Emancipation of Slaves" changed the freeing of slaves by an owner in their last will and testament altogether. My research led me to information stating that in 1850 in Charleston, only two slaves were recorded as earning their freedom through the courts. Slaves had no choice but to try to take their freedom.

In closing, I wanted to note that Olivia, as the sole heir of Livingston, would have inherited all properties (which included slaves) from her father. It's possible—and my story may reveal more on this in future novels—that Olivia's father set up a trust or arranged a legal settlement with Charles to protect Olivia's estate.

Having my novels stay as close to history as possible is of utmost importance to me. I've spent months researching and studying documents to make sure I line up with history as accurately as I can without actually living in the time period and with the limited sources I can find.

In *A Slave of the Shadows*, Mammy was purchased by Charles and Olivia after their marriage. It's quite possible that Olivia could have had the papers done up that would give Mammy and her daughter freedom upon her death. As an artistic choice, I decided to leave Mammy and her daughter freed upon Olivia's death.

On my website, under "Extras," I will post all articles I've found in my research, if you are interested in researching for yourself. Thank you for your understanding.

If you have enjoyed my work, please leave a review on Goodreads, or the platform you purchased the books from. Your reviews are crucial in spreading the word about my books, and I am sincerely grateful for this support from readers.

Book Two is available now.
A GUARDIAN OF SLAVES

# ABOUT *the Author*

Naomi is a bestselling and award-winning author living in Northern Alberta. She loves to travel and her suitcase is always on standby awaiting her next adventure. Naomi's affinity for the Deep South and its history was cultivated during her childhood living in a Tennessee plantation house with six sisters. Her fascination with history and the resiliency of the human spirit to overcome obstacles are major inspirations for her writing and she is passionately devoted to creativity. In addition to writing fiction, her interests include interior design, cooking new recipes, and hosting dinner parties. Naomi is married to her high school sweetheart and she has two teenage children and a dog named Egypt.

Sign up for my newsletter: authornaomifinley.com/contact

Made in United States
North Haven, CT
20 February 2022